SKI MASK WAY II

BY

RANDY "SKI" THOMPSON

Cover Design by Next Level Publishing
Interior design by A New Quality Publishing
A New Quality Publishing L.L.C. trade paperback printing 2010

For more information, or to contact author or publisher, send correspondence to:

A New Quality Publishing
P.O. Box 589
Plainfield, New Jersey 07061
anewqualitypublishing.com
facebook/randyskithompson

ISBN: 978-0-9817756-6-1

10 9 8 7 6 5 4 3 2
First Paperback Edition

Acknowledgements--

As always all praise and glory goes to my Lord and Savior Jesus Christ. Through him all things are possible.

2 my Mrs. Thank you for showing me what a REAL WOMAN and TRUE LOVE is. It's all about US!

2 my mother evangelist Barbara Butler there aren't enough pages in this book to tell you how much you mean to me and how much I appreciate you. I hope I am making you proud.

2 my brother David Terrell, and my lil sis Sable Butler Love y'all 2 death.

2 my brothers from another mother Scoob, and Bless- ya'll know once I kick this door down we rushing it. Ain't nuthin change. I want for y'all what I want for me.

2 Mabricio Wilson Good looking 4 all the help and support. Know that if and when the time comes you make that call to me I'mma step up to the plate no questions asked. When essence come calling I'mma be rocking a futbolr hoodie in the flick.

Coke, we coming to get you my nigga! Hold ya head. Waffle you my brother at the end of the day; Don't let nuthin or nobody come in between ya family.

Shout out to the all Long Island and especially Baldwin. Cheeba, Brukshot, Knucs, Frog, Vaughn, Han, Ed, Amy Andrieux. If I 4got ya name it's only because of a lapse of memory not a lapse of love.

2 my son Digga-U know I couldn't leave you out. U held me down on this one I ain't 4get.

Big shout out to my fellow authors for showing me support and giving me sound advice when I needed it. Kwan, Erick Gray, T. Styles, K.Elliot.

2 Nancey Flowers- Thanx 4 not holding me back and letting me spread my wings.

Special Shout out to my dude J.M. Benjamin and the entire A New Quality Publishing squad. J-Rod Nider, FiFi Cureton, Glorious, Nyema, Cherie Johnson and Pete. We got now we don't care who got next.

Last but not least I want to thank all of the readers that have supported from my first project to now. I do this 4 y'all. I'm not striving to be the highest paid author, I'm striving to be one of the best authors.

R.I.P. to my father Rudolph Clarence Thompson, Andrew Nalty, Madea Incardona, Lishy Mollette, Craig Espy, Roderick Campbell

Dedication

To my first born Randy Alexander Thompson Jr. When you were born a part of me was reborn. I'm gonna be the father to you that I always wanted.

SKI

MASK

WAY II

BY

RANDY "SKI" THOMPSON

Cooper

Chapter 1

February 03

BEEP... BEEP... BEEP...
When I opened my eyes all I could see was a bright white light shining down on me. I felt like I was floating on air. My first thought was that I had died and some how made it to heaven. But I shot that theory down quickly because I knew there was no way my evil ass could have made it to heaven unless God was grading on a mean curve. I opened and closed my eyes several times to see if I was dreaming but I wasn't. An incessant reverberating beeping sound could be heard in the distance. I had no idea where I was or how I had gotten there. Then suddenly I heard a voice.

"Mom look, he opened his eyes. Look, he's awake! " I heard a familiar voice cry out.

At first I could not place the voice but when I saw my little sister Sable's beautiful face peering down at me I knew I was still alive.

"Praise the Lord! Thank you Jesus! Thank you Jesus!" My mother shouted, kissing me on my forehead as tears rolled down her cheeks.

I tried with all my strength to talk and put my arms around her but my arms seemed to be frozen in place.

"Don't try to talk baby. You're still weak. Sable go and get the doctor, hurry up!" my mother said as she squeezed my hand ever so gently.

My little sister ran out of the room while I struggled to grab my mother's hand back and smile. A few minutes later my doctor, Dr. Mollette, a young black woman in her mid thirties, came to my bedside.

"Good afternoon sleepy head. We were wondering when you were going to wake up. You don't know how bad we wanted to see those brown eyes of yours," Dr. Mollette stated smiling down at me while raising the head of my bed.

Dr. Mollette checked my eyes with a bright light, and then checked my pulse, blood pressure, and reflexes.

"Mr. Thompson you are a lucky man. For someone who has been in a coma for as long as you were, you seem to be in good shape. I am going to schedule you for a M.R.I. and a CAT scan tomorrow. Try to drink some water but take it easy," Dr. Mollette said as she filled the pink hospital cup half way and handed it to me. "You two can stay for a little while but don't keep him up long. He's still weak."

The water I drank that day tasted like the best drink I had ever had in my life. My mouth and throat were so dry I thought they were gonna crack. The water quenched my thirst and made me feel alive again. I could actually feel it creeping through my entire body.

"Ma, how long have I been in here?" I asked in a barely audible whisper.

"Ten months baby, ten long months. I knew you were gonna pull through it though. God is good. Thank you Jesus, I never doubted it for a minute," my mother went on.

"Where's Michelle? What happened to the baby?" I asked.

"Isaiah was here yesterday. That boy looks just like you and he's already bad," she said. Her smile matched her tone.

"I have a picture of him right here," my sister said pulling out her wallet. "That's when he was six months. He's much bigger now. You should see your baby picture and his together. You two look like twins," Sable said handing me the photo.

I cannot even describe the feeling I felt when I looked at my son for the first time. I could not stop myself from crying. Tears of joy flowed as I glared at the photo. Then everything started to come back to me. Raphael. He tried to kill me. My tears of joy quickly turned into anger. I almost didn't make it to see my son. I made a decision at that moment that I would stop at nothing until I got my revenge.

Ten months prior I had took the FEDS to trial and beat two counts of brandishing a firearm in relation to a robbery. I was facing thirty years. While the jury was being brought in to announce the verdict my fiancée Michelle, who was then nine months pregnant, water had broke. She went into labor right there in the courtroom. No more than an hour later court resumed and I was acquitted on all charges. I was on my way to the hospital to see my fiancée and son when Raphael, who appeared to be a regular cab driver, pulled out a gun and proceeded to empty his clip out on me. He then pushed me out of the cab on to the street and left me for dead in front of the courthouse.

"Where's Michelle? How come she ain't here?" I inquired after a quick flashback.

"Michelle? She's probably at work. She's fine baby," My mother answered.

"Call and tell her to take off work. I wanna see her. I know she's been going crazy since I've been in here," I stated.

"Isaiah, take it easy. I'm sure Michelle will be here the first chance she gets," my mother responded.

"Well did you at least call her and tell her I'm out of my coma?" I asked with an attitude looking my mom directly in the eyes.

I didn't know what it was but something was definitely wrong. My mother was hiding something from me. I could see it in her eyes.

"Where's Michelle? What happened to her? Don't tell me she's… Don't tell me she's dead!" I shouted sitting up in the bed and snatching the heart monitors off my chest.

BEEEEEEEP! BEEEEEEP! BEEEEEEP!

Suddenly I felt a burning sensation in my chest and it became hard for me to breathe. The last thing I remembered before I lost consciousness was seeing the doctor and the nurse running into the room and then everything went blank.

***

The next day was a good day. My M.R.I. and CAT scan all came back negative. I was taken off the respirator, the I.V. peg tube that fed me, and had my catheter and neck brace removed. But the best part of the day was when my ten-month-old son Isaiah and I laid eyes on each other for the first time.

"Da…Da--," he yelled reaching out for me from my mother's arms.

I was still weak but after hearing my son try to call me daddy, I felt like I could run a marathon.

"No, Isaiah daddy is too weak to hold you right now. Daddy is still sick," my mother explained.

"I'm a'ight ma. Fix my bed so I can sit up," I said.

My mother sat me up on the bed and gently placed my son in my lap.

"What's up handsome? You know who I am?"

"Da…Da…Da…Da--," he responded clapping his small hands together and smiling.

I had never felt more alive in my life. I was so happy and excited that I didn't know what to do. I'd missed the first ten months of my son's life and I vowed to myself that I would never miss another day of his childhood as long as we both lived. I was going to be the father to him that I never had. I was twenty-three years old and considered myself grown a long time ago, but after having a child I felt different. I felt more mature and realized that I had a newfound responsibility.

"So where's Michelle?" I asked an hour later with my son sleep in my arms.

"I'm right here," Michelle, answered standing in the doorway.

"Here give me the baby so you two can talk," my mother said taking the baby out of my arms and walking out of the room.

Michelle looked exactly how I remembered her. Shoulder length hair, deep brown eyes, small gap in her teeth, and some big breasts. To everyone else she was just an average girl but to me there wasn't a woman in the world that could match her beauty. She stood in the doorway staring at me for a few minutes in silence.

"Baby, what's up? Come over here and give ya husband a hug?" I said enthusiastically with my arms outstretched.

"It's not that simple Isaiah. A lot has changed," Michelle, said walking towards me. I could hear her voice cracking and that put me on alert.

At first, I thought I was seeing things. At second glance I thought she just put on some weight but the closer she got the clearer it became.

"I know you ain't pregnant?" I asked already knowing the answer to my own question.

Michelle sat down in the chair closest to my bed and said. "I know it seems crazy Isaiah but I can explain. I didn't plan this…it…just happened."

"What the fuck you mean it just happened? What you just happened to fall on some dick while I was up in here dying!" I yelled sitting up in the bed.

"You're so selfish. You only see things from your end. What about me? What about me Isaiah? What about everything I had to go through?" Michelle asked raising her voice and standing up. "Ask your mother, I was here faithfully every day for months. Every day! You know why you don't have bed sores. Because I washed, you up every day and shaved your face. I even slept here some days. I was going through a lot. First, I lost my father…then my mother…and then all of this happened. I was lonely. The doctors were saying there was a chance you would never wake up. Then I met Darryn."

"Darryn? Who the fuck is Darryn?" I asked gritting my teeth unable to hide the disdain I was feeling.

"You don't know him. He drives trucks and he's from Troy. He's a good man Isaiah. He treats us good. I love him and Isaiah adores him too."

"Don't sit here and tell me about another fucking nigga. I don't give a fuck about him. How you got my son around another nigga? You ain't never give a fuck about me!"

"Don't you dare say that shit to me, you know I loved you. Look at all the things I did for you. I gave you my father's insurance policy money," Michelle was now standing over me screaming.

I cut her off. "What about all the fuckin' shit I did for you? The reason I'm laying in this hospital now is because of you. The reason I got caught up in that case was because of you. You forgot. You forgot that I was trying to get money for ya momz surgery?"

"Isaiah, I love you. I always will. I just moved on. I'm happy. I want you to be happy for me. Darryn just had a house built from the ground up in Ohio. What I wanna ask you-," Michelle tried to ask before I cut her off once again.

"You want my permission to take my son out there?" I asked finishing her sentence.

Michelle shook her head and wiped her eyes.

"Don't cry baby. Come here. It's a'ight come here." I said quietly motioning for her to sit on the bed.

Michelle sat down on the bed next to me. Once she got within arms reach, I put my hands around her neck and started choking the life out of her.

"Listen you triflin' bitch! If you ever try to take my son away from me, I will kill you! You understand me. Huh? You hear me?" I yelled continuing to choke her. "Now get the fuck out of here before I really strangle your stupid ass!" I continued, letting go of her neck and mushing her in the face causing her to fall to the floor.

Michelle remained on the floor for a couple of seconds to regain her breath all the while never taking her eyes off me. From the fear, I saw in her eyes I could tell that she knew I meant every word I said. She picked up her purse and jetted out of my hospital room. When she ran out the room, my mom must have noticed the marks on her neck. She came in immediately.

"Isaiah, what did you do to that girl? I hope you didn't put your hands on her. She's pregnant you know," my mom stated seriously with her arms folded across her chest.

"Mom...please leave. Just go. I don't want any more visitors today. Please just go," I said closing my eyes, trying to catch my breath.

My mom must've known I was heartbroken because she closed the door to my room and left without saying a word.

Heartbroken failed to describe how I was feeling at that moment. Never in a million years did I ever think that Michelle would've left me while I was on my deathbed. I'd never felt more betrayed in my life. Michelle was my heart. After the death of one of my closest homies, Snoop, during a robbery, I had decided to go back to school and play basketball. Right after I regained my scholarship and the first semester was about to start we found out that Michelle's mother needed corrective surgery for a brain aneurism and her insurance wasn't covering it. Being that her father had just recently passed I participated in one last jux to get the money up for the surgery. She was my fiancée and the mother of my unborn child at the time. There was nothing I wouldn't have done for her. I would have died for her and she betrayed me.

Lying in that bed that night I felt a plethora of feelings. I wasn't gonna be Mr. Nice guy anymore. It was all about me and my son. I was out for revenge. Everybody that betrayed me was gonna get dealt with one way or another. I was the last real nigga out of my crew still free and I was gonna take advantage of it. God had let me survive those bullets for a reason. This time I was playing for keeps. I was gonna get rich or die trying. My heart was cold and I had no feelings or emotions left.

Chapter 2

March 03

Tiesha felt like her insides were about to explode. The fire she felt building up in her stomach had her going crazy. She was in heaven. Sweat trickled down her brow and the veins in her neck protruded as she arched her back in ecstasy. She bit down on her lip and kept her eyes closed as she massaged her own chocolate nipple. It seemed like with every second the fire inside her kept building. She wrapped her legs around her lover's neck and began grinding her hips counter clockwise. Her love box was so wet her juices ran down her thick ebony toned thighs and soaked into the mattress. She had been breathing deeply and moaning softly as to not draw any attention but she couldn't hold back anymore.

"Ohhhh! Yes, Re right there mami. Don't stop!" Tiesha cried out.

Ranisha put her palms underneath Tiesha's soft thick coco brown ass and pulled her body closer to her as she continued flicking her tongue up and down her clitoris at a feverish pace. This sent Tiesha even closer to the edge of climaxing. Ranisha spread Tiesha's pussy lips with her index and middle finger and began licking her clit in circular motions. She sucked and licked at Tiesha as if she was the sweetest delicacy that she had ever tasted. She savored her flavor. She even loved the smell of Tiesha.

"Ohh...I'm about to cum baby. I'm about to cum!" Tiesha announced.

After hearing that, Ranisha stuck one finger in Ty's pussy and the other in her ass and began biting on her clit gently. Tiesha came so hard tears came streaming down her face. Her toes curled, her eyes rolled in the back of her head and her whole body convulsed as she released her orgasm. Tiesha had cum many times with men before, but Ranisha was the first person to ever make her achieve a climax. She touched her in all the right spots at all the right times. It was as if Ranisha knew her body better than she knew it herself.

"Damn Re you don't know what you be doing to me, ma." Tiesha replied out of breath pulling Ranisha up from between her legs and sticking her tongue in her mouth.

"Ty, do you really love me like you say you do?" Ranisha asked kissing and sucking Tiesha's neck.

"Re, you know I love you baby. Why would you ask me that?" Tiesha responded.

"I don't want you to forget about me when you go home. Since I've been down, I've heard many promises. All I want is for you to keep it real with me Ty. That's all I ask. If you don't wanna be with me after you get out lem'me know. We can still be friends," Ranisha said seriously looking Tiesha in the eyes.

Tiesha and Ranisha were in their cell at the Woman's Correctional Institution at Danbury in Connecticut. Tiesha was serving a year and a day sentence for perjury because she switched up her testimony to help Ski at his trial. She was to be released the following morning.

Ranisha was Tiesha's cellmate, best friend, and lover. Ranisha was a thirty-one year old lesbian from Brooklyn that was serving a five-year sentence for fraud. Ranisha was attracted to Tiesha from the first day that she saw her. Ranisha was a full-blown lesbian that had never did as much as kiss a man before. She knew she liked girls from the tender age of five. Tiesha on the other hand had never dealt with or been attracted to another woman before Ranisha. But, even a blind person couldn't deny Ranisha's beauty.

Ranisha was a 5' 10" redbone with long sexy legs, firm D cup breasts, and a behind that could cause accidents. She wore her hair in a low Caesar that she dyed blond. She had piercing hazel eyes and her face had an exotic look to it. She could've easily been a high-end runway model if she pursued it. She wasn't what you would call pretty or cute, she was beautiful. Both of her arms were covered with tattoos and she had a black panther tattooed on her left thigh. Her beauty was deceiving though because she was heartless. She would use anything and anyone she could to get whatever she so desired. She'd been in and out of jail since she was a teen. The five-year sentence that she was currently serving was her longest stint in prison and her release date was almost a year to the date of Tiesha's.

"Re, look at me," Tiesha said turning serious sitting up on the bed. "I love you. You, my son, and Ski are all I got. My son is in a foster home and Ski is still in the hospital. Right now, you are all I have. I told you I'mma loyal bitch and I meant it. By the time you come home I'mma have everything set up for us," Tiesha continued.

"I'm sorry boo. I just needed to hear you say that. I don't know what I'm gonna do in here without you. I'm gonna miss you soooo much," Ranisha said laying her head on Tiesha's lap while she cried quietly.

"Baby I'mma write you everyday. And, I know as soon as Ski gets healthy he gonna have a plan for us. Watch…I'mma pick you up in a Benz baby," Tiesha stated with a smile. "Wait till you meet Ski you gonna love him. That's my nigga! When y'all two put y'all heads together it's gonna be a wrap. We gonna be rich!"

"How you know he still gonna wanna do dirt? Didn't you say he's a college type nigga?" Ranisha asked with doubt.

"Trust me Re. If I know Ski the way I think I do that nigga already has a plan and he ain't even out his coma yet," Tiesha responded laughing at her own statement.

"Ty…I got a thousand dollars left on my account. And, I wanna send it to-," Ranisha started to say but got cut off.

"Re, I can't take ya money. It wouldn't be right. You still got a year left. You need it more than I do. I'll be fine, trust me."

"I want you to have it. It's hard out there girl. You don't even have anywhere to go. Ski, ain't even out the hospital. A thousand dollars ain't shit but it's a start." Ranisha explained.

"What about you? What are you gonna do for money?"

"Listen Ty I know how to bid. I've been doing this for a long time. I'll be a'ight. You got a son out there you gotta get back. I ain't taking no for an answer baby."

Seeing that she had no choice Tiesha gave in. "A'ight I'll take it but you gotta let me pay you back."

Ranisha smiled, rolled on top of Tiesha, and kissed her passionately. A few minutes later, she was back in between Tiesha's legs licking and sucking away. An hour later Tiesha was asleep in her arms.

Tiesha loved Ranisha and had every intention on being with her after she went home. But what Ranisha didn't know was that Tiesha had been secretly in love with Ski for years. There wasn't anything she wouldn't do to be with him. He was everything she ever wanted in man. She didn't know Ski's plan or if he even had a plan but finding him was her number one priority. Tiesha was a ride or die chick. There wasn't anything she wasn't ready to do to get rich. With Ski's mind, and Ranisha's skills on the computer, she knew there was no limit to what they could accomplish.

The next morning at 8:30, Tiesha Hilton was released with nothing but fifty dollars, a bus ticket, access to a thousand dollars from Ranisha, and a dream.

She took a deep breath of fresh air, and hopped on the bus to New York. She knew she'd be able to find Ski or hear about his whereabouts once she arrived. With that on her mind, she couldn't wait to get back to The Big Apple.

Chapter 3

July 03

It was 7:30 on a cool summer Friday night in Scranton, Pennsylvania. I hopped out the Cadillac Seville that I had brought for my momz a few years back and walked up the six steps into the house. The neighborhood was so quiet you could hear a mouse piss on cotton. All that could be heard was crickets chirping and the traffic light on the corner switching. Actually the neighborhood sort of reminded me of parts of Long Island where I grew up. I walked up the steps and knocked on the door.

KNOCK! KNOCK! KNOCK!

"Who dat?" a deep voice shouted with force.

"Ski," I answered.

"Ski?" he repeated. "Ski who?"

"Ski. I'm here to see Shaheim. He told me to come through here. Do I got the right crib?"

"Oh, yeah yeah. Hold on. One second."

The dude unlatched what seemed to be a hundred locks and opened the door. When the door finally opened and I saw the lame nigga standing in front of me I realized my plan was gonna be easier to execute than I'd expected it to be.

"What up fam?" The light skin stranger said extending his hand to give me dap. "Shaheim ain't here right now but he should be back in like a half hour. You could wait for him in the living room if you want. You know how to play Madden 03?" he asked.

I could not believe how stupid this joker really was. He'd just invited a stranger into a crack spot without patting me down and then had the nerve to ask me to play a damn video game. It took all the restraint I had not to smile.

I pulled out my Glock 9 and put it to his stomach. "Ayo, how many people up in there wit you nigga?" I whispered directly in his face.

The kid looked like he saw a ghost when I pulled out on him. His legs gave out, and he fell backwards onto the floor. I expected the bitch nigga to be shook but not how he was acting. Dude was acting like a broad so much that he was making me nervous. I didn't know who else was in the crib or if they were gonna, come to the door to see what was taking him so long. I was prepared to body something if I had to but I was hoping that it wouldn't be necessary.

I picked the dude up by his jean shorts, stood him against the wall and closed the door shut. "Listen to me nigga. Get ya-self together. I don't wanna have to kill your bitch ass, but I will if you make me. Just follow my instructions and you and whoever else that's in here will live to see tomorrow. You understand?"

He shook his head up and down several times to let me know he understood.

"Good. Now once again how many other people are inside?"

"It's just...it's just me and my twin brother Smiley. He's...he's...he's in the living room," He stuttered. This nigga was so scared that his bottom lip was actually quivering.

"A'ight good. Let's go. I'm telling you B don't try nuffin' cause I will pop you son," I warned him and put the gun to his back.

I followed him down the hallway.

While we were walking down the hallway, I started to smell a nasty ass odor. At first, I thought duke had passed gas but as we kept walking, I knew it had to be more than that.

"Ayo. I know you ain't shit on ya-self." I asked already knowing the answer to my own question.

"Yeah man. I'm scared yo and I was just about to take a shit before the doorbell rang," he answered.

When we made it to the living room, I saw his brother sitting in front of a flat screen television with a Play Station controller in his lap talking on the phone. The living room was not decked out in the least bit. It only had a cheap ass leather couch on one wall a small coffee table in the middle of the floor, a small flat screen television, and the Play Station. I didn't expect it to be laid out though; after all, it was a crack spot.

"Hang up the muthafuckin' phone right now nigga before I put ya brothers' brains on the wall!" I ordered.

"Smiley do as he says yo. Please! Just listen to him!" his twin brother pleaded.

"Shut the fuck up nigga! Don't talk unless I ask you a question!" I shouted gun butting him in the back of the head. The blow sent him crashing to the floor.

His brother was even more of a bitch than him. He hung up the phone, curled up in a ball, and started sniffling like he was ready to cry. I had no idea what type of hustlers these dudes were supposed to be. They had no heart. Usually if jokers don't show restraint during a jux it makes me take it easy, but for some reason these bitch ass niggaz were getting me madder by the minute.

The two twin brothers looked like they were between 18 to 20 years old. They were short stocky light skin dudes. One had cornrows, and the other had a baldhead. They had the thug look to a tee. If you didn't know them, you would swear they were super thorough.

"Both of ya'll bitch ass niggaz get the fuck up!" I yelled smacking the twin that was acting like he was about to cry in the back of the head. "Get butt ass," I commanded with the wave of my gun. "Take all y'all shit off and throw them in the middle of the room."

They followed my orders and stood in front of me ass naked.

"You…take these and handcuff ya brother to the radiator," I shouted tossing one of the brothers a pair of handcuffs.

After he handcuffed his brother to the radiator, I had him handcuff himself as well.

"Now I'm only gonna ask y'all niggaz one time. Where the fuck is the money and the work at?" I asked calmly.

"It's in the kitchen under the sink dog. We were running low so Shai had to go and re-up. He should be back in a few. If you wait, you can get everything. Just don't kill us."

"Bitch ass nigga!" I yelled in disgust kicking him in the mouth with my size twelve-construction timberland boot. "You ain't waste no time snitchin', huh."

I made my way to the kitchen and found the stash. There was $1200 and what looked to be a half ounce of base bagged up in twenties. I ran back in the living room infuriated.

"Who y'all niggaz think I am? Huh? That's my word if ya'll niggaz don't cough up that bread I'mma make this shit a crime scene!"

"Everything is right there dog. That's all we got. I swear to God man please! Don't kill us! I told you Shaheim just went to re-up. Please man, we telling the truth," one of the twins pleaded.

I believed them because I knew they were scared for their lives. And I was always taught that pressure busts pipes, especially with cowards. I knew they would've given me their mother's address to save their asses. It was because of pussies like them that I almost got twenty years and my manz and 'em was never gonna see the sun again. I got so tight I beat them cats beyond human recognition. I beat them so long I got tired. After an hour of waiting for Shaheim to come back with the work, I kicked back and began playing Madden 03.

By the time Shaheim finally came back to the crib, it was almost 10:00 at night. I made a promise to myself that I was gonna beat him for every minute that he kept me waiting.

I'd met Shaheim about three months prior at a barbershop in Scranton where I was getting my haircut. He was a loud ass, fronting ass dude who drove an Escalade. Every Friday like clockwork, this clown would be at the barbershop when I'd go to get my cut and he'd try to strike up a conversation with me. I ignored him for months but one week I started kicking it with him and he started running off at the mouth about all of his business. He told me how he was getting "crazy paper", how he just opened a spot and how he'd front me some work and whatnot. I took his number and he told me to come through. He had no way of knowing he had made the worst mistake of his life. He practically gave me an invitation to rob him.

Shaheim was a 5'6" cat in his twenties, with a baldhead, and a raspy voice. To me he looked like a bootleg Ja Rule but that's neither here nor there.

When I heard the front door locks being opened, I didn't move a muscle. I kept playing the video game as if I was a regular visitor. I had the twins handcuffed to the radiator in the far right hand corner so Shaheim didn't see them when he first came in.

"Oh shit! My nigga Ski! What's up dawg? I forgot all about you baby. My bad. Why didn't you have Y.B. or Smiley hit me on the horn?" Shaheim asked looking genuinely happy to see me.

"Nah, it's all good my nigga. I know you gotta handle ya B.I," I responded with a fake smile.

"Where them niggaz at anyway?" Shaheim asked nonchalantly putting a duffle bag on the coffee table.

"Oh, them niggaz? Them niggaz tied up in the corner son," I stated just as nonchalant never taking my eyes off the video game.

He let out a nervous laugh, then looked in the corner and saw that the twins were really tied up. His whole facial expression changed. But before he had the chance to re-act or say a word I had the ratchet pointed at his face. I was on him like a cheap suit.

"Oh shit! Yo, Ski what's good wit all this dawg?" Shaheim said looking at the gun and then at me square in the eyes.

"Fuck you mean what's good? You know what it is nigga! I'm trying to eat and it's looking like Thanksgiving in here. Where the work at?" I asked standing up putting two hands on the gun. "Matter of fact, get over there wit them two niggaz and strip! You got a ratchet on you son? You better not have a ratchet on you B."

"Nah…nah. I ain't got no weapon." Shaheim said starting to remove his clothes. After he removed his last piece of clothing, he asked. "Yo, why you doing this to me dawg? I was gonna look out for you man. We could've done business together. C'mon yo, don't do this."

"Lem'me explain the rules to you nigga. You only speak when spoken to. Is that understood?" I asked putting the Glock to his nose. "And, second of all nigga I don't know you and don't give a fuck about you. If you wasn't running around shooting off at the fuckin' mouth you wouldn't be in this situation right now," I explained pushing him to the floor. "Is this everything right here? And, don't lie cause I know you just came back from re-in' up," I continued.

"Everything's right there in the bag dawg. Just take it and go. I got a lil bit more work and cash under the sink…it's yours. Just leave," Shaheim stated.

I opened up the duffel bag and I couldn't believe it.

It looked to be two ounces of hard.

"A'ight son you startin' to try my patience. Where the fuck is the rest at? I'm counting to three. One...two-,"

"That's all I got dawg! I just picked that up. That's a little over two ounces right there, that's all you. Take it. That's what I picked up," Shaheim explained.

"Two ounces? Who the fuck you think you talking to? How the fuck you paying for an Escalade with two ounce money? You gonna make me have to show you that I ain't playing," I said cocking back the hammer.

"I swear to God man. On my son dawg! That's all I got. That Escalade ain't even mine. It's my stepmothers. She lets me hold it on the weekend's man. I ain't getting it like you think son I'm just starting off."

"What happened to all that big money shit you was kicking at the barbershop? Better yet how the fuck was you gonna front me work and you only picking up 2 ounces?"

"I was gonna give you a pack." he answered.

"A pack? Nigga is you stupid. Do you know who the fuck I am?" I shouted smacking him in the face repeatedly with the Glock.

I swear I must have the worst luck in the world. Here it was I'm thinking I got a sweet lick lined up and this cat was broke. I was so infuriated that I started beating on all three of them until I was sweaty. After that, I ransacked the crib looking for anything with value that I could take but there was nothing. That got me even more heated.

I sat back down in the living room trying to decide what I should do to them cats. I didn't feel like they were any threat so killing them was out of the question and I had already beat the shit out of them so I ain't know what to do. Then an idea popped in my head.

"Ayo. You know what? I'mma let ya'll keep the drugs. I'm just gonna take the money." I started to say but got cut off.

"Thank you dawg. Thank you. Thank you." Shaheim shouted out.

"But before I leave here I'mma make y'all niggaz smoke up all this work for wasting my time," I announced with a devilish grin.

"Smoke the work?" I heard one of the twins repeat.

"Yeah, you heard me right nigga. The three of y'all gonna smoke up all this shit tonight. It's y'all choice though. Smoke or die?" I asked.

"We don't smoke crack we blow trees?" The other twin stated matter of factly.

"I don't give a fuck if you smoke incense nigga! Tonight y'all niggaz is smoking crack. Period! Y'all got stems in here? I could've sworn I saw one under the sink."

"We ain't got no stems in here," Shaheim answered.

I went under the kitchen sink and found them just where I remembered seeing them.

"It's only two in here so y'all niggaz gonna have to pass these shits around in a cipha." I said spreading all the work on the coffee table.

I broke all the work down into big New York 50's, uncuffed one hand of each of them and made them all smoke until there was nothing left. In total them bird ass niggaz smoked up more than two and half ounces. They were on the moon. They were like zombies. I walked out of their crib at 7 a.m. the next morning with $1200 dollars, a Play Station 2, three guaranteed customers if and when I got work, and a hell of a story to tell. The whole thing was a waste of time. I was still at ground zero. Something had to give sooner or later and if it was up to me it was gonna be much sooner than later.

Chapter 4

July 03

About a week later, I was doing my daily five-mile jog around my mother's neighborhood in Bartonsville, Pennsylvania. Bartonsville was another small town in PA. It was even smaller than Scranton; the town where I had ran up in them niggaz fake ass crack spot. My mother's neighborhood was the prefect place to hide out. It was thirty-five to forty minutes from Scranton, which happens to be the biggest town in that section of PA. Houses were spaced out miles apart, and there was nothing in the town to do. The only people I saw were the people who lived there. And they were generally old retired white folks.

I'd probably been jogging for only half a mile when I noticed that a car had been slowly tailing me. At first, I thought I was imagining it all on some paranoid type shit, but after I made a couple turns down some streets I normally didn't turn down and the car was still behind me I knew something was up. My mind started moving a million miles per hour and my heartbeat wasn't too far behind it. *"Who could this be? No one even knows I'm up here-," I thought to myself.* Then panic struck. *"Either it's Raphael or them niggaz I just robbed," I reasoned with myself.*

Either way it didn't matter because I knew both parties would be trying to kill me. Call me what you want but after getting shot at point blank range eleven times, I did the only logical thing to do being that I didn't have a burner. I HAULED ASS! I cut through backyards, hopped over fences and ran around houses. Since I didn't know the neighborhood that well I didn't know where I was running, but it didn't matter.

After I was sure that the car that was following me was nowhere in sight, I slowed down and sat on the curb to catch my breath.

Just then, a car came screeching around the corner. When I looked up and saw the car that was following me reappear, my heart fell in my stomach. The car rounded the corner exceeding the speed limit posted for the residential neighborhood coming directly at me. I just knew I was a dead man. I was so tired I couldn't even move. It really didn't make any sense to anyhow since I was only delaying the inevitable.

The black tinted Dodge Neon came to a screeching halt just a few feet before me. When the window rolled down I knew it was a wrap. My body couldn't possibly survive any more bullets. I closed my eyes and turned my head in preparation for my fate. Suddenly I heard a familiar voice call out my name.

"Ski! What's wrong wit you boy? It's me!" Tiesha called out laughing as she unlocked the passenger side door.

I'd never been happier to see a familiar face in my life. Soon after the fear subsided, the embarrassment quickly replaced it and anger followed shortly after.

"What the fuck are you doing chasing me around like you the muthafuckin' police or something?" I asked standing up to get in the car.

"Nobody was chasing you boy. Stop tripping! What you thought? I was gonna kill you or something?" Tiesha asked with a smirk.

"Oh that's funny? That's funny huh? I bet you think this shit is funny too huh?" I yelled taking off my sweat soaked t-shirt to reveal the bullet wounds on my arms, chest, and shoulders.

Tiesha looked at my body in disbelief. I could see the compassion in her face. Her eyes began to get watery.

"Oh my God! Look at what they did to you. I'm so sorry. Are you a'ight?" she asked. Her eyes became wet with tears.

My anger quickly dissipated when I saw her reaction. I knew Ty ain't mean no harm. If it weren't for her, I would've been in the penitentiary somewhere doing football numbers. She had saved my life. She went against her rat ass baby father and testified on my behalf. She was a ride or die chick to the fifth power. I knew she had genuine love for me.

"Ty….Ayo Ty…my bad yo. I'm a'ight. I ain't mean to spazz on you like that. I just been mad high strung lately. I got a lot of shit on my mind right now," I apologized putting my arm around her and kissing her on the forehead as her warm tears ran down my bare chest. "How the fuck did you find me all the way up here anyway? Don't nobody know where I'm at. I never told anybody where I put my momz up at. Lem'me find out you got a lo-jack on a nigga or something," I said trying and succeeding at getting a smile out of Tiesha.

Tiesha wiped her eyes. "You don't even know the half. I've been looking for you for months now."

"Shit I ain't been that hard to find. I was in the same spot, in the same bed in the same hospital for almost a year. How come you ain't come visit me? My momz told me everyone who came by and sent cards and ya name wasn't one of them. What's really good wit that?"

"Nigga I just came home. What you thought, I wasn't gonna get time for that shit I pulled for you at trial?"

"They locked you up? Say word?"

"Word."

"How much time you get?"

"I got a year and a day but I did ten months of it at the Women's Correctional Facility in Danbury. All for ya stinking ass. You lucky I love you boy," Tiesha said proudly.

"Damn, that's crazy! They had my homey on lockdown?" I asked in disbelief then came back with a joke. "So tell me did any of those dikes rape you and fuck you with bananas?"

"Boy is you stupid? I was in there reppin'!" Ty replied flexing her bicep muscles jokingly. "Ain't nobody did nothing to me that I ain't want done. Put it like that. I got a wife that comes home next year but I'll tell you about all that later."

"That's crazy. Lem'me find out."

"Boy you just did."

Hearing that Tiesha was bi-sexual surprised the hell out of me. She never struck me as the type.

Tiesha changed the conversation to a more serious topic. "So do you know who it was that shot you?"

"Remember Raphael?"

She couldn't remember the name. "Raphael? Nah, where he from Long Island?"

"Nah, he from upstate. Candy's older brother." I explained.

"Oh, yeah I know that nigga. What about him?"

"He's the one who shot me." I stated.

"Raphael? That bird ass nigga. He ain't no killer."

"I can't tell. He damn sure seemed like it to me. I was getting money wit that nigga and Candy lied and told that nigga some bullshit and we started beefing. I ended up robbing that nigga. I should've killed him when I had the chance," I said remembering the incident as if it were yesterday pounding my fist for emphasis.

"So where he at? I know you gonna get his ass back for that shit."

"I don't know where that nigga at. Ain't nobody seen or heard from him or Candy since. I'm telling you Ty when I see that nigga it's over. I'm terminating him on sight. I'mma do that nigga dirty."

"I feel you baby. I feel you. But yo let's get from in front of these people house before they call the police on us. I need to sit down somewhere and holla at you about some serious shit," Tiesha replied cutting me off.

"A'ight, come on. We can go to my momz spot," I suggested.

It took us almost twenty minutes but eventually I remembered the way back to my momz house. Tiesha parked in the driveway and we both got out the car and walked to the front door.

When Tiesha got out of the car, I had to do a double take. She was looking like she just jumped off the pages of the XXL magazine Eye Candy of the month. She had on a pair of tight Apple Bottom Capri shorts, a wife beater with no bra, a pair of Jordan's. Her hair was in a ponytail and she sported some big doorknocker earrings with her name in the middle. She was an around the way girl for real.

Tiesha was 5'4" with a cocoa brown complexion, sexy full lips, a tiny waist, an ass fat enough to sit a drink on, and a mean bow legged stance and stride. She sort of looked like a mix between the actress Tichina Arnold who played Pam on the show "Martin", and the rapper Shawna who was down with Disturbing the Peace. Her skin was flawless and had this radiant glow about it and she had gained weight in all the right spots all the while maintaining her flat stomach.

"Damn girl you looking good. What were you eating in there besides pussy," I asked looking her up and down.

"I always looked like this Ski. You just never noticed," Tiesha, answered as if she was pleased I was taking notice of her appearance.

She was right I had never paid her any attention because she was the wifey and baby momz of one of my closest mans. But there was always an undeniable attraction between the two of us. One night she had almost seduced me into sleeping with her while her man was on lockdown. But me being the loyal dude I was I stopped it before anything could happen. But now after her baby's father Rule ratted on me and my peoples she was fair game. If she gave me indication that I could get that pussy I was taking it.

"You ain't looking too bad yourself Ski. That weight you put on looks good on you," Tiesha said rubbing my shoulders.

After I got out of my coma I had lost over twenty-five pounds and as skinny as I was I couldn't afford it. I came out the hospital looking like a Samolian. My doctor had me going to physical therapy and recommended that I exercise as much as possible and I started a vigorous workout regimen. I lifted weights, did calisthenics, and jogged every day. I gained back the twenty-five pounds I lost and added an additional twenty pounds of muscle. I was 6'2" and two hundred pounds solid and in the best shape of my life. I'd always been a fairly decent looking guy, but this exercise had me in the best shape of my life. I was tall, dark skin with a smooth complexion, with brown eyes and high cheekbones. People have told me that I looked like several people from Akon to Morris Chestnut. Personally, I never saw the resemblance to any of them.

Tiesha and I entered the front door of my mother's four-bedroom ranch style house and sat down in the living room. After we flirted with each other for a little while, Tiesha got down to business.

"Ski, listen you know I've always been attracted to you and I wouldn't mind at all if something happened between us, but that's not why I'm here," she said digging in her pocketbook.

She went in her purse and pulled out two chrome 45's and two ski masks and put them on the table.

I was shocked. "What you doing with those? You came up here to rob me?" I asked jokingly putting my hands in the air.

Ty ignored my joke. "Ski, I always respected you because you was always about ya business. You a real nigga, and by now you should know that I'm a real bitch. Remember that night we almost slept together and you told me that if you had a chick like me you'd be a millionaire?"

"Yeah…I think I remember saying something like that."

"Well I always felt the same way. I needed to be with a nigga like you. Rule is the father of my son and I used to love him but I don't respect what he did to y'all. I always knew he wasn't a real mu'fucka."

"So what you trying to say? You trying to be wifey?" I asked with a smile not knowing where she was going with the conversation.

"Ski, I'm not joking. I'm dead serious. I've been thinking about this for a while. I heard what happened between you and Michelle. She's a foul bitch. I'd never do anything like that to you. And no, I don't wanna be your wifey. I wanna be more than that. I wanna be your everything. I wanna be your best friend, your partner, your lover, and someone you know that you can depend on and trust no matter what the situation. I got a plan Ski let's do this," Ty ended. I could see in her eyes she was dead ass serious.

"Lets do what? I don't understand what it is you are asking of me. I'm fucked up right now. I ain't got a pot to piss in. I don't know what I'm gonna do but I know I ain't ready to jump into another relationship. And didn't you say ya wife comes home next year. What about her?"

"I understand and respect that. But we don't need nothing but what is on this table. Nobody ain't never gonna give us nothing. We gotta take what we want…The Ski Mask Way," Tiesha said throwing one of the masks on my lap. "I'm built for this shit Ski. I'm telling you. I'm down for whatever. Don't worry about Ranisha. She knows all about you. She's a real thorough bitch that's about her money and I think she could be a help to us. She's nice with them computers and white-collar crimes. We gonna get paid. I just need you on board with us."

Tiesha had a point. But the reason why I never considered pulling heists again because I didn't have anybody to rock with. My whole team was either in prison, dead or informants. A heist would be a quick and easy way to get on my feet but I had my doubts.

Running in spots sounds easy but it's not. You have to be comfortable and be able to trust the people you go in there with, with your life. And I wasn't sure if Tiesha was ready for that type of pressure.

"Yo, Ty I don't know B. I ain't trying to pull no more heists. That shit is dangerous. The Feds giving out time like party invitations." Tiesha saw right through my excuses.

"Stop frontin' boy! You just don't think I'm ready. And, besides what you gonna do sit up here in the boondocks and work a nine-to-five? Come on Ski that's not even you." She sat down next to me and put her hands on my face. "On some real shit if you just sit out here and let ya life waste away everything that me, Dro, Wise, Boota and Snoop did for you will be in vain. Mu'fuckas gave up their lives and freedom for you. It's too late to be thinking about getting out you already waist deep."

She was bringing up a lot of good points. Dro, Wise and Boota had to go through a lot to help me beat my case. Snoop, my closest homey, took a bullet for me and died from it during a botched robbery and Ty herself did a year in prison for me. She was right. I had no choice. I was knee deep.

"A'ight...I'm wit it. Let's do the damm thing. Gimme a minute to find us a spot. I wanna find something simple so you can get a feel for it. Then depending on how that goes we'll take it from there."

Tiesha smiled from ear to ear, jumped on my lap, and stuck her tongue so far down my throat that I almost gagged on it. Being that I hadn't had sex in over a year my dick was has hard as concrete. It was damn near busting out of my shorts. I rubbed my hands all over her soft skin and almost undressed her right there in the living room.

"Wait. Hold up," I said in between kisses. "We can't do this here. Let's go downstairs," I suggested.

I picked her up in my arms and carried her downstairs to the basement where my room was. Once we entered my bedroom, we were like wild animals. We practically ripped each other clothes off. Neither one of us wanted to make love. We both wanted to fuck.

I threw her on the bed roughly and tore her wife beater off her ripping it in half. As I was doing that, she was pulling my T-shirt over my head. After we were both bare-chested I took off her skin-tight Apple Bottom Capri's along with her panties exposing her neatly trimmed pussy. She was so wet her juices were running down her thighs and I hadn't even touched down there yet.

"Ski, you don't know how long I've been waiting for this," Tiesha whispered as I bit her on the neck while she removed my boxers.

Once my boxers were off and we were both completely naked Tiesha reached in between us and put me inside of her. Her love fit snug around me and was dripping wet. I could tell it felt good to her as well because as soon as I put it in she closed her eyes real tight, bit down on her lip and opened up her mouth real wide. Her thighs were shaking lightly as she moved real slow.

"Oh! Damn baby you got a big dick. You feel so good. I feel you in my stomach. Tiesha moaned grinding her hips in perfect rhythm with me whispering in my ear.

Maybe it was because I hadn't had sex in over a year and some change but that day her pussy was so good it had my eyes watering. I didn't know it then but she hadn't had sex with a man for just as long. She was so wet and tight that I could barely contain myself from being a five-minute man. Fortunately, she beat me to the punch. She began breathing heavily and moaning. Her sex was getting wetter and wetter with every stroke and she was throwing it back at me aggressively. I could feel myself hitting the bottom of her pussy. Her nails dug in my shoulder blades breaking skin and the only sound that could be heard was the squishing of her juices and her screams.

"Ohhh Yes…Yes! Don't stop! Fuck me! Fuck me!" Tiesha shouted as her whole body convulsed. She creamed all over my dick.

Tiesha was one of those women that came hard. Her eyes rolled back in her head and her whole body shook as if she was having an epileptic seizer. After she finished cummin', her pussy was wetter than a swimming pool. She pulled herself on top of me and rode my dick like it had never been ridden before. A lot of women think they know how to ride dick but they really don't. All they know how to do is go straight up and down. Tiesha on the other hand was going up and down; counter clockwise, clockwise and anything else she could think of.

"Sssss…Ummm…Damn that feels good ma," I moaned.

"Yeah? You like that? Cum for me daddy! Cum in this pussy," She whispered in a sexy voice slowing down and grinding on me.

I couldn't hold it. Between the sight of Tiesha's fat ass jiggling, every time she went up and down on my dick and the sound of her ass cheeks slamming down on my thighs I couldn't take it anymore. I let loose inside of her. As I was cumming she gripped my dick with her muscles and squeezed every drop of energy I had in my body as she licked my ear.

"Damn girl, I ain't know you had it like that," I said as she collapsed on my chest.

"Ski, I know you gonna think I'm crazy for saying this but I love you," Tiesha confessed.

"C'mon girl you know I love you too."

"Nah, not like that. I mean…I'm in love with you. I've been for a while Ski. I'll never cross you. I'd take a bullet for you baby," she shot back looking into my eyes and it felt like she meant every word with every fiber of her being.

I didn't know what to say. No one had ever told me some shit like that before. What do you say when someone says they'd die for you? Before I had the chance to think of a response she had my dick in her mouth.

We ended up fucking all day and all night. We substituted sex for food. Our sexual chemistry was off the hook. I just hoped our chemistry would be as good in a heist.

Chapter 5

August 02

"Yo, Ty you a'ight?" I asked from the driver's seat of a stolen Honda Prelude.
She nodded her head nervously up and down.
"Don't worry ma, it's easier than it looks. That feeling you got in the pit of ya stomach is natural. All that is, is anxiety. It's gonna go away as soon as we get inside. Seconds are gonna feel like minutes and minutes are gonna seem like hours. Time is gonna seem like it's moving in slow motion. You gotta stay focused though. Don't move too fast and don't move too slow. You gotta relax," I explained calmly to Tiesha, never taking my eyes off the jewelry store.
Once again, Tiesha didn't respond. She just kept nodding her head and kept her eyes closed. I knew exactly what she was going through. I felt that same anxiety when I went on my first jux years back.
Tiesha and I were in Scranton Pennsylvania, which was about a twenty-five minute drive from my mother's house, outside of Sapp's jewelers.
Sapps jewelers was a small jewelry store on the outskirts of Scranton. On the dimly lit side street there were only two stores. An antique shop that sold old furniture, lamps, vases and other assorted items. They also had an old movie theatre that looked like it hadn't been open since Clinton was president.
It was 5:40 p.m., twenty minutes to closing time. Inside there were two old men who I assumed owned the store and a middle-aged couple with a small child. Back in the days, we would run in a spot if there were twenty customers inside, but since I was unsure about Tiesha I wanted to wait until the customers left. She was gonna have the gun and I was smashing and grabbing and I didn't want her to have to focus on too many people.
The layout of the store was simple. The doors were regular, not

lock bolt doors, meaning they didn't lock from the inside. There were only three-display cases that were positioned to look like the letter "N". The first case to the left when you first entered the store contained women necklaces, earrings and beads. The second display case was where the money was located. It contained twenty-five men and women Rolexes. Everything from Yacht masters, to Presidentials. When I first found out the small store had such an array of watches, it seemed too good to be true. A spot like that in New York would have had better security. These people were acting like it couldn't happen. The third display case had three trays of engagement rings. The store had one camera in the middle of the store that didn't move and no security guard.

My plan was for us to run up in there around closing time and empty out the two display cases with the watches and rings. Tiesha's responsibility was to lay down the two old men in the middle of the store, keep an eye on the door and to keep track of time. One minute. Not a second more and not a second less. The getaway was smooth. All we had to do was make one turn, go through one light and we were on Interstate 81 headed to my mom's house.

"A'ight Ty. The time is now. Let's go," I announced as I watched the family that was in the store drive out the parking lot.

We put our mask's on, pulled our hoodies up and hopped out the car. I was armed with a gym bag and a mallet and she was armed with a chrome Glock 9.

When Tiesha entered the store all the nervousness she was feeling went out the window. She showed me a side of her that I never saw, and I'm sure she didn't even know she had.

"Y'all know what the fuck it is! Put ya fucking hands in the air, bring y'all old asses over here, and lay on the floor with ya hands behind ya heads! If you try something y'all are dead!" Tiesha yelled brandishing her ratchet as she entered the store.

The glass shattered, as I wasted no time smashing and grabbing the goods. I broke both display cases with my mallet and then started emptying them out. I'd done plenty of robberies in my time but that was the first time I was smashing and grabbing. Usually I was the gunman who was responsible for holding everyone and everything down. You wouldn't be able to tell from my performance that I was a rookie at smashing and grabbing though. I was snatching up watches and rings at a dizzying pace. My motivation was not only to make it out of the store with everything but to get out as soon as possible because I didn't trust Tiesha yet.

The two old men nervously walked to the center of the store with their hands up. Both men were in their sixties, with grey hair and wrinkly faces, and looked like they had one foot in the grave. I'm surprised they didn't have a heart attack or a stroke right then. They both wore cheap grey suits and loafers.

"Please don't kill us! Please!" one of the old men pleaded.

Tiesha gun butted him in the face immediately drawing blood from his forehead, and pushed him on to the floor.

"Don't move and don't talk. If you do that, you don't die. You understand me?" Tiesha explained placing her right foot in the center of man's back. "You-," she continued pointing the gun at the other man who was still standing. "Where the cash at?"

"In the back in the safe," the man blurted out.

"Yo, go wit him to the back and get that money!" Tiesha ordered. "I'll get the rings."

I looked at my watch and saw that we had been in the store for only twenty-eight seconds. She was deviating from the plan but we had time so I went with it. I'd already snatched up all of the watches so it would be easy for her to get the rings because they were all on trays. I threw her the duffel bag and walked with the old man to the office.

Once we got in the office, the old man was so nervous his hands were shaking. I knew there was no way he was gonna be able to open the lock in that condition.

Time was ticking. "What's the fucking combination nigga?" I yelled making him flinch.

"11-4-23." he recited.

After I opened the safe, I turned around and punched the man in the jaw knocking him out. The safe was stacked. I grabbed the garbage bag out of the trashcan by the desk, emptied the contents on the floor, and began putting the money in the bag. Just when I finished I heard Tiesha shouting out front. "Hurry up in there, we over our time by ten seconds. Let's go! Let's go!"

When I came back to the front of the store Tiesha had emptied the display case with the rings and had assumed the same position she had when I left. Gun pointed at the door, with her foot in the old mans back.

"You got everything?" I asked.

"Yeah. You?"

"Yeah. Lets' bounce."

I stuck my head outside the door to make sure there were no cops patrolling or surveillance walking by and gave the signal that it was clear.

We ran directly across the street in the now pouring rain and jumped in the whip with me in the driver's seat, and she laid out in the backseat. I made a few turns down some backstreets to where I had my mothers Caddy parked and we removed our masks, hoodies, jeans, boots and gloves then put the dress shoes on that we had stashed in the Caddy. Underneath our gear, we wore all formal clothes as if we were going to a wedding reception. I had on a plain white button up shirt, a pair of khaki pants, and some ugly ass wing tipped shoes. She had on a black strapless dress with four-inch heels. After we were finished dressing we got into my moms whip, this time with Tiesha behind the wheel and cruised to interstate 81 and all the way back to the crib. It was a perfectly executed plan.

Tiesha had impressed me. She showed me that she was a "Go Hard Bitch" for real. I couldn't help but smile as I glanced at her as she drove. We were like Bonnie and Clyde. Seeing her in action turned me on. I could not wait to get her in the crib so I could rip off her clothes.

We made it out with twenty Rolexes, close to sixty engagement rings, and fifty grand in cash. We weren't on yet but it was a start. I knew from that day on that me and her were gonna make a lot of money together.

That night I impressed myself. It was the first time that I had a plan and plotted out a jux by myself. Actually I don't know why I was surprised. I had learned from the best that ever did it.

***

"Ski, you just don't learn do you?" Ernesto said as he checked the clarity of the ice in one of the rings.

"You are a hard headed son of a bitch. I tell you what though you got balls man," Ernesto continued.

"Yo, you know what they say man. Winners never quit, and quitters never win," I said smiling.

"You've got some good shit here man. Real good," Ernesto replied.

I was on Jamaica Avenue in The Coliseum in Queens selling off the jewelry to our old fence Ernesto. Ernesto was a young Iranian dude in his thirties. He was good peoples. He stood about 5'6 with thick bushy eyebrows and a low cut fade like a black man. Ernesto was cool except for when you were doing business with him. He was like the P. Diddy of jewelers. He was as crooked as they came.

"So how much you want for everything?" Ernesto asked.

"What? Come on Nesto. Get off that bullshit man," I said sensing that the bullshit was on the way.

"What are you talking bout man, I asked you a simple question."

"A hundred fifty," I replied.

"Oh, okay. Here you go," Ernesto said. "I'll see you later." He continued pushing all the jewelry towards me.

It was something I went through dozens of times with Ernesto. I go high he goes low; I go higher he goes lower until we finally meet in the middle. It wasn't personal it was business.

"A'ight Ernesto I'm out. I'll get up wit you." I replied taking all of the jewelry and putting it in my bag.

As I was walking out of his office, Ernesto stopped me.

"Ski, I'll give you ninety for everything. That's all I can do," Ernesto lied with his arms outstretched.

"One twenty-five."

"One hundred and ten!" Ernesto shot back.

"Gimme my money you camel jumper," I joked putting the jewelry back on his desk.

After about a twenty minute wait. Ernesto came back with the money in a duffle bag.

"You ain't gotta count it Ski it's all there." Ernesto said as I inspected the bag.

"Yo, Nesto if a penny of my shit is missing. I'mma kill you."

"Why you wanna kill me daddy o'? All I've ever done is made you richer."

"Make me rich my ass. I'm making you rich."

"C'mon Ski let's go to lunch, my treat. It's been a long time," Ernesto suggested.

"I'll take a rain check on that. I gotta get up out of here. I got an appointment in Brooklyn at two," I said giving him dap preparing to leave.

"A'ight Ski, don't be a stranger. Oh, shit! I can't believe I almost forgot to tell you. Guess who came by here a couple weeks ago trying to sell me some watches," Ernesto blurted out.

"Who?"

"Roach."

"You lying," I shot back.

"Swear to God man. I damn near shitted in my pants. I thought he was trying to set me up."

Roach was the brother of my man Boota. He was the first one out of my crew the Feds picked up. He started the domino effect. The Feds didn't have evidence on him or anyone of us but he turned over and told everything he knew to protect his baby mother. Not more than a year and a half ago I watched Roach get on the stand and testify against me at trial. I was the only one that went on trial but he told on Dro, Wise, and his younger brother Boota. Since I had gotten out of my coma, I hadn't paid too much thought into thinking what happened to Roach, Danielle or Rule. Just the sound of Roach's name had my blood boiling.

"What he want?" I asked curiously.

"I told you, he was trying to sell me some watches."

"How many?"

"Only two. You remember his watches? The platinum Presi and the gold Yacht Master. He said something like he was trying to get up some money to get out of town."

"What did you tell him?"

"I told him I was short on cash and that he should come back. But,

I was only giving him the run around. You know I don't fuck wit rats' man."

"So he should be coming back then?" I asked.

"He said he was," Ernesto answered.

"Yo, Nesto if he comes back try to get a number or an address from him but don't tell him it's for me."

"No problem Ski. No problem."

"A'ight, Nesto I'm out. I'mma see you," I said giving him dap again and walking out the office with the duffle bag.

On the way out the door, I could not help but think about what I would do to Roach if I ever found him. He would be a dead man. It didn't matter where we were at, who I was with, or what was going on. I would do him dirty. I know it would not get my man's and them out of the Feds but it damn sure would even the score.

Later on that night about 1 a.m. I was back in P.A. at my mothers' house. I parked in the garage and went straight to my bedroom in the basement. When I came in the room I found Tiesha in the bed.

"What's good ma? I got good news," I announced walking into the room putting my bag down and sitting on the bed. "I got ten grand more than I expected. I got one hundred and ten. All together, that's one hundred and sixty. That's eighty apiece." I continued emptying all the money on to the bed.

She didn't respond or move. When I pulled the cover off her face, her eyes were bloodshot red. I could tell she had been crying.

"Ty, what's wrong? What happened?" I asked concerned.

She rolled over and handed me a picture. It was a picture of her son.

"Ski, I miss him. I try to block it out but I can't. I miss him," Tiesha explained crying.

"I know Ty. I know," I replied kissing her on the forehead.

Like I said earlier Tiesha had a baby by one of my ex-closest mans who rolled over and told as well. During the trial at the last minute Tiesha switched her testimony up to help me but he still ratted. She went to prison for perjury and he went to jail for the robberies, so there was no one to take custody of their child. Their son Amir was staying in a foster home somewhere in New York City.

"Ski, what are we gonna do? I need my baby back. I can't take it anymore," she inquired, her crying became hysterical.

"After this next jux we gonna get a crib somewhere and get a lawyer. You gonna have to get a legal gig for awhile though to make it look official a'ight?"

She nodded her head and within minutes had cried herself asleep in my arms. That night I missed my crew in the worst way. Here it was we had just hit a big score and she was crying. Women were too emotional I thought thinking about how hard my dudes were when they were here.

Chapter 6

September 03

It was a cloudy and breezy fall morning. Due to all the fog, it looked like it was nighttime. The sky looked gloomy as if something bad was on the horizon. And, it was.

Tiesha and I were sitting in a stolen Acura Legend in the parking lot of PNC Bank in Stroudsburg. We were both dressed in men's business suits, Air Force One's, bulletproof vests and ski masks. I decided to go with the suits to give the impression that we were both men so that when we were making our getaway we'd be in the clear because the police would be looking for two males. I can't even front, I was more nervous than I'd ever been before going on a jux. For one, I had never run up in a bank before, and two, I was not sure if Ty was ready for that type of pressure. A jewelry store is one thing but a bank was a whole different ball game. Running in a bank had a lot of variables. Anything can happen at anytime. You gotta deal with one or more armed security guards, a teller possibly pushing the button, electronic lock bolt doors locking you inside and dye packs. Timing was everything.

"Ty, don't try none of that shit you pulled last time. Stick to the muthafuckin' script. You hear me?" I stated from the passenger side of the Acura.

Tiesha was impatient. "Yeah, yeah I know. Let's go already. What we waiting on?"

"Chill it ain't the right time," I shot back quickly. "And turn that fucking radio off. I can't even hear myself think," I replied staring at the bank doors.

The time was 9:30 a.m. Everyday between 9:45 a.m. and 10 a.m. the security guard would go outside for a smoke break. The plan was to apprehend and disarm him outside and walk him into the bank at gunpoint. The only problem was that I was gonna have to run up on him barefaced because if he saw me approaching him with a ski mask on he most likely would draw his gun on me.

While I was outside dealing with him, Ty was to stay in the car and wait for my signal. I had to do it that way because it made no sense to let the security guard see both of our faces and I really didn't want anyone knowing that she was a female. Once we entered the bank I was to announce the robbery and lay everyone face down in the middle of the bank except for the three tellers and the bank manager. Ty's job was to have each teller clean out their drawers watching them closely to make sure they didn't hit the button. After all three tellers were finished, she was to leave the bank and pull the getaway car to the side door where I was to enter the vehicle. The reason for that was that we didn't have a secondary getaway car. We were gonna have to push the stolen Acura all the way from Stroudsburg to my momz crib in Bartonsville.

The security guard came out for his smoke break at 9:51. His timing was perfect. The bank was located on a main street and traffic was generally bumper-to-bumper but at that time the streets were relatively empty. One woman was using the drive thru ATM and she'd been there for a while so she was about to be on her way. "Ty, I'm out. When I give you the signal don't hesitate," I said getting out the car.

"I got you baby," I heard Tiesha promise as I closed the door.

I got out the car carrying the briefcase and wearing my cheap ass Burlington Coat Factory suit, gloves with my ski mask rolled on top of my head like a skully. I had a bullet-proof vest on my chest, a .45 on my waist and a .38 on my back. The nervousness I felt quickly dissipated as soon as I stepped foot out the car.

The tall, lanky white security guard paid me no mind as he saw me approaching. The stupid muthafucka even had the nerve to speak.

"How's it going buddy?" he asked.

"Great," I responded nodding my head in my white friendly voice walking by him. Pausing and turning around I said, "Hey, you wouldn't happen to have a light would ya?"

"Sure," he said checking his left pocket and digging in his right.

By the time he pulled the light out of his right pocket and started to pick his head up to hand it to me I had the .45 jammed into his rib cage. "Don't move pussy!"

The security guard instantly began having a panic attack.

"Please man don't kill me. I got a newborn man. Please," he pleaded raising his hands.

"Put ya muthafuckin' hands down nigga!" I yelled looking around the parking lot and the street to see if anyone had seen us. "Don't make a scene," I said taking the gun off his waist.

"If you try anything you're dead understand?"

He nodded his head.

I gave the signal for Ty to come through, pulled my ski mask down and entered the bank with one gun to the white boys head and the other to his back.

Once in the middle of the floor, I let off one in the air to get everyone's attention. "A'ight y'all know what this is. Don't start nuttin', won't be nuttin'! If the muthafuckin' police trap us inside here I'm letting you know now I'm killing everyone. All I need is sixty seconds of ya time. Follow my orders and you won't get hurt."

Just then Tiesha came running into the bank.

"Everybody besides the tellers and the manager come to me with ya hands up and lay on ya stomachs with ya hands on ya head," I ordered. Seeing that they weren't moving fast enough I yelled. "Quickly! Quickly! I ain't got all fucking day!"

There were only three customers inside the bank. A middle aged black heavyset woman in a pink nursing uniform, a white man a little older than me and a elderly white woman who looked like she was gonna die any minute. Two of the three tellers were old and grey and the third one was a black girl who was probably a few years younger than I was. Besides the three tellers and the bank manager there was only one other employee. A middle-aged white woman who I assumed was a Bank Representative and did not seem to be pose a threat.

PNC Bank was a robbers dream. It was small and compact. When you first entered the bank to your right were two Bank Representative's desk, one of which was empty. The tellers were located to the left and they did not even have bulletproof glasses. You could reach out and touch them with no problem. If you kept walking straight you'd run right in to the safe. To the right of the safe was stairs and if you walked up them they took you straight into the manager's office. The set up made it all too easy.

The four men and women followed my orders and laid down a few feet away from me on their stomachs.

I gun butted the security guard in the back of the head, and pushed him on the floor with the rest of the hostages.

"You three over there; empty ya registers out and pass them to my good friend Mr. Black over there," I said waving my gun in the direction of the tellers. "And, you Mr. Dempsey come here I ain't forget about you. Come here," I yelled over to the Bank manager who was stuck on stupid standing on the stairs.

The old white man with the wrinkled face and hair the color of salt and pepper walked over to me. I thought he was about to have an epileptic seizer. I knew I wasn't gonna get too much restraint from him.

"How you doing this morning John? I don't want no shit out of you. If you follow my instructions, you'll be able to see ya daughter Carolyn graduate from Penn State this summer. If you don't, not only will you die but ya wife Lynne and Carolyn will go with you. Do you want that?" I asked waving the gun around in his face.

He shook his head no. I could tell he was surprised to know that I knew so much about him. While I was staking the bank out, I had Ty follow him home and watch him. We stole his mail and found out everything about him from his daughter's school, his wife's ovarian cancer and his fetish for underage porn.

"Take this briefcase and fill it up with nuffin' but big bills from the safe and make it quick," I ordered putting the briefcase in his hands.

The manager wasted no time in following my orders. He was in the safe in a matter of seconds. Meanwhile, the tellers had finished emptying their drawers and were handing the money over to Tiesha. After she received the money from the last teller, I ordered the three female tellers to the middle of the bank floor and told them to lay down with everyone else.

"What's the time Mr. Black?" I asked Tiesha.

"Fifty-eight seconds Mr. Brown," Ty responded in a deep male sounding voice.

Just then two people entered the bank; a white man in his mid-thirties and a white girl in her mid-twenties. When the man walked in he didn't know what was going on until the girl screamed. Tiesha turned around and put the gun on him immediately. The man grabbed her hand and looked like he was about to take the gun when shots rang out.

At first, I could not see who had been hit but when the white man's body slumped to the ground, I took a deep sigh of relief.

"AHHHHH!" the young white girl screamed running out the bank.

Ty tried to grab her but she was too late. The woman was out.

"Mr. Black get the car. I'll be out in a few," I told Ty.

By the time Tiesha ran outside, the bank was in chaos. Women were crying, the men were fidgeting and the man that she had shot was dying in front of our eyes.

I let off three shots.

"Everybody shut the fuck up! Next nigga who makes a sound is dead!" I yelled calming everyone down.

The bank manager came out seconds later and handed me the briefcase.

"Get on the floor. Nobody move while I make my way out!" I screamed locking the bank.

When I made it outside it was really pandemonium. Sirens could be heard in the distance, traffic was backed up on Main Avenue staring at the bank and there were at least ten spectators in the bank parking lot. I hopped in the whip and Tiesha sped off like a bat out of hell. The sirens seemed like they were getting closer and closer. My mind was racing. There was no way we were gonna make it all the way to my mother's house in a stolen car. There were too many witnesses that saw us. I knew the police would have the make and color of our car in matter of minutes. As we were making our way to the parkway, I was stripping out of my suit replacing it with jeans and t-shirt. We passed by a bus terminal when an idea shot through my head.

"Make a right down the next block Ty," I said still breathing heavy. "Pull over."

I had Tiesha change out of the suit she had and slid into a long flower patterned grandma dress.

"Take the money and walk around the corner to the bus terminal and take the bus to Port Authority."

"What? What are you gonna do? I ain't leaving you," Tiesha responded.

"Ty, just do it! This ain't the time to be fucking arguing wit me! Do it!" I yelled.

Her eyes began to water. She kissed me on the cheek and got out the car with the money.

I dumped the car a few miles away and took off on foot. I strolled casually down the street as the police cars zoomed pass me in pursuit. After about fifteen minutes of walking, I saw a sign that read East Stroudsburg University. I followed the signs and was walking around campus like a regular student. I sat in the cafeteria for a while, and then called my mother to pick me up. I made it to my mother's house at about 1:30 that afternoon. The plan didn't go as smooth as I planned but we had gotten away and that was the most important part. What we got away with, I didn't know. But I knew it had to be a nice piece of change.

Chapter 7

November 03

My Tupac ringtone "Never Had A Friend Like Me" woke me up out of my sleep.

"This is a pre-paid call from an inmate at a Federal Prison. You will not be charged for this call. This call is from- Boota. To accept this call press five. To decline this call press seven or hang up. To block calls from this caller press seven-seven." the automated voice stated.

I pressed five. "Yo, what's popping my dude?" I asked excitedly as soon as the phone connected us.

"Geese neck what's crackin?" Boota said jokingly.

"Yo, I know you ain't tryna snap? I got them pictures y'all niggaz sent. I see you slimming down and toning that shit up," I replied.

"Yeah, you see me son. My shit getting right," Boota said proudly.

"What you gonna do about that Big Benjamin Franklin face you got? They got exercises for big faces B. I'mma get you a subscription to Big Face Magazine. Every time I spend a new hundred I think about ya big face nigga!" I said snapping back.

Boota started laughing.

"Yo, you still use ya neck as a stash spot?" he shot back.

"You still using that crooked front tooth to open up can food?" I asked laughing at my own joke.

It felt like old times. Boota was one of my best friends since Junior High. Him and two of my closest mans were all doing time at Lewisburg penitentiary. Boota and Wise each had thirty years and Dro had life. We all went way back. From playing freeze tag on playgrounds to becoming one of the best, stick up crews in recent memory. Originally, it was five of us up until Snoop's death. When I went to trial Dro, Wise and Boota faked the District Attorney out into thinking they were gonna testify against me but went up there and exonerated me. I loved them niggaz. There wasn't a thing in the world I wouldn't do for any of them. I felt incomplete out on the streets without my dudes.

"What's good though son? Y'all a'ight in there?" I asked seriously.

"I'm good. We maintaining. We soldiers my dude. This shit ain't really nuffin'. It's just like the streets. Only the strong survive. If I could see my kids more and get pussy once a month I wouldn't even care," Boota explained.

"You crazy son. They ain't got conjugal visits?"

"Nah, the Feds ain't got trailers, only the state. I'm in here feeling like a bird ass nigga beating my dick to magazines," Boota replied.

"Fuck all that though. What up wit you? You takin' advantage of your freedom or what?"

"Nigga you knows' this! Y'all niggaz would be proud of me. Yo, y'all got that paper I sent?"

"Yeah good looking."

"I got subscriptions to the Source, XXL, King, Smooth, Essence, Ebony, Jet and Straight Stuntin magazine for each one of y'all niggaz. They should be on the way any day now."

"A'ight. I'll be on the look out for them. You must be doing it real big out there. You put a lot of bread on niggaz books B."

"Son, that wasn't nuffin. Trust me. I got it poppin' out here. Shit is crazy B. I wish y'all niggaz was here to enjoy it with me," I responded.

"You be seeing any of my old bitches?"

"Nah, son. I just moved back to New York a couple months ago. I was in PA. I haven't been around the way like that. I'm on some low shit."

"Ayo, how's ya lil man?"

"He's chillin' son. I got him and Tiesha's son wit me right now. I'm about to take them to Chucky Cheese."

"Tiesha? What Tiesha? Not that rat ass nigga Rule's seed? Son, I know you ain't out there fucking wit Rule after all this?" Boota asked angrily.

"Nigga is you stupid? When I catch Rule that nigga is-," I paused realizing that our call was being taped. "C'mon you should know better than that. Rule ain't even home yet. I still fuck wit Ty though. She's a rider," I explained.

"You beating that?" Boota asked starting to laugh. "That's my nigga! Bust in her face, take some pictures and send it to me. Send some panty shots too. That bitch had the fat ass."

"Nah son you buggin', I can't do that."

"I know you ain't wife that bitch up?"

"It's a long story but shorty is on the team. I'll explain it to you when I come up there."

"Oh, yeah son. I almost forgot. I need you to bring Shamika and the kids up here to see me on Thanksgiving."

"I'm supposed to go to mom dukes crib but I'll give her the money to get up there," I explained.

"Nah, I need you to come up here. I got something very important to tell you. Something real important that I can't talk about over the horn," Boota was saying but got cut off.

"This is a call from a Federal Prison." the automated voice stated.

"Yo, I only got a minute left. Wise wants you to bring his chick up here. Store this number in ya phone, 516-555-1796. Her name is Pam. Call her and tell her you bringing her up."

"A'ight I got it," I said saving it into my phone.

"Ski, don't bullshit. This is important. It can't wait. Don't miss this visit son," Boota said seriously.

"Say no more my nigga, I'm there."

"A'ight. One."

"One," I responded hanging up my cell phone.

I had no clue what could be so important that Boota couldn't wait to after the holidays. But, whatever it was I knew it was important. There was no way I was gonna miss that visit. Not because I had to or because I felt obligated to, but because I wanted to. I loved my niggaz. There was nothing I wouldn't do for them, and I knew there was nothing they wouldn't do for me.

The past few months' life had been good to me. Tiesha and I made it out the bank with one hundred and seventy-five grand in cash. The man that Tiesha shot in the bank died and the police were on the hunt. It was a bank so you know the Feds were automatically on the case. That area in PA had never seen anything like that before and it was front page on the paper and top story on all the local new channels. The police had a sketch of me from the security guard but it was nothing remotely resembling me. My plan also worked, the Feds believed that two men had robbed the bank. We were in the clear but I decided it would be best to pack up and get out of dodge. We moved back to New York into a three-bedroom townhouse in Bayside, Queens. Between the first and the second jux we had almost three-hundred grand combined.

Tiesha was working on Jamaica Avenue in Queens at a clothing store named S & D's as a front for BCW because she had just gotten custody of her three-year-old son Amir. Ty was ecstatic. I was on the grind. I had three more juxes planned for after the New Year. I had money but I wasn't comfortable. I didn't buy any jewelry or clothes. The only thing I spent money on was the house and a 2000 745i BMW that I used.

As I pulled into the driveway of our house, I sat there for a while thinking about Dro, Boota, Wise and Snoop. I was getting money, fucking broads and partying, but it wasn't the same. Things were never gonna be the same.

***

Thanksgiving Day 2003

When we pulled up to Lewisburg Penitentiary in PA, I got the chills. I knew I could've easily been there with them if things turned out different. Lewisburg didn't even look like a prison. It looked like a big ass castle. If it wasn't for the huge wall surrounding it, you wouldn't even have known what the building was. The only thing that shit was missing was a draw bridge. It looked scary as a muthfucka, like vampires or something lived up in there.

I parked the car in the lot that read visitor parking only. It was me, Boota's baby mother Shamika and their two kids, my eighteen month old son Isaiah and a petite light skin girl named Pam that was coming to see Wise.

I was surprised that they hadn't searched us more thoroughly. They didn't pat us down or anything. All we had to do was walk around one punk ass metal detector.

The visiting room was a large room with square metal tables, vending machines, a background on the wall where you could take pictures at and an officer's station with three C.O.'s watching our every move like hawks.

Dro, Boota and Wise came down at the same time. They were all wearing blue jumpsuits that were freshly ironed and sneakers. They also all looked healthy and well rested. Besides having their weight up, they had this glow to them that I can't really explain. After we all exchanged daps and hugs everybody sat down with their visitors. Me and my son with Dro, Shamika and the kids with Boota and Pam with Wise. Since we were all not allowed to sit at one table, we sat at three tables close to one another so we could all talk.

"Yo, look at ya man Ski. Nigga got his weight up!" Wise exclaimed.

"Yeah, no bullshit, all he need now is a neck reduction." Boota said starting up already.

"I know you ain't tryna snap with that big ass garage nose you got. It look like you can sniff up a eight ball of hard nigga!" I snapped back.

"You ol' go-go gadget neck. Telescope neck, Akon in the face nigga. I know you don't think you can fuck wit me in snapping. I've been doing you dirty for years," Boota responded.

Everybody started dying laughing but my man Dro was laughing extra hard.

"Yo, Dro that shit wasn't that funny nigga. Wit that big ass head you got. It looks like you got a fucking brain tumor nigga. Ya head looks severely swollen B. Word to mother," I stated laughing as everyone followed suit.

"Wise, what you laughing at?" Dro asked with a smirk.

"I'm laughing at you, you big coconut head ass nigga!" Wise replied laughing so hard that his face was turning red.

One thing about us was we loved to snap on each other. If you couldn't take a joke around my way, you might as well stay in the house. Jokers would focus on your one flaw and make a million jokes off it. Niggaz was always snapping on me about my long neck. Everyone was good sports for the most part but every now and then someone would really get mad and all that would do is make niggaz snap on him more.

"C'mon B. Enough with the jokes I ain't in the mood for that shit today," Dro said getting salty because everyone was laughing at him.

"Niggaz don't give a fuck if you ain't in the mood nigga! You ain't scaring nobody but the kids. You ol' medicine ball head ass nigga. Wit a head like that you should be able to read niggaz minds," Boota added laughing at his own joke and getting a laugh out of everyone including Dro.

Boota hadn't changed one bit. He was dark skin with a baldhead and in the face he and Shaquille O'Neal could've passed for twins. He stood 6'4 and weighed over 250 pounds. He was a big funny nigga. When you were around him you always had to stay on your toes because he was always trying to clown somebody. I was amazed that they all were in such good spirits and able to laugh being in the predicament that they were in.

"Yo, ya lil man looks just like you B." Dro said smiling at my son.

"Word. Let's just hope he don't end up having a long neck like his daddy," Boota joked.

I began to introduce my son to the crew. "Isaiah-the light skinned Christopher Williams/Al B. Sure looking nigga over there is ya Uncle Wise, the big face African looking one over there is ya Uncle Boota and this big coconut head nigga in front of you is ya Uncle Dro. Say hi."

"Whuz up!" Isaiah said waving at them and putting his head in my chest shyly.

Everyone laughed.

"I know he ain't just say what's up," Dro asked.

"Yeah you heard him. My son is smart as hell," I said proudly.

"I heard about Michelle," Dro whispered.

"Yeah you know how it goes. Bitches ain't shit," I stated nonchalantly. "What up wit Danielle? You heard from her?"

Danielle was Dro's wifey since junior high. She was down with our crew too. She was far from being a hood chick though. She was a upper class white acting Puerto-Rican that Dro turned on to the street life. She was the one that Dro sent inside the jewelry stores to find out what they had and where it was located. She eventually graduated to get-a-way driving and once Dro even took her on a jux with him. When the Feds came knocking Danielle told everything she knew. Her testimony at my trial by itself almost got me convicted. We all expected her to tell but the worst thing she did was get married to her so called best friend Jamal. That was the cherry on top of it all.

"Nah, I ain't heard nuffin from her B. I know she's on the street though," Dro explained with a sad look on his face. All of the sudden he switched the conversation up. "Yo, you ever find out who it was that tried to pop ya top?"

"Yeah, I know exactly who it was. Remember that Dominican nigga I use to get money wit upstate named Raphael?" I asked.

Dro was more than surprised. "Hold up. That's the nigga that shot you B? That bitch ass nigga?"

"Son was playing for keeps. He wasn't bullshitting at all my nigga," I stated lifting up my shirt to show him my scars.

"Damn son," Wise responded shaking his head.

"Right after they read the verdict I hopped in a cab to go see him," I said pointing to my son. "And the nigga was the cab driver. He turned around dumping and then pushed me out the cab and took the fuck off," I explained.

"Where is this nigga at now?" Boota asked.

"Hell if I know. He's hiding somewhere. But if I catch him or his stinkin' ass sister I'm giving them straight face shots," I promised.

We all continued to catch up and talked in a group for almost two hours. After that, Boota focused on his kids and Shamika, Wise focused on Pam and I was telling Dro about what I had been doing on the streets.

Dro shook his giant head in disbelief. "Ty going hard like that? Damn B!"

"Yeah shorty go hard," I assured him.

"You fucking her?"

I didn't answer.

"You dirty muthafucker. You fucking her ain't you?" Dro replied giving me dap and laughing. "So how's the pussy?"

"The pussy is blazing son. She gets it in for real for real. She in love wit ya boy and all that. She be getting her little attitudes when I be coming home with other broads."

"Damn my nigga. You living it up out there. What up wit that rat ass nigga Rule?"

"He's still locked up. But as much as he was telling he should be on his way home soon. Ty don't communicate wit him at all though."

"You could use Ty to find out where he's at when he touches down. You know he gonna come home looking for his bitch and his seed," Dro explained.

"Word," I agreed shaking my head.

"And speaking of rats, here," Dro replied handing me a piece of paper he took out of his sneaker.

I was dumbfounded. "What's this?"

"That's this address to this Dread out in Philly that Boota pops is cool wit. Roach staying out in Philly now. That Dread is gonna help you find him. You know Boota's pops is a gangsta. He don't respect or tolerate ratting. Only reason he not handling it himself is because it's his child. That's why we wanted you to come up here today. We need you to go up there and handle this nigga before he relocates again and we lose him for good. You wit it?" Dro asked.

I was definitely down. "What kind of question is that?"

"A'ight listen up B. The number on that paper is to a Dread named Prince. Call Prince and he'll set you up wit everything you need. He's a good nigga B. You can trust him." Dro clarified.

"Visiting hours are now over. All inmates report to the officer's station to retrieve your I. D.'s" the C.O. announced.

"Consider this shit done my nigga," I assured Dro as we exchanged daps.

"Be careful B. You know Roach plays wit guns so be smart," Dro whispered.

I nodded my head and gave Wise and Boota daps and hugs and waited for the C.O. to escort us out the visiting room. When I looked over at my boys I saw the sadness in their faces for the first time. My eyes started getting so watery that I had to turn away to keep from shedding tears. I wanted to get them the fuck out of that hell hole and bring them back to the hood with me where they belonged, but I couldn't. The sadness I felt in my heart that day slowly turned into anger. All I could think about was revenge. Killing Roach wasn't gonna get my niggaz out the Penn no sooner but it sure was gonna make me feel a whole lot better. Wherever he was he was a dead man walking and he didn't even know it.

Chapter 8

December 03

"Shakedown! Shakedown! Everybody outside the housing unit! Hurry up! Let's go! Let's go!" I heard a voice calling out.

Initially I thought I was dreaming but when I pinched myself and I was still awake I knew I wasn't. I glanced over at the alarm clock on the side of my bed and saw that it was fifteen minutes after 8:00 in the morning. I didn't know what the fuck was going on and truthfully I didn't care. I was tired as hell. I put the covers over my head and went back to sleep.

A couple of minutes later, Prince's three-year-old daughter came running into my room tapping my bed.

"Shakedown Mr. Ski. Hurry up before my daddy writes you a shot," she said running out the room.

I was in a daze. I had no idea what the fuck was going on. Soon after his daughter left my room, Prince came in himself.

"Shakedown! Shakedown! Put ya shoes on and go to the back of the building!" Prince shouted pulling the covers off me.

"What? What is you talking bout B? Do you know what time it is?" I responded still half sleep.

"I ain't gonna tell you again son. Get ya ass up and exit the housing unit. Shakedown!" Prince said forcefully.

I didn't know what the hell he was talking about but I knew that whatever it was he was dead serious about it, and after all it was his house. If he wanted me to go outside I was gonna have to go outside.

I got up and tried to go in my duffel bag to get some clothes to throw on but he stopped me.

"No time for that now! Just put ya shoes on and step outside!" Prince ordered.

When I put my sneakers on, he had me put my hands against the wall and patted me down. When he was finished his search and was sure I had nothing on me he sent me outside with his wife, three-year-old daughter, live in maid and eighty year old mother.

It felt like I was in Alaska when I stepped outside. It couldn't have been no more than twenty degrees outside and this negro had me outside in nothing but a t-shirt, boxers and a pair of sneakers. Prince's wife, a modest looking woman in her early forties, saw me shivering and gave me her leather jacket to wear.

"What's going on in there?" I asked still shivering.

"Routine shakedown. He does these about once a month. If he doesn't find anything he'll be done in a half hour." Prince's wife replied as if what was going on was completely normal.

I was staying in a suburb just outside of Philly called Sheltonham Township on Old York Road in a five-bedroom Colonial style house with Boota's father's childhood friend Prince. Prince was a 6'6", 250-pound Jamaican giant who had dreadlocks down to his back. He had just come home from doing a twenty-year Federal bid for drug trafficking and conspiracy. When he got locked up he was eighteen years old and he didn't come home until he was thirty-eight. At that time he'd been home a little over five years and was forty-three but looked to be ten years younger. Prison preserved him in a major way. But, it also left some lasting effects on him. To say that this man was institutionalized was an understatement. He actually ran his household as if it was a prison. He did counts, inspections, ate all of his food off of trays and didn't allow anyone to leave their rooms after 11 p.m. or talk on the phone for more than fifteen minutes at a time. He even had everyone in his house submit visiting forms and telephone lists for their friends. He had a law library and constantly referred to his house as "The Compound". He was burnt the fuck out for real. I had only been in jail for a few months during my trial but being in his crib made me feel like I was doing a bid in the Feds. I don't know how his wife put up with him.

I was mad that I was outside in the freezing cold half-naked, but I realized that Prince didn't discriminate when I saw that he had his eighty year old mother outside in nothing but her nightgown. He didn't bend his rules for anyone.

After about forty-five minutes, he came out and announced that the shakedown was over. When I got to my room, Prince was inside waiting for me.

"Report to the lieutenant's office in ten minutes, and don't be late," was all he said to me before he walked off.

"Lieutenants office? Oh, a'ight. Whatever, I'll be there in a minute. Lemme just throw some clothes on and brush my teeth," I responded.

Fifteen minutes later I was in a room with a desk and two chairs that Prince called the Lieutenants office. He sat across from me staring at me in the eyes without saying a word. He was starting to make me feel nervous. I knew that nigga was a couple fries short of a happy meal so I ain't know what to expect. With niggaz like him, you never knew. For all I knew he was about to kill me.

I had to break the silence. "Yo, Prince what's good B? I know you ain't call me down here to stare at me. What up?" Holla at me," I said nervously.

"Listen up youngin'. I agreed to let you stay here because Brooksy told me to take care of you. This right here is my compound ya understand? I'm the Warden, Captain, Lieutenant and Ruler of this compound. Don't nothing get pass me up in here." Prince was so close to me I could smile the toothpaste still on his breath.

He pulled out a plastic bag and pulled out my two .45's. "I found contraband in ya room. Do you know anything about these?" he asked showing me the guns. "Why you bring these weapons inside of my house? Do you know you are endangering the security of my compound?"

"C'mon Dread you wildin'. You know what I came here to do. How else would I push this niggaz shit back if I ain't got no hammers?" I shot back.

"Brooksy knows how I run my compound. He didn't tell you that I said not to bring anything?"

"Yeah, but he ain't say not to bring no heaters. How else am I supposed to do what I gotta do?" I repeated again.

"I got everything you need right here. Come here lemme show ya something," Prince said taking me to the corner of the room.

Once there, he pressed a button underneath his desk causing the wall to turn counter clockwise revealing a arsenal of weapons. He had Techs, shotguns, M-16's, Glocks, 38's, 357's, bullet-proof vests and even grenades. I was impressed. I'd never saw no shit like that except for in the movies.

"See youngin' I got everything you need right here," Prince replied proudly.

"Word. You wasn't bullshitting," I stated picking up an M-16.

"You like that? You probably don't even know what to do wit that," Prince smirked.

"Yeah. A'ight. I'mma show you how I get down. You'll see."

I put the M-16 back on the shelf, he closed the wall back and we went and sat back down at his desk.

"You know Ski. I like you man and I don't like many people. I'm a good judge of character. I have run into every type of blood clot nigga there is in my years. Brooksy told me all about you."

"Brooksy told me all about you too. I respect you and ya household. I would never do nuffin' to disrespect you or ya rules. The whole thing was a misunderstanding."

"Misunderstanding," Prince, repeated rubbing his chin. "Yeah, I like that youngin'. I'm gonna throw out ya shot. This one is on me. I'mma keep the guns until you leave. I can't have guns laying around my house. I have a three-year old. You know Ski. A lot of people think I'm crazy but every successful society needs rules and regulations. And, these are mine. You don't think I'm crazy do you?" He asked.

In my mind I was thinking HELL YEAH! But I played it off. "Crazy? Who? You? Nah, you ain't crazy. Far from it," I lied.

"Okay good. Get some rest. I got my people bringing in that rat tonight. Tonight is the night."

"Word? Yeah, that's what's up!"

"I'll tell you the details after chow," Prince said standing up to shake my hand. "I'm glad all this worked out. I would've hated to have to put you in the hole."

That last comment threw me off a little bit but I let it ride. I was just happy that I could finally take care of business and get the fuck away from that crazy nigga. I was starting to think that I was gonna have to do him in.

***

Later that same night I was in a Jamaican club called the Upper Deck Lounge in Germantown in between Germantown Avenue, and Shelton. The Upper Deck Lounge was a straight death trap. There was only one way in and one way out. The club was located on a main strip on the top floor of a two-story building. On the bottom of the Upper Deck Lounge was a bar. Right next-door was Vernon Park and across the street was strip mall that housed a supermarket, clothing store, and a jewelry store. Regardless if I shot Roach in the club or outside it, it was gonna be in front of an audience, and I was gonna make it a show worth watching. I took two 357's from Prince filled with hollow tips, and had on a bulletproof Kevlar vest. I was ready for whatever.

Since Prince was a known face in Philly, he couldn't come in the club with me but he agreed to be my getaway driver. Truthfully, I think the sick muthafucker just wanted to watch the murder game get put down though.

Besides Prince running his crib like a penitentiary, he was a cool nigga. Boota's father Brooksy told me all about him. Prince and Brooksy were both part of a Jamaican crew called the Echo posse. The Echo posse was legendary. In the eighties, they were killing up everything on the East Coast from Philly to Brooklyn. Prince got knocked off when he was only eighteen but his name still rang bells. In his day, he was a hit man for the echo posse. He had only been home five years but the story was that he had already made 10 million dollars. He had spots in East Germantown, Summerville, West Philly, and in Brooklyn. He sold everything from dope to ecstasy. He was definitely a powerful man and I knew I could use his friendship. I just needed a way in. He wasn't the type of nigga who you could just step to and ask for work if you know what I mean.

I had been in the Upper Deck Lounge for more than an hour and I still had not seen Roach. Roach was running with some young Jamaican crew and Prince got the word that they would be at the Lounge so I just waited patiently.

Finally, my patience paid off. At about 1:00 in the morning, I spotted him. Roach was up stairs in the V.I.P. grinding on some Jamaican girl with one of the hottest short haircuts that I had seen in a long time. Roach still looked the same. Medium height, medium built, brown skin, with the same small afro. He was really a regular nigga. He had no features that made him stand out in a crowd and that was always something he used to his advantage. Just the sight of him infuriated me. His mustache looked like whiskers, and when I saw him all I saw was Dro, Wise and Boota's sad eyes staring at me as I left the visiting room. I decided right then and there that I was gonna do him outside so I could run down the alley and make it to the get-a-way car.

I exited the lounge and chilled outside smoking cigarettes and talking to broads for close to an hour before he finally came out. Roach had on a N.B.A. leather coat, jeans and timberland boots. He was rocking Boota's Cuban link with the Virgo sign hanging from it and what looked to be a Rolex on his wrist. I recognized the chain instantly because I was there the night that he won it from Boota at a dice game on our block.

Outside the lounge was crowded as hell. Niggaz were parked up flossing their whips trying to holla at all the women, other niggaz were posted up chillin' smoking trees and women were everywhere. None of the scenery made a difference to me because I didn't know any of them people and they didn't know me. If it was up to me that was gonna be the last time I ever came to Philly again.

I was posted up on the corner when Roach came out with his little entourage. I don't know if he was drunk or what but he strolled pass me like he never saw me a day in his life.

I walked up behind him and tapped him on the shoulder. When he turned around and our eyes met, I saw the fear of God in his pupils. I'd never saw so much fear in someone's eyes before and I loved every second of it. I pulled out my two 357's and started dumping in his face. My first shot hit him directly in the eye. His eyeball popped out of the socket and blood squirted all over my face and shirt. The next shot landed in the side of his head and the impact of the bullet spun his body around. The wound that the shot created was so large I could have placed my hand inside of it. I continued shooting at him with reckless abandonment hitting him with all face shots. Roach's head barely remained on his shoulders. His brains flew all on the side of the building, on me and the sidewalk. His body crashed to the ground with a loud thud.

The block was in an up roar. Car alarms were going off, women were screaming, niggaz were running. It was pure pandemonium. I stood over Roach's lifeless body and fired one more shot in his face.

"I never liked ya bitch ass!" I stated spitting in his mutilated face.

His face didn't even look human. It looked like burnt pizza cheese. I grabbed Boota's chain off his neck and darted down the alley to where Prince had the getaway car parked. When I got there, Prince already had the passenger side door open for me. He started to peel before I had the door closed.

"Blood clot! Mi neva know yuh so dangerous! Boi yuh jus lick down da man star! You cold!" Prince shouted excitedly in his native West Indian tongue.

"I told you I was gonna show you how I get down. I told you!" I responded out of breath with my adrenaline pumping.

"A man like yu me wan pun side me. Mi respect dat. Wait tu mi tell mi bredren bout yuh. Yuh wicked my youth. When mi first see yuh I check seh you couldn't handle dat job deh. But now mi see it. Yuh a dangerous mon!" Prince continued giving me praise.

I can't even front I surprised myself that night. I'd killed before but it was nothing compared to what I'd just done. What I did that night is what you see gangsters do in the movies. It was some straight cold blooded shit. And the illest thing about it was that I didn't feel any remorse. It was the first time I'd killed and actually enjoyed it. I didn't know it then but that night was the night that changed my life forever. There was no turning back. I was who I was.

One thing I noticed on the ride back was the newfound respect and admiration Prince had for me. I knew he was excited because it was the first time I had heard him speak in his natural Jamaican accent since I'd gotten to his house two weeks ago. The whole ride back he kept glancing over at me with a sick grin while he rubbed his chin. It was the right thing to do, and I felt proud of myself. It was truly my pleasure.

We pulled up to Prince's mini mansion at about a quarter after 4:00

in the morning. I was still pumped with adrenaline and I knew I wouldn't be able to sleep so I decided it would be best to leave then.

"Ayo, Prince. Thanks for ya hospitality man. I appreciate that yo. You a real nigga B, but I think I'mma slide out tonight. Get back home na'mean?" I said.

"For what? Nah, mon yuh release date from the compound isn't till tomorrow," Prince replied.

I gave a faint smile but when I looked at Prince and saw he was dead serious I realized there was no use fighting it.

"Yeah big Dread I guess you right," I stated beginning to get out the car.

"Mi know it. Before yuh release mi hafi cook mek yuh a big meal. Seen! Yuh like dat? Some goat meat, some red snapper, and curry chicken. Yuh 'ere mi say?" Prince stated in patoise.

I wasn't half as excited as he was. "Yeah. That sounds good. I'mma take it down now big Dread . I'll see you in the afternoon," I responded giving him dap and making my way into my room.

That night I went to sleep as soon as my head hit the pillow. To me that meant my conscience was clear and was proof that I'd done the right thing. Roach was where he belonged.....IN HELL.

***

At about 9:00 in the morning I was awoke by loud screams and yells. I stayed in the bed for almost a half hour listening to all the commotion. It seemed like there were two or three Jamaican niggaz downstairs arguing with Prince. The more I laid and thought about it, the more I started to worry because I knew Prince wouldn't allow anyone yelling in his crib like that. I tried my hardest to concentrate and listen to what was being said but I couldn't understand them. Their accents were too thick.

I got out of bed, put some sweats on, and walked down the long hallway to see what the commotion was. Now that I was in the hallway, I could understand little bits and pieces of what was being said and it definitely didn't sound nice.

When I made it to the steps and looked over the rail I immediately crouched down to keep from being seen. Two Jamaican niggaz had Prince, his wife, his three-year-old daughter, maid and his eighty-one year old mother tied up in the living room. I wondered how I was lucky enough not to have been snatched up. I was also wondering how the fuck they made it in the house without Prince detecting it. That nigga had all the surveillance equipment money could buy. What I didn't know then was that the robbers had followed the maid out to the grocery store, and held her at gunpoint as they forced their way into the house.

"Weh de blodclot money de bwoy?" one of the robbers with dreadlocks shouted waving a pistol.

"Go suck you mudda! Me know se ah de bwoy Trevor sen unu fe com rob me. Uno hafi kill me to rass ka. Me na gi unu nuthin'. Bad mon lik me nah bow down to batty bwoy like unu!" Prince refused, not showing an ounce of fear.

"Yo, pussyhole…..you tink se yuh bad. Mek me see how bad yuh is! Since you na tell mi weh de bloodclot money, den me ago shoot you mudda in her face," the dreadlocked robber announced.

"Prince gi dem de money. It not worth life," Prince's mother pleaded.

"BOOM!"

The light skin dreadlock shot Prince's mother at point blank range splattering her brains on the face of Prince's three-year-old daughter. I was in shock. That was the most heartless shit that I'd ever witnessed in my life. Prince's wife, maid and young daughter were crying hysterically as his mothers lifeless body hit the ground with a thud still tied up.

"Pussy se wa yuh mek mi do? Heh? Look pon you mudda! She dead cause ah yuh. Yuh wan you bumba clot daughta dead nex?" The dreadlock threatened.

"Pussyhole y'all mit as well kill mi! Yuh know if you don't kill mi, mi come kill yuh mudda, yuh pupa, aunty, yuh puss! Everybody ago dead!" Prince yelled out furiously.

I realized I had to do something and I had to do it quick. Prince wasn't giving up a dollar and the robbers looked like they were prepared to kill everybody in the room to get what they wanted. I cursed myself in my mind for letting Prince take my two .45's. I didn't have a weapon. Then I remembered that amidst all the excitement from the night before that Prince had forgotten to take back the two 357's he loaned me to put it in on Roach. I crouched as low as I could and practically crawled back to my room to retrieve the guns. When I made it there luckily, the guns were right where I had left them. I checked each barrel, cocked back the hammers, and darted out the room.

When I reached the steps, Prince and I caught eye contact. He gave me a slight nod of the head to acknowledge that he saw me and it was then that I realized that the reason he had been arguing and making such a commotion was to alert me. The couch that the robbers had him and his family tide up on were facing them, meaning that the robbers back was to me. I took a deep breath and came down the steps blazing.

My first two shots were dead on target. Both shots hit the Jamaican closest to me square in the neck knocking him to the floor and killing him instantly. My next five shots missed. The dreadlock robber that had killed Prince's mother spun around quick, got low and returned fire.

Neither one of us had any type of aim because none of our shots came close to hitting one another. Finally, I got lucky and shot him in the hand, knocking the gun out of his hand. I walked up to him and finished him off. Two shots to his head killed him instantly.

"Hurry up en untie me bwoy! Hurry up!" Prince shouted.

After I untied him, Prince grabbed the guns from my hand and shot the robber who killed his mother ten more times in the face.

"Dead pussy! Dead pussy! Yuh kill mi mudda! Yuh kill mi mudda!" Prince yelled out in tears as he continued shooting the dead man.

While Prince was wildin' out, I untied his daughter, wife, cook and dead mother. They were all crying, shaking and hugging each other.

"Take everyone upstairs while we clean up down here," I said softly to Prince's wife.

Three hours later Prince's crew had came, cleaned up and removed the bodies. It was then that Prince called me into the backyard and we spoke for the first time.

"Star you sav mi and mi family life. Mi owe you fe mi life star. Anyting star. Anyting you need mi de fe you! Don't faget dat!" Prince said seriously hitting his hand against his chest.

"C'mon man you ain't gotta thank me for that. It was my pleasure," I responded modestly. "I wish I would've came a little sooner to save ya momz na'mean?" I continued.

"Don't worry star. Mi ah go tek care of dat pussyhole tonite. Mi know de pussyhole who ah send da man dem. It would be a blessing fa you fe spend the holiday wif mi wife and mi family."

"Big Dread I appreciate the offer but I'm gonna have to pass. I'll definitely take a rain check though my nigga. I got a lil son that needs to spend Christmas wit his daddy. Feel me?"

"Yeah, mi respeck dat. Mi respeck dat. Come bak soon ya hear? Yo mi ago sen yo home en style bredren," Prince said handing me a first class plane ticket.

"Good look Big Dread," I responded giving him dap and a hug.

After I packed all my things and I was headed out the door with a couple members of his crew Prince stopped us.

"Hole on. Hole on de bredren mi haf sumthin' fa giv you," Prince announced.

He walked up to me and handed me a platinum necklace with an iced out cross. Just by the weight of it, I knew it had to be worth at least a hundred grand. I wanted to refuse it but I knew Prince wouldn't have it so I said my goodbyes to his family and headed out to the airport. I had come to Philly to rid the world of Roach and ended up killing two more people. At the time, I didn't know it but I had just made the biggest connection of my life. Prince would be one of the people who would change my life forever. There was nowhere to go from the bottom but the top. Everything was just starting to come together slowly but surely.

Chapter 9

January 04

The sight of Tiesha's ass bouncing and shaking as I pounded away at her doggy style was enough to make a grown man cry. Her ass was so fat it smacked against my stomach with every stroke. Her ass was big but her waist was damn near invisible and even though I'd seen her naked numerous times I couldn't help but be in awe of her body. I pulled her ponytail as hard as I could making her neck snap back and her back arch as I continued to pound away at her fiercely. Tiesha loved when I fucked her hard. She was gritting her teeth and talking shit the entire time.

"Fuck this pussy nigga! This pussy is good ain't it nigga?"Tiesha shouted in ecstasy bent over the bathroom sink as I pounded away at her.

Her talking shit only made me fuck her faster and harder. I began smacking her on the ass and playing with her clit simultaneously. She was going crazy.

"Who's pussy is this?" I asked not breaking rhythm or missing a stroke.

"Yours! It's all fucking yours daddy!" Tiesha shouted grabbing the sink for dear life.

"What's my muthafucking name? Say my name! Say it!" I demanded.

Tiesha must've been about to nut because she couldn't even get my name out completely. She was grunting, and screaming for me not to stop and calling for the Lord.

Me and Tiesha were in the bathroom of our crib in Bayside, Queens getting it in. Ever since her live in girlfriend Ranisha got out of jail and came to live with us, we had to sneak and fuck whenever she left out and that was rare. Ranisha was possessive as hell over Tiesha. Wherever she went, she made sure it wasn't far enough where she couldn't keep an eye on Ty. Ranisha had been home three weeks and she already suspected something was going on between us. It wasn't hard though because anyone with eyes could read our body language and tell that we were more than friends. Ranisha acted like everything was all-good when Tiesha was around but I knew she didn't like me. She rarely ever said more than two words to me and when she did, they were always with an attitude. Truth be told, I didn't like her either. I didn't trust that broad at all. She had this sheisty look about her that I just could not get past. She was keeping a close eye on me but what she didn't know was that I was keeping a close eye on her as well.

The only reason I was home alone with Tiesha that day was because Ranisha had to complete an outpatient drug program as part of her supervised release. I was glad she was gone for the day. I missed being able to fuck Tiesha as I pleased. Our sexual chemistry was off the hook, and now that we had to sneak around to get it in, it made the sex ten times better.

"I'm…I'm…I'm about to come baby!" Tiesha cried out as she was near climax.

"Get that nut girl! Get it! Get that nut for daddy!" I replied standing still making Tiesha back herself into me to make her pussy nut.

After Tiesha got her nut, she sat me down on the toilet, put her legs around my waist, hands on my neck and rode my dick slow and sensually.

"You like that? Huh? Come for me daddy! Come inside me baby!" Tiesha replied picking up the pace.

Just as I was getting ready to nut, the bathroom door flew open. Before I even turned my head, I already knew who it was.

"What the fuck is going on in here?" Ranisha shouted.

"Re, what are you doing home?" Tiesha asked in shock.

"I knew it! I knew you were fucking this nigga!" Ranisha yelled out.

Tiesha hopped off my dick and fell on her knees in front of Ranisha.

"Baby please….Lem'me explain….it's not what you think ma," Tiesha pleaded.

Ranisha cocked back and smacked Tiesha so hard in the face that my ears were ringing. Tiesha fell back almost hitting her head on the back of the toilet.

"Get the fuck up you nasty bitch! I knew you wasn't shit!" Ranisha yelled out picking Tiesha up by the hair.

Tiesha tried to fight back but it was of no use. Ranisha was bigger, stronger, and the better fighter. She punched Tiesha in the face a few times and then began stomping her out. That was when I had to intervene. Enough was enough. She was going to fuck around and really hurt Tiesha.

"A'ight….A'ight. That's enough! What the fuck is wrong wit you?" I asked pushing Ranisha away from Tiesha and pulling my pants up at the same time.

Ranisha pushed me off her and landed a kick directly to my nuts with her timb boots.

"Fucking bitch!" I shouted as I doubled over in pain.

When the pain began to subside, I grabbed Ranisha by the neck and started choking the life out of her. Ranisha's high yellow ass was turning colors. She was almost out for the count. If Ty didn't stop me, I probably would've fucked around and killed that chick.

"Ski! Let go! You're gonna kill her!" Tiesha shouted.

When I heard Tiesha yell my name I came back to reality. I had blacked out that quick. I let Ranisha go and she fell on the bathroom floor holding her neck and gasping for air.

"Bitch is you crazy? Don't ever put ya fucking hands on me! I'll fucking kill you," I threatened.

Tiesha's stupid ass ran over to try to help Ranisha up. Once she was up, Ranisha ran into the bedroom that she and Ty shared. Tiesha followed her. About no more than a minute later Ranisha came back in the bathroom with a revolver pointed at my face.

"Don't move you bitch ass nigga! Who's a bitch now? Huh? Say something crazy and see if I don't put a hole in ya black ass! You better never put ya fucking hands on me again," Ranisha said just as calm. Ty was the one screaming at the top of her lunges.

"Re, put that shit down before you make a mistake. Put it down!" Tiesha pleaded.

As I stood motionless with my hands at my side staring down the nose of the revolver I realized that the gun she had was the gun that I had given to Ty to protect her in case someone ran in the crib.

What Ranisha didn't know was that the previous day I had cleaned the gun for Tiesha and took out all the shells just in case her son Amir found it.

Since I knew the gun wasn't loaded I decided to see where her heart was at.

"Yo, you heard Ty put that shit down. You ain't trying to do nuffin' wit that. You ain't got it in you. Go ahead....shoot me...come on. What you waiting for?" I urged Ranisha on staring at her in directly in the eyes.

One thing I couldn't front on Ranisha about was her looks. Shorty was bad. She was a 5'10 inch thick ass redbone, with big titties and a fat ass. She was easily one of the sexiest chicks I had ever laid eyes on in my life. She had this exotic look to her like she was mixed with something, and her face was drop dead gorgeous. Anywhere she went she was always the center of attention. I'd never saw a dyke that looked or dressed like she did in my life. Most of them I had encountered tried to be very masculine and dress like niggaz, but this broad dressed as if she was a model. If you didn't know her there would be no way, you'd ever guess that she was a dike. When I went to the prison with Tiesha to pick her up and she walked out I couldn't believe my eyes. I couldn't stop grinning. I thought I was the luckiest man in the world. No one couldn't tell me that I wasn't gonna be getting threesomes left and right, but that couldn't have been further from the truth. Ranisha barely even looked at me. Tiesha had told me that Ranisha had never been with a man in her life.

Besides being drop dead gorgeous, Ranisha was hot to death. Everything about her screamed "Come Fuck Me". I had pleasured myself a time or two fantasizing about her after I saw her walking around in her panties and bra.

"Ski, stop it! Don't listen to him Re. Gimme the gun baby. Gimme the gun," Tiesha asked.

I disregarded Ty's plea. "Yeah, you heard her....Give her the gun. You ain't gonna do shit wit it. And after all this is over I'm still gonna be putting this dick in ya bitch. That plastic shit that you use will never be able to compare to this," I replied smiling as I grabbed my dick.

I tried to read Ranisha's face but I couldn't. She had a hell of a poker face. The next thing I knew I heard a noise.
CLICK...CLICK.....CLICK....
The crazy bitch had actually pulled the trigger. If there had been shells in the revolver, she would have killed me that easily. I realized that afternoon that she was a cold-blooded bitch. I figured she had to have killed before by the way she pulled the trigger with such ease.

"Damn shorty, you go hard like that? I definitely respect ya gangsta ma. You got heart," I said snatching the gun from her. "But, yo I'm about to slide off. Ty, make sure her ass is out my crib before I get back. I can't sleep under the same roof as this muthafucka."

"Fuck you nigga! Fuck you! I ain't wanna stay here wit ya petty ass anyway. I ain't doing no business wit this bird ass nigga," Ranisha stated talking to Ty.

Ranisha was supposed to have had a counterfeit money heist lined up for us, but personally I didn't give a fuck if she wanted to do business with me or not. I had a decent amount of change stacked up and I knew she needed my business much more than I needed hers. Or so I thought.

"And, matter of fact Ty, you gonna have to choose between me and this nigga right now! Fuck that yo! Either it's him or me!" Ranisha demanded to know.

"Re....please don't do this to me. I love both of y'all-" Tiesha tried to explain but got cut off.

"ME or HIM?" Ranisha repeated herself crossing her arms over her chest.

Tiesha's eyes got watery and she said. "Ski, please don't be mad at me but I gotta go wit Re. I can't leave her alone. I'm all she has."

When Tiesha chose her over me, Ranisha was grinning from ear to ear like she'd won a big war. Little did she know that I didn't give a fuck who Tiesha chose because the reality of the situation was that she loved both of us, and neither one of us were gonna be out of her life for good. I couldn't figure out for the life of me how Ranisha had gotten such a strong hold on Tiesha so fast, but whatever it was it had to be serious because she had Ty feeling like she owed her big time.

"A'ight enough wit all the soap opera shit. It's all good Ty. I gotta go handle some business. I'll hit ya phone up when I need you for the next jux. But make sure this bitch is out my crib by the time I get back." I said to Tiesha making my way down the steps then remembering I forgot something. "Ayo Re. That time was on me. The next time you pull out a gun on me, Tiesha is gonna be picking out a nice pretty dress for you to wear in ya casket," I continued walking down the steps and leaving the house.

Truth be told after that situation I respected Ransisha's gangsta. She was definitely a killer. She was like Tiesha to the tenth power. She was definitely the type of chick that I could use on the team. She could've been very useful; I just had too much pride to tell her.

Chapter 10

February 04

The visiting room at Lewisburg Penitentiary was filled to capacity. There wasn't an empty seat left in the house. That visiting room was the most depressing place I'd ever been. Teary-eyed women and children said their goodbyes to their sad looking husbands and fathers. Even the color scheme was depressing. The walls were beige, the seats were plastic blue chairs, the tables were wood, and the prisoners wore dark blue jumpsuits. Every time I went to visit my niggaz it reminded me how lucky and blessed I was to still have my freedom. I could've easily been right there with them behind that wall in the Belly of the Beast with them.

Me and Boota's baby mother Shamika sat at two separate tables adjacent to one another, waiting for Boota and Dro to come out. Wise had gotten caught with a knife in his cell and lost his visiting privileges so he wasn't able to come down.

Dro and Boota both came out at the same time and each one of them wore serious faces, and I knew exactly why too. They were anxious to hear if I had gotten to Roach or not. In every phone call, and letter they each asked me in a roundabout way if I handled it and every time I evaded the questions and told them, I would tell them when I saw them face-to-face. After I made it home from Philly, I called Boota's father Brooksy and made him promise to let me be the first one to tell the fellas. It had been going on two months since they gave me the information on Roach and I knew they were anxious to hear the outcome. I also knew that they probably didn't think I'd gotten it done.

Before they sat down Boota and Dro each came over and gave me dap and a hug. Boota didn't waste any time getting down to business. As I was hugging him, he whispered. "Did you get him?" "Nah, son I couldn't. It wasn't the right time or place so I left. I was out there damn near a month and I had to get back home. I got y'all though son. I'mma go back out there sometime this year and get em'. Trust me I got this," I lied looking at Boota directly in the eyes.

Boota was disappointed. He turned his head sideways and shook his head. "I told you this nigga wasn't built for that. I told you Dro. Damn! We should've just got ya cousin to pay somebody B," Boota said loudly going over to sit with his baby's mother.

"Yo, Boota chill out B. You making a scene. He said it wasn't the right place or time. You want this nigga to get knocked off on some stupid shit?" Dro replied trying to diffuse the situation sitting down at the seat across from me.

Boota sat down with Shamika and completely ignored me. The whole thing was funny to me. He reacted just how I thought he would. I could barely keep a straight face. See, I was the youngest in my clique. I got into the streets late. While all of them were putting in work, I was going to school and playing basketball. In the middle of my freshman year in college shit happened, and I ended up trading in my hoop dreams for street dreams. I went back home snatched Dro up and we started hustling upstate New York in a town called Kingston. Kingston was the same town where I had an office campus apartment that my basketball coach had gotten for me. When shit got hot and the Feds started sweeping, Dro convinced me to switch up our hustle from drugs to robberies. Boota knew I wasn't a sucker, he just didn't think I had it in me to kill. No one from the crew besides Dro knew that I had ever killed someone before and the only reason he knew was because he was there. Afterwards Dro told me to never tell anyone about it and I never did. So in everyone's mind but Dro's I had never slumped nothing. Boota had no clue that my gun went off crazy like it did. Up until a couple months prior, I didn't even know I had it in me like I did. I didn't keep the bodies from my niggaz a secret because I didn't trust them. I kept it to myself because there was no need to tell anyone. It wasn't something to brag about or something I was proud of. It just was what it was.

Dro sat down in the seat across from me and studied my face. He still looked the same. He was 5' 10" and weighed a little over 220 pounds. He was light skin with a goatee and had a baldhead. On the streets he had begun to get fat, but since he'd gone to prison two years prior he'd cut himself up and got his old football build back. He was a quiet person by nature and he was always thinking. He definitely listened more than he spoke, but when he spoke, he always said something worth listening too. Most people took his quietness for shyness but it was really arrogance. Dro believed he was smarter than everyone else was and thought that no one deserved to be spoken too by him.

Dro had a sneaky look to him like he was always up to something and he usually always was. He was the mastermind of our robbery crew. He found the spots, scoped them out, came up with the plans, and sold the jewelry to the fence. Everything I knew about pulling heists I had learned from him. He was a genius when it came to shit like that. If I had to pick a celebrity, he looked like it would be Dame Dash.

"What's good nigga? What you staring at me like that for?" I asked with a smirk breaking the silence.

"You got him didn't you?" Dro questioned me suspiciously.

"What you talking bout? Get who?" I shot back trying my hardest not to smile.

"C'mon B cut the bullshit. How did you do him in? What he say when he saw you?"

"Damn Dro. How did you know?" I asked disappointed that he saw through my act.

"Well first off you got that stupid ass smirk on ya face and secondly I noticed that Shamika had on Boota's chain. And, I know for a fact that Roach had that chain because I was there when he beat Boota for it that night on the block."

Dro was sharp as a number two pencil. That nigga didn't miss anything. It was no use fronting anymore so I started to spill the beans.

"Yo, son I did that nigga filthy," I said leaning up in the chair closer to Dro to be sure that I wasn't being overheard.

"I was only in Philly like two weeks before I got him. Prince got word that Roach and his peoples were going to this Jamaican club called The Upper Deck Lounge," I explained.

"How he knew Roach was gonna be there?"

"Son, the Dread Prince is a heavyweight. That nigga is paid. You should see his crib. He got mad clout in Philly," I went on.

"Oh, yeah Prince. I heard of him. You need to keep that nigga close to you. You might need him down the road."

"You think I don't know it. I'm already two steps ahead son. Prince owes me a big favor."

"Yeah. Yeah. That's a good look but tell me about how you got Roach."

"Oh, my bad son. Like I was saying-," I started off telling Dro everything that happened that night with Roach.

After I was finished, Dro was impressed. "Damn like that B? Who was driving the getaway car?"

"Prince was. Did ya man come through or what my nigga? That nigga is a dead issue my nigga," I said proudly.

"That's what's up my nigga. That's what's up. So you officially a gangsta now, huh?" Dro asked.

"Nigga I been a gangsta," I shot back as we both laughed.

"So when you gonna tell Boota the good news?"

"Trust me by the end of the visit he'll put it all together," I assured Dro.

Dro shook his head and sat back in his chair. He was the type of nigga who didn't show his emotions but me knowing him like I did I could tell he was happy that Roach got what he had coming to him. He switched up the conversation.

"So what's popping out there? How you supporting ya-self? You still getting it the ski mask way or what?"

"I got a couple spots lined up. Nuffin' big," I answered.

"What up wit Ty?"

"Oh shit!" I shouted not believing I almost left without telling him the latest news. "I'm glad you mentioned that. Ty fucking wit this dyke bitch who she met in prison. I can't front though son, this bitch is bad. Tall, redbone, beautiful and super thick. She's a waste of a bad bitch."

"Why you say that?"

"Cause she's a dyke. She don't fuck wit niggaz at all and never have. Ever!" I explained. "I can't even get no pussy from Ty no more. Ranisha came home and fucked up my whole situation."

"Yo, what did you say her name was again?" Dro asked curiously.

"Ranisha."

"She got blond hair and mad tattoos?"

"Yeah, how you know?"

"Her name is Ranisha Watkins if I remember correctly. I read about her in the Don Diva. She's a real bitch B and she's known for getting mad bread. Nigga if you think Ty go hard, you ain't seen nuffin. That bitch is the next level. She's down for whatever. You need to try and get her on the team," Dro explained.

"Word?" I asked waiting to hear more.

"Have I ever lied to you before B? I'm telling you B this bitch gets busy. She does it all. Hustle, rob, kill, white collar… you name it. She's been in jail most of her life and I think she's like 31 or 32. She's thorough. She never told the police shit. The Feds had been trying to get her for years but they couldn't. That's how she got bagged for that bullshit fraud charge. I'm telling you B get her on the team."

"Man fuck that bitch. I had to choke her ass out a couple weeks back. She caught me and Ty fucking in the bathroom and started spazzing. Bitch even pulled out the ratchet on me."

"Ski, let her have Tiesha. You gotta think out the box B. It's no limit to what you can do wit this bitch. She's ill on them computers. She can break into anything."

"And?" I replied still not getting it.

"For instance you won't have to go in a jewelry store with guns. You could have her disable the alarms, and go in there when that shit is closed and clean the whole shit out. You'd have to put major footwork in to make it happen but if you could pull it off you'd be a millionaire after ya first job."

Dro was the illest nigga I knew. He never ceased to amaze me with the crazy shit that he came up with. As he sat there and broke down his plan to me in further detail, I listened to every word he said intently only stopping him to ask questions. When he was done, I felt like hugging him. He had just given me the million dollar plan.

"Visiting hours are now over!" the C.O. announced over the microphone.

"Yo, good look my nigga. I owe you for this one son. I'mma put that in motion ya-heard?" I said giving him dap.

"Details Ski. Make sure you cover every detail," Dro suggested.

"I got you."

Just then, I heard Boota asking Shamika where she had gotten his chain from.

"Told you," I whispered to Dro.

"You know Boota is slow," Dro joked.

Before Boota gave me dap, he looked me up and down and asked, "Where you get my chain from?"

"I found it on a dead man," I answered coolly.

It took a minute for it to register but when it did Boota's whole face lit up.

"You frontin' ass nigga! Bout time you put some work in!" Boota replied giving me a hard dap and hug.

That day when I left the visiting room Dro and Boota's faces weren't as sad as they were the last time. This time they were all smiles and even though I knew those smiles were temporary, it still made me feel good. I had a different type of smile on my face. I had the smile of a man who knew he was about to be rich.

After the visit I dropped Shamika off at her crib and took Boota's two daughters to the mall to see a movie and to shop. By the time I made it back to my crib in Queens, I was dead tired. I'd been up since six in the morning. I didn't want to do anything except curl up in the bed and go to sleep.

I parked the Beamer in the driveway, got out of the car and staggered to my front door. My three-bedroom apartment seemed empty without Ty and Amir. I had gotten use to coming home to them. I went upstairs, jumped in the shower and fell asleep shortly after. Almost an hour later, I heard the bell ringing at my front door. As I was walking down the steps to answer it, panic struck me. "Who could be coming to my crib at this hour?" I thought to myself. I ran back upstairs and grabbed my hammer. If there was someone on the opposite side of that door trying to kill me I had to make sure it was gonna be a fair fight. I had no idea who it could be. For all I knew Raphael had found me and was coming back to finish the job. I looked through the peephole and didn't see anything.

"Who dat?" I asked cocking back my 9.

"F.B.I. open up! We have some questions for a Mr. Isaiah Thompson." a voice said flashing a badge so I could see it through the peephole.

My heart was racing. What could the Feds want to talk to me about? Whatever it was I knew it had to be serious because everything I did was major and had a possibility of a long sentence if I was caught.

"One minute," I said running upstairs to my bedroom to put the gun away.

After I made sure that all my guns were put up in my safe in the wall, I got dressed, went back downstairs and opened the door.

"What seems to be the problem?" I asked.

"We'd like to bring you down to the station to ask you a few questions."

"A few questions? I repeated. "About what?"

"Do you know this man?" The other agent asked showing me a picture of Roach's mutilated body.

"Nah, I don't even know if that's a human."

"Well how about this one?" The agent asked showing me a mug shot of Roach.

"Yeah, I know him. And?"

"Mr. Aaron Henderson was murdered on December 17 of last year outside of a club in Philly," the agent stated.

"And?" I responded flaring my arms out in the air.

"And, we think you might know something about it."

"Well you thought wrong," I said about to slam the door in their faces.

"Mr. Thompson you are making this harder than it has to be. All we want to do is ask you some questions. If you refuse we'll be back with two warrants. One for your arrest and one to search your house." the agent explained.

"Lem'me get my coat," I replied grudgingly.

I didn't wanna go to the station but even more than I didn't want them people searching my crib. At least by going to the station I could call my lawyer and I knew they couldn't have much on me because if they did they would've been arresting me not questioning me.

I grabbed my coat and took the ride with them to a nearby precinct. The whole ride I just stared out the window wondering if that was gonna be the last time I saw the streets. I didn't leave any evidence but with the Feds you just never knew. All they needed was a witness and there were plenty of people out there that night so I had no idea how the whole thing was gonna play out. If they wanted me bad enough they were gonna get me and that was the bottom line. Plus, I knew they were still mad that I beat them at trial last time.

I made sure I enjoyed the scenery because I didn't know when I'd see it again. With the Fed's you just never knew.

Chapter 11

March 04

Ranisha Watkins walked out of her probation officer's office in downtown Brooklyn and breathed a sigh of relief. She thought her P.O. was gonna violate her because she hadn't reported in three weeks and she had changed her place of residence without his permission. She had already decided that if she was violated she was gonna kill Ski the first day she got out. In her mind, it would have been all Ski's fault because he kicked her out his house. She felt like Ski was jealous of the relationship that she and Tiesha shared. Tiesha had told her all about Ski, and stories of how thorough he was suppose to be, but Ranisha didn't see it. She felt like Tiesha didn't know what a thorough nigga was. All Ski was to her was a stupid muthafucker who was destined to go to jail and Ranisha was trying to see to it that Tiesha would not be going down with him. Ranisha didn't like Ski or respect him. She was a hustler and she knew it was only a matter of time before she was back on top and Tiesha wouldn't have to depend on Ski anymore.

Ranisha put her Yves Saint Lauren sunglasses on and flagged down a cab to her and Tiesha's two-bedroom apartment in the Bedford Stuyvesant area of Brooklyn. Once in front of the two-story brownstone, Ranisha paid the cab driver, walked up the steps and opened the door.

"Wham!"

As soon as she stepped through the door, someone punched her in the face knocking her to the floor. Ranisha was in a daze but as she started to pull herself up off the floor, she saw that she recognized her unwanted visitor's face. It was one that she had not seen in six years and was hoping not to see for the rest of her life.

"What's good Re? Long time no speak. Nice for you to drop in." M.U. stated calmly chewing on a toothpick while sitting on the couch.

The blow had Ranisha's sight blurry but she still had enough instincts to reach in her boot for her gun only to find that she was not strapped. Ranisha began cursing herself in her head. She always kept her .22 in her boot for situations just like the one she was in right now. The only reason she didn't have it on her that day was because she had went to see her probation officer. Ranisha knew she was assed out. Her thoughts quickly shifted to Tiesha and Amir.

"Where's Ty and the baby? I swear to God y'all better not have done nuthin' to either of them! Where they at?" she shouted.

This made M.U. laugh. "God? The devil herself swearing to God. That's some shit," he commented then spoke to one of his peoples. "Abe bring the bitch and the kid out here."

M.U. was a 5'9 inch dark skin, stocky cat from the Bronx. He had long dread locks that fell to the middle of his back, and he had four tears tattooed under both of his eyes. And, unlike many others with similar tats his weren't for decoration or to make a fashion statement. Each tear represented a body he had caught or was responsible for. He was a live wire who was known all over New York for putting his murder game down and robbing niggaz. He was not to be fucked with.

A year or so before Ranisha had caught her Federal fraud beef, her and M. U. were out in Connecticut getting money together. Ranisha ended up crossing him for over seventy-five grand and skipping town. After she crossed him, M.U. was on hunt for her. When he heard she had been knocked he vowed to catch up with her after she was released. A week ago, one of his peoples spotted Ranisha leaving the P.O.'s office and followed her home. When M. U. got the news, he couldn't have been happier. He was out of state in North Carolina but came back up top to New York just to pay a visit to his old friend.

One of his peoples brought Tiesha and Amir out. Both of them were tied up and gagged. The sight of that sent Ranisha into hysteria.

"He's a fucking baby. How y'all got him tied up? What the fuck is wrong with y'all?" Ranisha yelled at the top of her lungs getting up and trying to run over to them.

M.U. punched her in the nose knocking her back on her ass and causing her nose to begin leaking like a faucet. Even with her feet tied together and her hands tied behind her back Tiesha tried to run over and aid Ranisha. M. U. backhanded her in the mouth and dropped her as well.

"Is y'all bitches crazy? What the fuck y'all think this is?" M.U. shouted pulling out his ratchet. "The next one of you ho's act up is getting a slug."

"Let them go yo. This ain't got nuthin' to do with them. This our beef. Please let them go!" Ranisha said busting out in tears as she watched Tiesha rolling around on the floor crying.

"Oh...I see it now. So this is ya bitch huh? Y'all bumping pussies ain't y'all?" M. U. asked with a laugh. "You still dyking? Some shit just never changes. What a waste," he said standing over Ranisha smacking her on the ass.

"What the fuck y'all want?" Ranisha asked.

"Bitch don't play dumb. You know exactly why I'm here. I want my muthafuckin' money. My two hundred grand," M.U. responded.

"Two hundred grand!" Ranisha repeated in shock.

"Yeah, you heard right bitch! The seventy-five grand that you stole from me and a hundred twenty-five grand tax for my fuckin' trouble," M.U. declared

"I ain't got it. Gimme a week or two and I'll have it for you. I swear," Ranisha promised.

Tiesha was trying to talk through the tape on her mouth. To M.U. it sounded like she said something about money, which immediately got his attention. He ordered one of his manz to remove the tape from her mouth.

Once the tape was removed, Tiesha shouted out, "Ranisha just give them the money. Theses niggaz ain't playing."

"Fuck these niggaz. We ain't givin' them shit," Ranisha yelled out defiantly.

M. U. was tired of playing games. "Y'all got 10 seconds to tell me where the money is at or everybody is dead. One, two, three."

"There's seventy-five thousand upstairs in my son's closet in a Prada shoe box," Tiesha blurted out.

M. U. immediately sent one of his manz upstairs to see if there was any truth to what Ty was saying. A couple minutes later, he came downstairs with the box and handed it to M. U. After looking over the box, he put it on the coffee table walked over to Ranisha and stood over her.

"You tried to hold out on me bitch? Huh?" M.U. shouted punching her in the face repeatedly.

Ranisha tried to fight back but it was to no avail. He was way too strong for her.

He walked back over to Tiesha and put the barrel of the gun to her temple. "Is there anymore money in here? And, if I find out you lying I'm killing everybody!"

"No, that's all we got I swear," Tiesha answered truthfully.

The seventy-five grand that Tiesha gave them was every penny she had left from the two robberies she had done with Ski. She didn't care about the money though, she just wanted for them to make it out of there in one piece.

After watching Ranisha roll around on the floor in pain and getting a view of the thong she had on, M.U. came up with a good idea.

"You know what Re... I was gonna kill you but I changed my mind. I'm gonna spare you. I'mma do something that I've been dying to do for years," M. U. said with a sinister grin unbuckling his pants.

He stood over and began ripping her clothes off piece by piece until she was in nothing but her bra and thong. Ranisha fought back the entire time but nothing she did helped. She did however, mange to dig her nails into his face. After realizing he'd been scratched M.U. got up and put the barrel of his gun to Amir's head.

"I'm done playing wit you bitch! If you fight back, I'm killing the kid. Now come here and suck this dick. And, I'm warning you, if you bite my shit I'm killing shorty!" M.U. threatened with his gun pointed at Amir.

Amir had been crying the entire time but now he was screaming his lungs out. The tape couldn't even muffle his screams completely. Tiesha was crying as well. There was no doubt to anyone in the room whether or not if M.U. was bluffing, and no one was surer of it than Ranisha. She'd witnessed him doing heinous shit numerous times. She blamed herself for the whole situation. If something happened to Tiesha or Amir, she wouldn't be able to live with herself. If it were just her life, she would've took a bullet rather than sucking a dick. But, since it was Tiesha, and Amir's lives at stake she knew what she was gonna have to do. She loved them and they were the only family she had. So, although her decision wasn't an easy one, it was the only one. Her hand was forced.

M.U. took his pants off and took his already erect dick out of his boxers. He was so excited that he had pre-cum all over his tip. Ever since the first time he laid eyes on Ranisha, he had fantasized about her. He had practically dreamed of this day.

Ranisha grabbed his dick with one hand and felt like throwing up, but she kept on. She closed her eyes and began sucking it. Within seconds M.U. had came in her mouth. Being that he was so excited, he was still hard. He pushed Ranisha down on her back.

"Yeah. Lemme see what that pussy hitting for," he said ripping her thongs off.

Tiesha and Amir were crying hysterically, but Ranisha on the other hand was numb. She was there but she wasn't there. One single tear crept down her eye as M.U. entered her insides roughly popping her cherry and stealing her virginity. Seeing that she was really a virgin only excited him more. He plowed in and out of her with reckless abandonment with no regard to the pain she was feeling. It felt like he was ripping her insides apart with every stroke. M.U. on the other hand didn't notice or care about her discomfort. He turned her over in the doggy style position and pounded away at her, as if she was a porn star. Ranisha wanted to scream and shout from the pain that she was feeling but she didn't want M. U. getting off more to the fact that he was hurting her so she stayed quiet and took it like the trooper she was.

After about fifteen minutes that felt like hours to Ranisha, M. U. climaxed. After ejaculating inside of her, he put his clothes back on. Seeing how his two soldiers were staring at Ranisha's flawless body, he said. "What up? Y'all niggaz wanna piece of that too?"

They nodded their heads eagerly and began disrobing. At that point, Ranisha was completely numb as they ran a train on her.

M.U. was laughing and cheering them on apparently getting just as much satisfaction watching as he did participating. The two young boys did a number on Ranisha. They did everything you could think of to degrade and violate a woman. After they were done, Ranisha lay on her back and stared at the ceiling a complete bloody mess. She felt as if she was paralyzed from the waist down.

After all three of them were completely dressed and prepared to leave M.U. grabbed the shoebox off the coffee table and said. "I'll be back this same time next week. If y'all ain't got my money, not only are we gonna take Re for another spin. We gonna have you join the party," he commented referring to Tiesha and walked out the door with his peoples.

As soon as they were out the door, Tiesha still tied up, hopped over to Ranisha and fell on top of her crying uncontrollably. Ranisha couldn't cry. She just laid there in the same spot staring at the ceiling blankly. Ranisha, Tiesha, and Amir stayed right there in the same spot in shock and horror for hours. There was no doubt in either of their minds that the men would be back and the million dollar question was how were they gonna come up with one hundred twenty- five thousand dollars in one week.

That day Tiesha lost every penny she had and Amir lost his innocence watching Ranisha get raped and beaten, which was probably going to scar him for the rest of his life.

But out of everyone Ranisha lost the most. She lost something that she never planned to give anyone and she lost something else that day, her sanity.

Chapter 12

March 04

"What the fuck happened to you?" I asked Ranisha walking into my bedroom and seeing her lying in my bed.

Ranisha looked twisted. She had a deep gash above her eye that looked like it had stitches, her nose was busted, she had an ice pack on her head, and she had big bags under her eyes like she'd been crying all night.

"Get out! Get out! Don't touch me. I swear to God I'll kill you," Ranisha shouted at the top of her lungs while attempting to cover her-self with all the sheets.

"Bitch is you crazy? You lying in my muthafuckin' bed in my muthafuckin' house threatening me? Matter of fact didn't I tell you not to bring ya ass back here? I would beat ya ass but it looks like somebody already beat me to it!" I spat back with venom.

It was seven in the morning and I had just gotten home from the precinct. If I hadn't had heard the shower running I wouldn't have even knew anyone was in the house. When I came upstairs, I checked Amir's old room and found him asleep on the bed so I assumed the person in the shower to be Tiesha. I figured her and Tiesha had gotten in to one of their intense arguments, and she came to my crib for the night. I couldn't have been more wrong. I was tired as hell and I couldn't lie down in my own bed. I really wasn't in the mood to be getting into it with Ranisha. My head was throbbing, I was tired, hungry, and on top of all that, this bitch was laying in my bed and had the nerve to be talkin' shit to me. I felt like there were a hundred midgets in my head banging hammers against my brain.

The Feds had questioned me for hours non-stop. Not only about Roach's murder but also about a couple jewelry store robberies that had taken place in the area that I didn't have anything to do with. They wanted me bad but they didn't have shit on me. The straw that broke the camel's back was when they sent my mug shot to Philly and it wasn't identified. God must've been watching out for me because they could've railroaded me. But, I was in the clear and they couldn't touch me. My lawyer threatened a lawsuit if they so much as looked at me wrong.

Ty must've heard us arguing because she came running out the steaming hot bathroom with nothing but a towel on dripping wet.

"Ski. Wait. Lemme talk to you for a minute," Tiesha pleaded trying to pull me out into the hallway.

Right before I went out in the hallway with Ty, I had one more thing to say to Ranisha. "I don't know what the fuck you still lying in my bed for. You might as well get up and get ya shit cause you ain't staying here."

Once we got into the hallway, Ty began explaining. "Ski just chill, she's been through a lot. Please… we don't have anywhere else to go. Niggaz are looking for us."

"What niggaz?" I asked.

"A few years back Ranisha had these dudes set up and robbed. Yesterday they came to our crib while Re was out and told me they were her cousins. My stupid ass let them in and they tied me and Amir up and waited for Re to come home," Ty stated taking a deep breath then continuing. "When Re came home that's when they really started wildin' the fuck out. They said that if we didn't come up wit the money they were gonna kill Amir."

"How much money?"

"200 thousand."

"Damn that's a lot of fucking money!" I responded.

"No that's not it," Tiesha stated with tears rolling down her eyes.

I was becoming worried. "They touched you? What happened? What they did to you?"

"No… They ain't touch me. I had to give them all the money I had stashed so they wouldn't kill us."

"How much was that?"

"Like seventy-five grand. I can't remember exactly how much I had but it's all gone."

I felt terrible for Ty. "Got damn," I said shaking my head.

"After I gave them the money they put the gun back to Amir's head and told Re that if she didn't have sex with them they were gonna kill him. They raped her Ski!" Ty announced beginning to cry. "All three of them. They all took turns while me and Amir watched. They said they'd be back every week until the debt was paid off. I know you said you didn't want her back here but we had nowhere else to go. I don't have anymore money to paying them people and who knows what they gonna do next time," Tiesha finished wrapping her arms around me and sobbing.

"Damn that's foul," I replied hugging Tiesha tightly. "Is she a'ight?" I asked genuinely concerned.

"I took her to the emergency room and they stitched up her ass, vagina, and her eye and they said her nose is fractured. One of her ribs is bruised and she was having a hard time breathing but it's getting better. She's been shaking and crying all night. "You know she's never been touched by a man before this Ski. She might never be the same. I feel so bad all I could do was sit there and watch."

I left Ty in the hallway and walked back into my bedroom. Ranisha was sitting up in my king sized bed fully dressed with her head in between her legs crying. When I walked in she wiped her eyes and tried her best to put on a brave front but I saw right through it. She was hurting, mentally, physically and most of all emotionally.

"Ayo Ranisha. Ty told me what happened and uhhh... I'm sorry for what I said to you. I ain't know. And uhhh... I know we don't get along but that was some foul shit them niggaz did and you welcome to stay here as long as you need to. Y'all can use my room," I stuttered.

"Nigga I don't need ya pity. Fuck you and this bullshit ass house. Ty, what you tell this nigga all my business for?" Ranisha spat with an attitude.

"Listen bitch I don't give a fuck about you-," I started to say but got cut off.

"I don't give a fuck about you either," Ranisha shot back.

"Good. We have a mutual understanding. But know this. I'm only letting you stay here on the strength of Ty so you better learn your fuckin mouth," I yelled back slamming the door as I left the bedroom.

It seemed like I had a dark cloud following me. No matter where I went or what I did, trouble always found me. Nothing ever went smooth. The Feds had just questioned me about a body that I actually had caught and I didn't know if they were gonna be watching me or not, plus I had inherited Ranisha's beef by association because if them niggaz found her and I was in the crib I was sure they would do me greasy too. It was time to get low and change the scenery. I had to come up with a plan B and come up with it fast.

***

The next morning I was up early. I drove to Jamaica Avenue in Queens and copped three burnout phones for each of us. I did that because it was no telling if the Feds had my phone tapped and I was going to need to be able to get in contact with Ty and Ranisha and talk freely. After I copped the phones, I made the most important move of my whole plan. I called Prince. He answered on the second ring.

"Hello," he answered sounding like I had woken him up.

"Prince what's good Big Dread?" Sounds like I just woke you up."

"Wha? Who ah dis?" Prince asked.

"This is Ski. What's good?"

Once he heard that it was me he immediately sprang to life. "Ski! Wha gwan? Yu good? Wha wrong bredren?"

"Too much to discuss right now. I'm in a jam. Yo, remember you told me that if I ever needed something to holla at you?" I reminded him.

"Yes mi tell you dat cause mi mean it. Whu you need?"

"Is this line safe to talk?"

"No. Lem'me call you back. Wha da numba?"

"718-555-1279."

"Mi call you right back star," he promised.

Ten minutes later and just when I was starting to think he was full of shit he finally called back.

"Wha you say?" he greeted me.

"Ayo. Big Dread no offense but I need you to speak regular English. I barely be able to understand you when you talking that shit." I responded.

"Nuff said. Whu you need?"

"Yo, Prince I hate to ask you this and I'm only asking you this because I need it." I started with my rehearsed lines. "I need you to front me some work. I'm fucked up right now but I'm good for it. I just need to get on my feet." I explained.

"That's all you need. Notta problem. Mi neva know you move drugs. Yu shoulda been ask mi."

"I was sort of into something else at the time but I gotta take a break from it right now. Shit is kinds hot right now, you feel me?"

"So whu you need and how much you want?"

"I don't know," I replied realizing that I hadn't put too much thought into what I wanted to push. "Gimme a little bit of everything. Hit me wit a lil starters kit," I said.

"No problem," Prince answered.

"So what I gotta do? You want me to come back out there, meet you somewhere or what?"

"No mi wouldn't make you do that. Everyting ah come to you. Four days, a week the most. I'll call you wit an address to pick it up from."

Hearing that was music to my ears. I definitely didn't want to have to travel with all the work. "Yeah, that's what's up!" I said excitedly. "Prince good looking baby, I appreciate the opportunity. I won't let you down," I promised.

"No problem Ski. You save mi and mi family life. Mi owe you still. Mi glad to help you."

"No doubt my nigga. You just saved my life and you don't even know it. Good looking again my nigga."

"No problem star. Talk to you in a few days."

"A'ight one," I said hanging up the phone.

Step one of my plan was complete. I secured a connect. From Jamaica Avenue, I took the Cross Island Parkway to the Whitestone Bridge and took Interstate 87 all the way upstate to Kingston.

Kingston was my old stomping grounds. It was the place where my life of crime was birthed. Before I got into the game, I was an All Long Island High School basketball player with good grades on his way to college. After High School, I went upstate to a college called Ulster to play ball and ended up balling in a different game. Me being the square I was I had no clue that I was in Crack Town USA. After all, before then I had never sold drugs a day in my life. I ended up going back around my way to Long Island to convince my peoples that their was money up there and that they needed to come up there and get it with me but no one took me seriously, except Dro. He came upstate a week after I told him about it and we got it popping immediately. We opened up a crack spot and was making close to ten gees a day. That may not seem like a lot of money but for me just getting in the game it was a fortune. When our spot got raided Dro convinced me to switch hustles and the rest is history. The Go Hard Crew was born.

Kingston was about 30 miles from Albany. I nicknamed it Candy Land because it was so sweet. Drugs went for double and triple the amount they did in the city, houses were cheap, the chicks were ho's and the niggaz were soft. I hadn't been in Kingston since the Feds knocked me in 2002. As soon as I hit the town, I bought a newspaper and started looking for apartments. Up there rent for apartments was between five to six hundred dollars a month, compared to twelve to fifteen hundred in the city. All the landlord's wanted was first months rent and security. They didn't even do credit or background checks. I rented two 2-bedroom apartments, one uptown and one downtown. I got Tiesha, Ranisha and myself two suites at the Holiday Inn.

From upstate, I drove to Baldwin, Long Island the hood where I grew up in. I grabbed five of the dirtiest, grimiest, hungriest little niggaz I could find and asked them if they were interested in getting money with me out of town. Being that my crew and I were like legends in our hood for all the Fed drama, they all jumped at the opportunity to get down with me. I told them I would send for them in two weeks.

From Long Island, I made my last and final stop, home. I knew Tiesha would be down with anything I came up with but the hard part was going to be trying to get Ranisha on board.

By the time, I made it home it was almost one in the morning. I'd been gone all day. I went upstairs to my room and found Ty and Ranisha in the bed watching a DVD. My bedroom looked nothing like the bachelor's room that it was. Nail polish, make up, perfume, brushes and combs were all over my dresser. My Nautica sheet set had been replaced with red satin sheets and big ass fluffy red pillows. It smelled like mad feminine products. Panties and bras were all on my floor and my timberlands had been replaced by Jimmy Choo stilettos. I had to bite my tongue not to wild on them. There were more important issues to discuss.

"Ayo. I need to talk to y'all. It's real important. Come downstairs to the dining room," I suggested from the doorway.

"Ski, can't we just talk here. You know Ranisha is stitched up," Tiesha reminded me.

"Oh yeah my bad," I shot back snapping my fingers.

I sat on the edge of the bed, took a deep breath, and began. "Yo, we gotta get out of here. Pack y'all shit up tonight cause we out in the morning. It ain't safe here."

"I'm good right here. Don't nobody know we here. I thought you were suppose to be a real nigga. Lemme find out you shook," Ranisha said with an attitude looking me up and down.

"Listen... The same night that them niggaz ran in y'all crib, the Feds came here questioning me about a homicide. I ain't have nuthin' to do wit it so they let me go," I lied.

"Ty you know them niggaz already got it out for me. I don't want them niggaz knowing where I rest my head at. If they ain't watching me and tapping my phone now, they will be soon. Matter of fact I'll be right back," I stated running downstairs to retrieve the phones I had copped earlier. "Here. The numbers to each of ya'll phones and mines are stored already. They burnouts," I said handing both of them a phone.

"Now listen I'm figuring that them niggaz that Ranisha got beef with found y'all at y'all crib they could find y'all here. And, we definitely don't want them knowing where we stay at," I continued.

"What you keep saying we for? Them niggaz don't know you or give a fuck about you. They got beef wit me. I owe them niggaz," Ranisha interjected.

"Because like it or not we on the same team. We live together and I'm inheriting ya drama and you inheriting mines. If them niggaz run in here you think they won't pop my top too?" I asked Ranisha. Ranisha didn't say a word. She just nodded her head. I knew she knew I was right.

"And, I hate to have to tell you this but you gonna have to forget about ya P.O. that's a done deal. Them niggaz probably got niggaz posted out there everyday of the week waiting for you to show up," I continued.

"So, where do you wanna move to?" Tiesha asked.

"Kingston," I answered looking them in the eyes.

"Kingston?" Ranisha repeated scrunching up her face. "I ain't moving to no damn Kingston. What's up there?"

"Money. And, we gonna get it! All of it! Next week I got some work coming in from outside of the country. It's supposed to be some official shit. I went around my way, snatched up some foot soldiers, went upstate and got apartments for them to pump out of. We gonna split everything evenly but everybody gonna have a different role to play," I explained. "Ty you gonna have to 9 to 5 it for a while but we gonna get rich."

"So what am I gonna be doing?" Ranisha inquired.

"Good question. You got the biggest job. First I'mma need you to make us all two fake drivers license, and passports a piece. You can do that right?"

"Yeah... That ain't shit. Why is that so important?" Ranisha shot back.

"For one it's important because you ain't gonna be reporting to ya P.O. no more so you gonna have a warrant. You gonna need I.D. to get around and me and Ty need them just in case shit gets hot and we gotta get out of dodge feel me?"

Ranisha nodded her head. I could tell she respected how I had thought so far ahead.

"But the most important job you got is- Yo, can you hack into security systems and break those shits down? I'm talking about big security systems," I said.

Ranisha seemed interested in where I was going with it. "How big?"

"A jewelry store. A big one."

"Yeah. I never did it but that ain't nuthin'. What you need that for?"

"I'mma clean the whole shit out and take everything. I found the perfect spot. I got my man putting in a good word for Ty to work there so I'mma need you to make a fake resume for her. Once she gets in, we in I'm telling y'all... This shit is gonna get us rich. Fuck just taking watches and rings we gonna take everything. Just the diamonds alone are gonna make us millionaires," I explained. "Fuck running up in there wit guns we gonna get on some Ocean 11 type shit."

"You think you could pull that off?" Ranisha asked me.

"No question. As long as you down. I can't do it without you," I responded. "You down or what?"

Ranisha thought it over for a second before she answered. "I'm wit it. Fuck it. I ain't never scared. Let's get this bread," Ranisha replied with a weak smile shaking my hand.

"Good. Then we all set. Get some sleep. We out tomorrow," I stated getting up from the foot of the bed and walking out the bedroom. "Oh yeah Ranisha... You ain't gotta worry about me pressing ya wife. That's you and I'mma respect it ya heard?" I turned around and said before closing the door of the bedroom behind me.

Everything was in place. Nothing was gonna stop me from getting rich. For the first time in a long time, all of my plans went smooth. If I had it my way by next year I was gonna be filthy rotten rich.

Chapter 13

September 04

I had upstate jumping. Money was coming in like clockwork. When I asked Prince to front me, some work all I had asked for was a starters kit. I was expecting at the most a brick or two of Coke, and few pounds a weed but I had Prince fucked up. This niggaz definition of a starter kit was ten bricks of powder, twenty-five pounds of hydro, and twenty-five hundred e-pills. Shit got so critical that I had to go back around my way to draft some more young niggaz to work for me. I had a weed spot in the Franklin Apartments, another one downtown in Roundout Gardens, six young niggaz pumping cracks hand to hand on Van Buren street, another one of my manz selling weight, and two bitches from around my way knocking the E off at New Paltz college in New Paltz. In a months time we finished everything. Prince couldn't even believe it. The next shipment he doubled everything and he was charging me next to nothing. In addition to all that, I had Tiesha working in a big jewelry store in the Diamond District named Zales. Zales had everything in it from Rolex's, Cartier's, Movado's, engagement rings, bracelets, chains, pendants, and most importantly diamonds. But this time the plan was different. I wasn't going to take some of the shit, or most of the shit, I was going to take all of the shit. The plan was to rent out the small office space directly upstairs from Zales and dig a hole through the ventilation system so I could enter the store from above undetected. However, going through and digging just to get to the ventilation it self was like trying to figure out an aerobics cube. It took me months just to find my way. Now, that I had the vent mapped out, and the digging completed all I was waiting on was for to Ranisha to break down the intricate security system. It was a slow grind but in the end, it was all going to be worth it. Everybody was playing his or her part. The best part of it was that my hands were clean. Niggaz upstate had no idea that I was the mastermind behind it all. I copped a 4-bedroom house in Scarsdale, a suburb of the Bronx and rarely went to Kingston.

One day I was eating lunch at Juniors in downtown Brooklyn with my man Cheeba. Cheeba was one of my closest friends from around my way. He was up north doing a flat seven for manslaughter and missed our first run. When I went home to grab up some more foot soldiers, I ran into him and brought him and took him back with me. He was my main lieutenant and my eyes and ears in Kingston. I trusted him with my life and besides running all the day to day operations in Kingston he was also the only person I had selling weight.

"Ayo Ski. We gonna have to re-up again by like next week B. Shit is jumping. Both weed spots down to like a pound apiece. Ziyah and Merl just gave me all the money from the pills, and I got like four or five of them things left myself. And, most likely them shits gonna be gone by tonight," Cheeba explained lighting up a Newport.

I was genuinely surprised. "Word? You moving weight like that? I ain't even think Kingston niggaz was copping heavy like that."

"You'd be surprised B. But, 4real Kingston niggaz ain't the only ones copping. Niggaz is coming out of everywhere son. Poughkeepsie, Newburgh, Schenectady, Middletown... When you got good work like we got word travels. We bringing city prices to them. Who wouldn't want to save a trip?" Cheeba stated pausing because his phone was ringing. "Pardon me for a minute fam." he said before he picked up his phone.

"Yeah... yeah...No doubt...I could definitely do that...I ain't far. Ya sister? Yeah, I remember her...That's cool...What time is it now? eight it is then," I heard Cheeba say talking on his phone.

"Who was that?" I asked as soon as he disconnected the call.

"That's my number one customer right there. Son, spends that bread B. He copped five of them things in the last three weeks and now he want my last five," Cheeba stated putting his Newport out in the ashtray.

"Where son from?"

"I don't know where he from, but he getting money in Middletown. I'm supposed to meet up with his sister tonight.

I'mma push up on her too. Shorty is bad-," Cheeba was saying before I cut him off.

"Damn Middletown must be poppin'. We might need to set up shop over there and see what it's hitting for. Cut them niggaz straight out the picture na'mean?"

"You know I'm wit whatever B. Show me the strip and I'll make it flip." Cheeba responded giving me dap as we both started laughing. "So what's on the agenda for the day playboy?" he continued changing the conversation.

"Can't call it my nigga. Why? What's good?"

"Take this ride wit me back up to K-town," Cheeba proposed.

I yawned before I spoke. "Nah, you bugging son. I was thinking more of the lines like laying up wit a bitch watching a bootleg or something."

"Yeah...we could still do that. It's still early son. Lemme just make this last sale and we can get up wit them chicks we met at the 40/40 Club," Cheeba said trying his best to be convincing.

After he saw I wasn't going for it he really started going in. "C'mon B. I hardly see you nowadays. We don't even chill like we use too. The whole fam is in the pen. We the last one's left. I'm still fresh out. What's good? I miss you my nigga!"

"A'ight man damn!" I agreed unwillingly just to shut him up.

Cheeba smiled. "Why I always gotta lay on the guilt trip?"

From Juniors we hopped on the Brooklyn Bridge and headed uptown to go shopping for clothes and sneakers. We copped an ounce of purple haze from Autobahn Avenue in the Bronx for the hour and a half trip upstate back to Kingston, and once we got there Cheeba snatched up the work from the stash spot and we headed to Middletown so he could make his sale. We were waiting in a park somewhere in Middletown when a red 600 Mercedes Benz sitting on 22's pulled up bumping some old Foxy Brown.

"Ayo. Don't let her come to you, go to her. I don't want this bitch seeing my face," I replied sinking down in the passenger seat.

"A'ight cool. Gimme a minute. I'mma try to push up on shorty. I think she wanna gimme some pussy," Cheeba remarked getting out the car.

He got out the car and flagged her down to let her know where we were at, came back to the car, and got the work out the stash box and bopped over to baby girl riding in the Benz.

Cheeba was a brown skin, chinky eye, pretty boy type nigga. He stood 5' 10" and had a stocky build with cooly jet-black hair. He was one of them niggaz who really had Indian in his family. I had never laid eyes on the chic in the Benz in my life, but I would've bet a stack that he'd bag her. Cheeba was like my man Wise. They were bitch magnets. If I had to say, he resembled a celebrity it would have to be Noreaga from the rap group CNN.

I was slumped down in the car trying to hide my face, but for some reason curiosity made me look up to see how the chic looked. Cheeba was kicking it to her from the driver's side window, and he was all in her face so all I could see was the back of his head. But when he opened the door for her to get out and go to her trunk I recognized her immediately. She looked exactly how I remembered her. I cocked back my nine and got out the car. The trunk was her blindside so she didn't see me coming. But when she did see me it was like she had saw the grim reaper in the flesh. Her eyes damn near fell out their sockets with surprise.

"Stinkin' bitch!" I yelled gun butting her in the face as hard as I could busting her nose open and knocking her unconscious.

Cheeba looked like he was in just as much shock as Candy was. "What the fuck you doing B?"

"Go pop the trunk!" I ordered.

Cheeba did as I told him and popped the trunk from the driver's side of the Benz. I took the duffel bag full of money out the trunk and put Candy in it.

"Take all the work and money with you and follow me. I'll explain everything when we get there," I stated slamming the trunk down.

I can't even front on my man Cheeba he kept it all the way real with a nigga that night. He had no idea what type of shit I was on, and he was still riding out with me. In his mind, he probably thought I kidnapped and assaulted an innocent woman. I couldn't think of anywhere to take her so I ended up driving all the way back to the Manhattan. I found an abandoned building on the Lower East Side on 6th street and parked up. I was nervous the whole ride back to N.Y.C. because Candy had woke up mid way through the trip and she was screaming, punching, and kicking at the trunk the whole trip. If a cop would've pulled me over, it would've been all she wrote.

As soon as I popped the trunk all the screaming and banging I had heard the whole ride ceased.

"What the fuck were you making all that noise for?" I shouted punching Candy in the mouth opening a deep cut on her bottom lip.

I put her over my shoulder and carried her into the basement of the abandoned building. The basement of the building was fucked up. It looked like some homeless crack heads took shelter there because there were a few blankets on the floor, a lamp without a shade, and mad stems on the ground. The building itself looked like it had not been occupied for years. There were holes in the floor and ceiling and the sounds of rats scurrying about was prevalent. The worst thing about the basement was the odor. It smelled like a mixture of death, shit, and crack smoke. To put it in simple terms the basement looked like hell on earth. And, that was exactly what it was going to feel like to Candy.

I had some rope and a baseball bat in the trunk of my car so I sent Cheeba out to get them. By the time he came back I had stripped Candy naked, and tied her up to the ceiling by her hands.

Cheeba looked at Candy then looked at me and asked the million dollar question. "Yo, Ski you better have a good explanation for this shit because you starting to scare me. What the fuck is this all about?"

"Remember I told you about the nigga that hit me up in the cab outside of the court house?"

"Yeah. What he got do with all this?"

"This is his sister," I explained. "She started everything. The whole situation went that way because of her."

"So what you bring her all the way up here for? You should've just popped her in the park and ended it right there."

"Nah it ain't that simple. I need to find her brother Raphael," I said.

Candy was a pint sized Puerto-Rican chick about the same age as me. At one time, she was my live in girlfriend. She was 5'2, 130 pounds with olive skin, light brown eyes and the body of a video model. She was far from your average hood chic though. She was the most spiteful, grimy, lying ass bitch that I had ever encountered in my life. Four years ago when I was just fucking her casually, I ran into her brother Raphael at a bar in Kingston. Before that night, we spoke when we saw each other, but we were far from what you would call friends. That night he was pissy drunk and I noticed two cats plotting on him and ended up saving his life. After that night one thing led to another and we started getting money together. Rapheal had been pushing me from day one to get serious and settle down with Candy and after a little while I gave in. I ended up buying a crib for us and everything. Shortly after, her jealous ways pushed me away and we broke up. But, she being the vindictive bitch she was, she started doing any and everything she could to ruin me. Eventually she succeeded when she lied and told her brother that I beat her up. Raphael believed her because somehow, she managed to get her eyes black and bruised and he severed ties with me stopping me from getting money and threatened to kill me. I let my anger get the best of me, and I ended up running in their crib, robbing and beating them both. The biggest mistake I made was not killing them because two years later Raphael caught up with me and almost killed me. I hadn't laid eyes on Candy since.

"Ski you did this shit all wrong son. You should've let me make the sale and then let me call that nigga Ra and ask him to meet me somewhere on some business shit. He usually always meets me alone. It would've been easy to get him. Now you got the heat on me. This nigga sent her to meet me, when she don't show back up he gonna think I robbed and killed her and come after me," Cheeba explained after I had given him the rundown on the whole situation.

"So the fuck what nigga! Is you scared?" I shouted.

"C'mon son don't try to play me," Cheeba replied.

"That nigga ain't no fucking killer man. Trust me he don't get busy like us," I said angrily.

"I can't tell nigga. The scars on ya body say otherwise. And, who is you to say that this nigga won't go to the cops?"

Cheeba was right. I had reacted too quickly. I'd let my anger get the best of me again. The funny thing about it was I couldn't even remember having such a bad temper. I had changed so much that I didn't even know myself anymore. I was doing shit that I never thought I was capable of doing and looking back on it things definitely could've been handled better.

Cheeba saw that what he had said was sinking in and said, "Fuck it now son! We here. Ain't no going back. How you wanna do this"

"I'mma beat her ass for awhile until she coughs up his whereabouts."

I walked over to her and began smacking her in the face to wake her up.

"What's up Princess? Did you sleep well?" I asked sarcastically.

Candy looked around dreary eyed trying to process what was going on.

"You wasn't dreaming bitch. It's me. You missed me?" I yelled smacking her in the face.

"Fuck you punta!" Candy shouted spitting in my face.

I grabbed the baseball bat that was leaning against the wall and hit her directly in her knee. The cracking sound of her bones breaking echoed throughout the basement. It sounded like one of Barry Bonds home runs. Candy let out a piecing scream that was so high it could've cracked the windows. I could see the pain in her face. It was scrunched up and every vein in her forehead was visible.

"Bitch you ain't in the position to be talking to me like that. Apologize before I break ya arm next. Say sorry," I demanded.

"I'm sorry! I'm sorry! Please! No mas!" Candy pleaded.

"That's what I thought bitch. Now tell me where I can find ya brother."

"I don't know where that nigga at. Nobody knows where he's at," Candy lied.

I hit her in the same knee again with the bat. Her knee was now facing the opposite way and her leg was black and blue.

"Ahhhhh! Ohmigod! Help me God! Please save me Lord!" Candy cried out in pain.

"Save ya-self shorty. Just tell us where ya brother is staying and we'll let you go!" Cheeba said trying his best to sound sincere.

Candy didn't respond. She just hung there crying and shaking. I didn't feel an ounce of remorse for her. I began beating her whole body up with the bat until her whole body was swollen, and black and blue. I hit her everywhere but above the neck. I didn't want to kill her because I needed information from her. I was sweating profusely and had stripped down to my wife beater. Candy was falling in and out of consciousness but still not talking. She was much tougher than I gave her credit for. I remembered seeing a curling iron in her trunk so I sent Cheeba to the car to go get it. When he came back, I plugged it into the socket and waited for it to get steaming hot.

"Candy, this is ya last chance to cough up some information. Don't make me do this to you," I warned her.

Once again, she did not respond. I took the sweltering hot curling iron and stuck it between her legs. Instantly, you could smell her silky pussy hairs burning. Her whole body convulsed and her eyes rolled back into her head as if she was being electrocuted. The scream that she let out that night was the most horrific sound a human being could make. The smell of her insides burning smelled like burnt rubber. When I took the curling iron out of her, I could see pieces of her inner walls stuck to it.

Still she gave up no information and that angered me. I stuck the curling iron back in her pussy, up her ass, on her face and her nipples but it was to no avail. She wasn't talking. I hated her with a passion but after that night, I respected her gangsta. She was a trooper. A burned up trooper nonetheless.

"Just get it over with and kill me! Kill me! I ain't telling you shit! I called my brother while I was in the trunk and told him that it was you. Don't worry you'll be joining me in hell soon punta. Next time you won't survive bitch!" Candy yelled frantically.

"Good. Now he knows it's real," I responded.

Right then, I concluded that Candy was not going to come off any information about her brother's whereabouts. It had been well over two hours of torture. It was time to take her out of her misery. But a bullet was too good for her. I wanted her to die a slow agonizing death.

"Cheeba go to one of these bodega's and get me two jars of peanut butter, duct tape and some plastic gloves." I said with an evil smirk.

"Peanut butter? What the fuck you gonna do wit peanut butter? You a sick nigga," Cheeba shot back.

"Just hurry up and go get it. I'mma show you," I answered.

When Cheeba came back, I took Candy down from the ceiling, covered her mouth with black Duct Tape, taped her hands to her feet and spread the peanut butter all over her entire body and face. When I was done, I cut the lights off and left her for the rats to devour. I don't know where I got the idea from but it was the perfect way for a bitch like her to go out.

All I had to do now was find Raphael before he found me because I knew he would be coming. Raphael and Candy were tighter than the average brother and sister. They were each other's best friend and the only family they had. Cheeba was right I could have handled the situation better. I had let my emotions get the best of me. I'd made a similar mistake the last time and almost paid for it with my life. I hoped this time would be different. I would definitely be better prepared this time though. The only satisfaction I felt was knowing that Candy suffered before she died. She deserved every second of it and I enjoyed every minute.

Chapter 14

November 04

"Ilk! Look at you looking all dusty! You need to get in the shower! You stink too!" Tiesha replied scrunching up her face looking me up and down as I came out the vent.

"All for the love of money girl. Come gimme a hug," I said playfully extending my arms.

Tiesha ran behind my office desk laughing. "Stop playing I got my work clothes on. I gotta go back to work," she pleaded.

I stopped chasing her. "Oh, so that's how it is? I bet you when I come out that vent with all that jewelry you'll gimme a hug," I replied jokingly.

"So, did you finish the hole or what?" Ranisha asked with an attitude obviously jealous of how I was playing around with her woman.

I was feeling cocky. "C'mon what's my name? Everything is a go! The hole is finished. I'm waiting on you now."

Tiesha, Ranisha and I were all up in the office I had rented out above Zales. I had finally finished digging the cement out of the vent that had been previously covered in the safe room. Ranisha had already cracked the code for the safe and hacked into the security cameras and all she needed was to find a way to stop the alarm from sounding. She had already found a way to mute the alarm but she hadn't figured out how to stop the silent alarm from being sent to alert the police at the nearest precinct. The display cases and all the safes were set on time alarms. Even if the code was punched in correctly, as soon as the safe or display cases were opened the police would be notified, and we definitely didn't need that. Ranisha was on her computer 24/7 trying to hack into the police's phone system but she hadn't found a way yet. I had no doubt that she was more than capable of figuring it out. It was just a matter of when. She was an animal on the computer.

"I don't know what it is but I'm overlooking something. It's some simple shit I ain't doing. I know it," Ranisha said frustrated.

Tiesha stood behind her and began massaging her shoulders. "Don't worry mami you'll get it baby."

My cell phone rang. "What's good?" I answered.

"Are you busy?" a sexy voice asked.

"Nah, who's this?" I asked curiously.

"You don't remember me baby?" The voice asked. "How about this?"

After that, I heard nothing but juices being squished around and the sound of her moaning. I recognized who it was immediately.

"Kia, what up? I didn't recognize this number, where you calling me from?"

"I'm in room 203 in the Waldorf Astoria laying in the bed naked playing with myself in the mirror above my bed. You wanna come?" she responded teasing me.

Just the sound of her voice got my dick hard. Kia was a sexy ass brown skin married woman in her mid thirties. I had met her at Justin's a month earlier and smashed it the same day. She was who Rick James was talking about when he made the song Super Freak. She took it anywhere-anyhow. I hadn't spoken to her or saw her since the first day we met and I didn't expect to hear from her ever again. I was pleasantly surprised to be hearing from her. Her pussy was blazing.

"Do I?" I shot back. "I'll be there in twenty minutes," I responded.

"They'll be expecting you at the front desk," Kia told me.

"A'ight cool," I said hanging up the phone.

After disconnecting the call, I hopped in the shower and changed my clothes. The office space wasn't big at all. In total it had two rooms the smaller of two rooms was completely empty. The bigger of the two had a bathroom and I furnished the office with a desk, flat screen TV, computer, and a couch.

Tiesha was being nosey. "Damn, where you in a rush to?"

"None of ya business. And, don't be questioning me. Save that shit for Ranisha," I stated grabbing my car keys.

"Well excuse the fuck out of me nigga," Tiesha exclaimed. "I was asking because I need you to do me a favor."

"What up? Make it quick," I answered not even bothering to look her way.

"I need you to take Ranisha to Brooklyn."

No way was that going down. "Brooklyn?" I repeated. "For what? Why can't she hop her ass on the train?" I asked then thought about it some more. "Nah, fuck that. I got something to do."

"She gotta go back to our old crib to get her laptop. She has an email address stored in there to someone who she thinks might be able to help her with that code problem we having. And, the reason why she can't go there alone is because them niggaz might be out there posted up," Tiesha explained.

"I didn't even know you still paid rent there. Damn! Why now?" I complained.

Ranisha jumped into the conversation with her shitty attitude. "Ty you ain't gotta beg that nigga. I'm good. I can handle it by myself. Fuck him."

"It been almost eight months since all that shit happened. Trust me them niggaz ain't out there," I stated. "And what I tell you about your mouth?"

Ranisha just rolled her eyes. Her mouth had gotten better but it was still vicious.

"Ski, fuck that bitch man. This is about money. That ho can wait," Tiesha got on me.

Tiesha was right. No pussy was worth more than money.

"C'mon Ranisha let's bounce. But, you gonna have to take the train home. I ain't driving ya ass all the way back home."

Ranisha rolled her eyes for a second time. "Whatever."

Tiesha went back to work and Ranisha and I hopped in my BMW Brooklyn bound. We'd all been living together for more than eight months and Ranisha and my relationship was still strictly business. If it wasn't about money we ain't speak. She didn't like me, and I didn't like her and that was just what it was, but we put up with each other. We did however develop a mutual respect for each other. I even had kept my word and stopped fucking Tiesha.

Two months had past since we did Candy filthy and there had been no type of retaliation yet. I knew Raphael had to of known it was me who was responsible, and I knew that he knew that I was the one flooding upstate with drugs. Honestly, I was shocked that he hadn't made a move yet. For the first month, I stayed out of Kingston and moved carefully. I was still on point but I'd just began to relax again. The money was rolling in and the heist was about to go down. Life couldn't be sweeter. Deep down in my heart I knew that eventually there wasn't enough room for both Raphael and I to co-exist on earth and that one of us was going to have to go. And, I was praying that when we did cross paths that I would be the one who had the drop.

It took us an hour to get to Brooklyn. Traffic was backed up for miles. By the time we made it there, it was almost nine thirty at night. We would've made it there quicker if we hopped on the train. I was steaming. There was no way I'd be back in time to get it in with Kia. Every time I looked over at Ranisha, I got more upset. She had the nerve to have an attitude and I was the one doing her a favor. There was absolutely no conversation between us the entire ride. I didn't even let her hit my L.

When we pulled up to the brownstone that Ty and Ranisha use to live in, I let her out and circled the block looking for a parking spot. I couldn't find a spot so I ended up double parking across the street. I was lighting up a cigarette, when I happened to have noticed a cat closing the door of the brownstone behind him. I thought it was a neighbor at first so I let it go and turned up the music. But after a couple minutes passed and Ranisha still hadn't come back I knew something wasn't right. I got my thirty-two shot .38 special out the stash box and got out to investigate.

I jogged up the steps of the brownstone and slowly opened the door. My instincts were right. Three niggaz had Ranisha on the floor stomping, kicking, and trying to tear her clothes off. I couldn't see her face clearly but I could tell she was bleeding. She was doing her best to fend them off by flailing her legs and kicking at them but there were too many of them and they were too strong for her. She kept trying to reach in her boot but she couldn't get to it. It was no time to waste. I came into the living room firing.

I let off seven shots but none of them hit anyone. I did however manage to hit the TV screen and break a lamp and vase. My shots startled the dudes for a second, but all three of them quickly recovered and returned fire.

The bullets came at me in rapid succession. One bullet flew by me and was inches away from my head. My adrenaline was pumping. Them niggaz were not playing. While I was running to take cover behind the kitchen wall, I was hit in my left shoulder. The impact of the shot spun me around and I immediately hit the floor. My shoulder was on fire and leaking like a faucet. The complete left side of my body was temporarily paralyzed. My grey Yankee's warm up jacket was almost red. I lay on the floor in pain as shots continued flying into the kitchen hitting everything from the refrigerator to the cabinets. When Ranisha saw that all three-niggaz attention was on me she went into her boot, pulled out a revolver, and started letting off. Ranisha was a marksman. She let off four shots and all of them landed. The first shot hit one of the niggaz square in the forehead and killed him instantly. He fell to the sofa and his limp body slid down to the floor. Her next two shots hit one of the other cats arm and he hit the floor as well and dropped his gun. The third dude saw two of his manz drop and let go a few shots in Ranisha's direction and tried to run out the crib. In all the madness he must've forgot that I was still in the kitchen. When he ran by the kitchen, I let off numerous shots at him but it looked like only one of them hit him in the leg. My shot was already off and now that I'd gotten hit in my shoulder, my aim was really off. The kick-back from the gun felt like it was tearing my shoulders into shreds. Once the nigga who I'd shot in the leg fell, I gathered all my strength and got up and finished him with headshot. His body jerked once and his head jumped off the floor and crashed back down. While all that was going down Ranisha ran over to the cat that she had shot in the arm, kicked the gun away from him, and started wildin' out.

"You bitch ass nigga! What now? I'mma kill you! You raped me you faggot ass nigga! Who's the bitch now? Who's the bitch now?" she shouted with tears rolling down her face and her shirt ripped exposing one of her titties.

I ran over to her and grabbed the gun.

"Chill. Don't kill him yet. We can't let him off the hook that easy," I stated putting my arm around her after I took the gun.

"He's the one that made them rape me! I should put my strap on and rape him! " Ranisha yelled.

I definitely didn't want to see that. "Nah, don't do that," I said quickly cringing at the thought. "He gonna die with his manhood, but then again he's still gonna lose his manhood. Y'all got some tape or something in here?" I asked.

Ranisha nodded her head.

"Go get it."

Ranisha hesitated but followed my instructions. When she came back with it, we stripped him naked; duct taped him, and beat the shit out of him. Ranisha was putting most of the work in. She kicked him repeatedly in his head until blood was leaking from his nose, mouth, and various spots on his face. His face began to bruise immediately. He had cuts and scrapes everywhere. She then began slamming his head to the hardwood living room floor by his dread locks until he was in and out of consciousness. The entire time she was screaming, crying, and carrying on so bad that she almost passed out. As for me, I was losing so much blood from the wound to my shoulder that I felt like I was going to pass out. I grabbed my cell phone and called Cheeba. He picked up on the second ring.

"What's good Ski?" He answered casually.

"Meet me in the Sty son. I'm on Halsey and Patchen. It's the block over from my grandmomz crib."

"Brooklyn?" he repeated as if he wasn't trying to make the trip. "For what? Let's just get up tomorrow in the hood."

I was becoming impatient. Shit was critical. My shoulder was killing me and I was in a house with two dead bodies. Who knew if someone had called the police. "It's an emergency son. When you get off the Belt Parkway and get on Atlantic Avenue call me, and I'll give you directions."

Cheeba peeped the urgency in my voice. "I'm on my way B."

"A'ight. Hurry up and bring some rope," I said before I hung up the phone.

Me getting off the phone must've temporarily distracted Ranisha, because she looked over at me and said. "Oh my God! You're losing mad blood. I didn't even notice that you got hit! Come on sit down."

She ran into the bathroom, got some sheets out the line closet, and started applying pressure to my shoulder. It was the first time she ever did anything to show me she cared.

Twenty-five minutes later Cheeba was in the crib walking over the bodies shaking his head.

"Son, you out here wildin'. You gotta slow down B. How this happen? And, who the fuck is these niggaz?" He looked at me and saw that I'd been shot. "Where you hit at?"

"I'm good my nigga. Way to be here though son. Help me put this nigga in the trunk," I replied.

Cheeba and I carried the nigga to the car and threw him in the trunk. Thanks to Ranisha, he was in dreamland. After that, we all headed to Jones Beach in Long Island. Cheeba was in his whip with the body, and Ranisha and I were in the BMW. It was past one in the morning on an icy cold Sunday night in November so the beach was empty. Perfect for what I had in mind.

We dragged the nigga M.U., onto the beach and tied him to a tree ass naked. After we were sure he was secured, I had Ranisha tie another rope around his dick, and tie the other end to the bumper of my car.

Cheeba was baffled. "Where do you come up wit this shit son?" he asked shaking his head in disbelief. "You a sick nigga B. You got issues. When did you get like this Ski? Fuck it don't matter, I don't even wanna watch this shit."

I wasn't fazed. "Good. You can be the driver."

I threw some water on his face and smacked him up until he regained consciousness. He came too slowly but when he did, he looked down at himself and his surroundings bewildered. His entire body was shivering and his eyes were as big as quarters. He tried to see if he could manage to get out from being tied to the tree but after he was unsuccessful, he began to plead for his life.

"What? What's going on yo? Why y'all niggaz- doing this- shit- to me?" he asked with his lips quivering. "I don't even know y'all niggaz man. Please! Lemme go. You don't know this bitch B. She's-she's foul. She's gonna cross you at the end," M.U. stated.

M.U. was visibly shaken. He was in pain from the beating and the gunshot he received; he was freezing cold and scared for his life.

"You bitch ass nigga! I hate you! I hate you!" Ranisha shouted punching him in his face repeatedly.

I let Ranisha get all of her anger out on him. It was important to me that she got all of the get back she wanted.

"Son, you already know what it is man. You got caught wit ya pants down," I said looking down at him. "Literally."

He hadn't noticed that his dick was tied to a rope until I said that. He looked down at his dick, and then followed the rope to where it ended and saw that other side was attached to the car bumper. He immediately began to panic.

"Agh!!" he let out with a gut wrenching scream. "C'mon man don't do this shit to me. Please," he pleaded using all his strength to try to escape.

"It's a done deal daddy," Cheeba stated.

"Raping chicks ain't cool son. I don't know where you going in the after life but wherever you going you won't be getting no pussy," I joked.

"Re, I'm sorry. I'm sorry. I was high when I did that shit. I felt fucked up about it. But you owed me. You did me dirty. You would've done the same shit to me," M.U. tried to explain.

That sent Ranisha over the edge once again. She pulled out her ratchet and shot him in the leg. The force from the shot damn near ripped off his knee. I could see the cartilage and ligaments dangling by a string. After that, she shot him in his other knee and then, she began shooting his arms. M.U. let out gut wrenching scream after scream. I had never seen a man in so much pain. It was as if Ranisha was possessed. Just when I thought, she was finished she'd do something else to him. She punched him, kicked him, shot him, and even spat in his face. I wanted him to be conscious for the main event so I stopped her.

"Re, chill out ma. That's enough. We want him alive and conscious to feel everything," I suggested.

She punched him one last time in the face and stopped.

"Yo, Cheeba start that car homey," I ordered.

When Cheeba started the car M.U. started screaming in anticipation of the pain. He looked terrible. His face looked like raw meat and his body was badly beaten, bruised, riddled with gunshots wounds, and dried up blood.

"You got anything you wanna say to this nigga before we do it?" I asked her.

"I hope you rot in hell bitch!" was all Ranisha said.

Cheeba revved the engine up a few times and peeled off. After he got about twenty feet I watched as M.U.'s limp dick drag behind the car like cans on car of a couple that had just gotten married. Blood came squirting out in waves and he let out the most piercing scream that a man could make. Cheeba couldn't help but to get out and walk to the back of the car to view the scene.

"This has got to be the craziest shit I've ever seen in my life," He replied covering his mouth as if he was about to throw up.

His penis lay on the ground covered in blood and his balls were still attached to his body. I even had to turn my head. Ranisha watched the whole time defiantly as if she was putting an end to a terrible chapter in her life.

"Let's get the fuck out of here," I suggested.

"What are we gonna do about him?" she asked.

"Oh, yeah." I answered pulling my gun and walking over to him.

I picked his head up, opened his mouth, and stuck my ratchet inside putting him out of his misery. M.U. was a goner.

As we were getting back into our cars, Ranisha gave me a hug and a kiss on the cheek. "Thank you. Nobody's ever defended me like this before."

All of the hardness was completely out of her. I could tell that she was sincere.

"No problem ma. It was my pleasure ya heard. C'mon let's roll out," I responded.

"Ski, you need to go to the hospital ya shoulder looks bad," she advised.

"No hospitals. The last thing I need is to be questioned by the jakes. They'll probably check my hands for gunpowder residue and all that. Let's just go home," I stated.

I un-hooked the rope from the back of my bumper and sent Cheeba back to Tiesha and Ranisha's house to clean up. Me and Ranisha drove back to our crib. 10 minutes into the drive the whole right side of my body got numb and I started getting light headed.

Before I knew it, everything was in total darkness. I had blacked out.

"Ski! Ski! Come on Ski open ya eyes! Ski!" Ranisha shouted frantically.

Ranisha was scared, but she couldn't panic. She checked his pulse and it was light, but he was still alive. She got off the Southern State Parkway stopped at 7-Eleven and bought a first aid kit. From there she drove to a motel and carried Ski into the room. Once they got into the room Ranisha went to work. She went to. She stripped him naked and removed the bullet from his shoulder with tweezers and a knife. After the bullet was out, she cleaned the womb, gauzed it up and tied a sheet around it tight to stop the bleeding. Ski was still not conscious but his pulse rate sounded like it had gotten stronger. Twenty minutes later, Ski woke up shivering and shaking uncontrollably. He was sweating profusely and his temperature was 103 degrees. Ranisha wrapped all the sheets and blankets that they had in the room around him, laid next to him, and wrapped her arms around him tightly trying to use her body heat to warm him up.

"C'mon Ski. Fight it. Don't die on me baby. Don't die on me," she cried out as she rocked him back in forth.

Before that night, Ranisha respected Ski as a thorough nigga but after that night, she had genuine love for him. No one had ever done what he'd done for her, nevertheless a man. He risked his life to save hers when he could have just stayed in the car and let them do her dirty. If Ski died, she would never get the chance to show him how much she appreciated it.

Since she was a child, Ranisha had been deprived of love and affection. No one ever gave a fuck about her, her entire life and in turn, her heart grew cold and stopped caring about anyone as well. The "Fuck the World" tattoo she had on her neck was the motto she lived by. Her mother was a dope head who sold her body to support her and her boyfriend's habit. Not only did her mom's boyfriend pimp her mother, but he also use to beat up Ranisha and touch her in sexual ways. When she tried to tell her mother, she accused her of trying to steal her man and kicked her out at the tender age of twelve. Ranisha lived on the streets for a while and eventually moved in with her Aunt Netta and her cousin Lorenzo.

Netta was Ranisha's mother's sister. Her husband Lorenzo use to sneak in her room at night and eat her pussy. She ended up running away from there and started boosting, robbing, transporting and selling drugs and anything else she could to survive. She built a reputation as a being a thorough female and got down with various crews but at the end they always took advantage of her and did her dirty. When she was eighteen, she was in the car with a dude that she thought was her peoples who she was getting money with and they got pulled over. The nigga convinced her to take the weight saying he had a record and the most she could get was probation. Being that she was young and somewhat naive, she agreed. She ended up getting a 1 to 3 year sentence for the gun and never heard from or saw the cat again.

Ski was the first nigga who came into her life that ever kept it all the way real with her. She realized that the main reason that she hadn't liked him up until that point was because of the relationship that he and Tiesha had. Ranisha was a loyal person when she knew someone's heart was true, and after what Ski had done there was nothing she wouldn't do for him. For the first time in her life, she felt physically attracted to a man. She wondered what it would be like to make love to him. She decided that when Ski woke up she was gonna give him something that she never gave any man.

***

When I woke up the next morning, I felt weak and disorientated. I didn't know where the fuck I was at or how I'd gotten there. My shoulder was sore as a porn star's pussy after a gangbang. All of a sudden I realized that someone was sucking my dick and sucking it well.

"Damn!" I yelled out gripping the sheets.

Whoever it was that was sucking my dick was underneath the covers so I had no clue. My first thought was that it was Tiesha but when I pulled the sheet off I couldn't believe my eyes. It was Ranisha.

The head I was receiving was so good I could barely talk. "What? What iz you doing?" I asked.

She put her index and middle finger on my lips. "SSHHHH!!"

I didn't know what had gotten into Ranisha but I didn't give a fuck. For a woman who had never messed with a man before her head game was on one thousand. She was spitting on it and jerking it off in a circular motion as she sucked the tip of my dick, and moaning as if she was really enjoying it. The vein in the middle of her forehead popped out as she took my entire eight and half inches down into her throat. Her mouth was so warm and moist that it almost felt like pussy. I began moving my hips forward and fucking her face. I pulled the sheet completely off her so I could get a glimpse of her banging body. Her body was even sicker than I imagined it would be. She had the softest skin and her body didn't have an ounce of fat on it. Looking down at her sucking my dick with her fat yellow ass propped up in the air, and her titties bouncing on my thighs I felt like I was in heaven. She was a dime. My dick was so hard that it felt like I could hit a homerun with it. I wanted to get in that pussy badly.

"Yo, Ranisha chill. Are you sure you wanna do this?" I asked.

She looked me in the eyes and stuck her tongue down my throat. After that, she ran her tongue all the way down from my ears to my balls. As we were kissing and fondling each other, I stuck my hand in between her legs and began rubbing her clit in fast circular motions. This drove her crazy. Her pussy was drenched. I stuck two fingers inside her and she let out a soft moan.

"Lemme do this," I whispered taking control and laying her on the bed on her back.

She laid back on the bed as I slid in between her legs and started kissing and licking her belly button. I could tell she felt a little uncomfortable at first but she relaxed and went with it. First, I teased her by licking the inside of her thighs and then I ran my tongue lightly against her clit. This drove her crazy. Sweat was pouring down off her face, her love juices were running down her legs, and she was shaking uncontrollably. I've never been big on eating pussy but she was so bad I felt obligated too. She didn't have a flaw. She had beautiful firm natural 36 D breasts, long legs, thick thighs a dimed out face and a flat stomach.

Being that it was her first time having consensual sex with a man I wanted to make it special so I took my time with her. After I was done eating her pussy, I turned Ranisha over on her stomach and started kissing and sucking the back of her neck. From there I ran my tongue down her spine making goose bumps appear all over her body and spread open her ass cheeks and did something I never did in my life. I licked her ass. Ranisha held on to the bedpost for dear life. She was bucking and screaming wildly. I had to hold her down to continue.

"Ski, put it in. I wanna feel you," Ranisha pleaded.

I climbed on top of her and kissed her. "You sure you wanna go through this? We can stop right now if you want?" I asked double-checking.

"I've never been surer of anything in my life," she responded reaching in between us and guiding my dick inside her love cave.

Being that she was so tight, it took a second for me to get it all the way in. Once I got it in, it was so wet and tight that I couldn't contain myself. Ranisha came instantly. She grabbed a hold of my shoulders and squeezed them with all of her strength as she arched her back with her eyes closed. The pain from my shoulder meant nothing at that point.

"You feel so good inside of me," she cried out with tears in her eyes digging her nails into my biceps.

"I'm about to cum," I announced shortly after.

That morning we didn't fuck, we made love. We didn't stop to eat, drink, or to go to the bathroom. We made love all day. After the

third and final time I rolled over exasperated staring at the ceiling.
"Ski, I love you. Promise me you'll never do me dirty and shit on me. I want you to be mines," Ranisha declared.
"What about Ty?" I asked.
"What about her?" Ranisha shot back. "It's us three to the death! We all love each other so why not? Me, and Ty are gonna be everything you need. You might as well call all of ya little ho's and dead them because if I catch them around you I'mma pop they ass."
"Yeah?" I responded with a chuckle. "So you just gonna Deebo me like that," I asked referring to the popular character from the movie Friday.
"Yup. You mine now. Ain't nothing no other bitch can do for you that we can't. Shit you gonna have every nigga's dream, two wives. Two bad ass wives."
"How you know Ty gonna be down wit it?"
Ranisha made a face as if to say I sounded stupid. "C'mon Ski stop it! You know Ty is crazy about you. This is what she always wanted."
She laid her head on my chest and fell asleep. As she slept, I stayed up all night thinking about everything that happened. My life never ceased to amaze me. Ranisha was talking about she was in love with me after one night, and I'd caught more bodies due to beef that wasn't mines. I didn't know what the future held for me but I just hoped the drama would come to an end. I just wanted to live my life and be happy. Maybe I could be happy with Tiesha and Ranisha. For one thing, I knew the sex was going to be off the hook and they were both down ass chicks so it was a win-win situation for me. Before I went to sleep, I made up my mind and decided that I was going to try it. I didn't know it then but I had broken one of the oldest rules of the game. Never mix business with pleasure.

Chapter 15

December 04

"Surprise!" everyone shouted in a deafening tone scaring the life out of me as I walked through the door of my crib.

"Oh shit! Y'all scared the shit out of me!" I said with a smile holding my chest. "Y'all tryin' to give a nigga a heart attack on his born day?"

"Watch ya mouth boy! Don't be cussing and carrying on like that while I'm here. You grown but you ain't grown enough to be speaking that type of language in front of me. I brought you into this world-," my mother replied with fake anger.

I cut her off. I knew all of her lines by heart. "And you will take me out. I know ma. You've been running those lines for the last twenty-five years. When you gonna switch it up?" I responded as my mother walked up to me, smacked me in the head playfully, and gave me a hug and a kiss.

"So who's responsible for damn near killing me?" I asked everyone in attendance putting my arm around my mother.

Everyone pointed at Ty and Ranisha and they were pointing at each other.

"Oh, so that means y'all both responsible," I replied before bear hugging both of them at the same time and lifting them off the ground. "I should've known something was up cause y'all was acting real strange today. Thank you though on some real shit, I'm mean real stuff. This is what's up," I continued kissing both of them.

It was December 27 at 8:30 at night. There had been a big snowstorm in New York a few days prior so besides the wind chill making the temperature seem like it was ten below zero, snow covered the sidewalks and the roads were icy. All day long Ty and Ranisha were taking turns keeping me out of the house. For the two previous hours, I'd been waiting for Cheeba out in Hempstead, Long Island. He called me on some frantic shit like he had beef and told me to meet him as soon as possible. I was out the door as he was telling me but when I made it, there he was nowhere to be found. His phone was going straight to voice mail so I didn't know what was up. I looked everywhere for him and called around but no one had seen him. Two hours later, he called me and told me to meet him at my crib. I'm assuming that's when they were setting everything up.

As I was making my way around the party giving hugs, kisses, and daps I ran into Cheeba.

"So you gonna turn on ya man like that? Lemme find out you was down wit the conspiracy too?" I asked jokingly giving him dap.

"Ty and Re made me do it son. I was forced into that shit B. Them bitches had me under pressure," he joked back.

The surprise party at my crib was small but my circle was small so it was all good. Everyone besides my niggaz that were locked up was there. My mother, little sister, Cheeba, my son, Ty's son, Boota's baby mother Shamika and their two daughters, the six little niggaz I had hustling for me and Ziyah and Merl the two chick's I had pumping E pills for me at the college. My mother cooked all of my favorite foods and that was a birthday present within itself. My momz made it do what it do when it came to the kitchen. It was all love. Dro, Boota, and Wise all called me up separately wishing me a Happy Birthday, and everyone got me little gifts. Cheeba and the rest of the team chipped in and copped me a pair of 2-karat earrings. My son drew me a picture, my sister got me a pair of throwback Jordan's, and Ty and Ranisha spent like ten stacks on clothes for me. For the first time in a long time, I was completely happy. Everything was going my way. We had upstate on smash, and everybody was eating lovely. My mother and sister were straight. We were getting closer and closer to being able to pull the heist and shit was good on the home front with Tiesha and Ranisha. On top of all that, I was getting more money than I ever had gotten in my life. Life was sweet.

At about 10:30 at night I got another surprise. My mother called me to my front door and there was a white man there waiting for me.

"What's good?" I said when I got to the door.

"I have a deliver for a-" he paused looking at his clipboard. "Mr. Isaiah Thompson. Are you him?"

I was leery. "What kind of delivery?"

"Are you Mr. Thompson sir?"

"Yeah."

"Sign here."

I signed my name and the white man didn't hand me shit. He just stood there with a dumb look on his face.

"Where the fuck is the delivery nigga?" I barked making him jump.

He went in his pocket and pulled out a funny looking key.

I was puzzled. "What is this to?"

He nodded his head towards the driveway and that's when I saw it. A big ass 22 inch white World Craft speedboat with a ribbon on it.

"Who the fuck sent me this?" I inquired.

"Uhhhm, it doesn't say but enjoy." he said with a smirk and walked off.

My mother came back to the door and asked. "Where did this boat come from?"

"I don't even know," I answered still not knowing what to make out of the situation.

"Hey, everybody get your coats and come outside. Somebody bought Isaiah a boat," my mother announced.

Everyone put on their jackets and ran outside to check it out.

"Who bought you this?" Ranisha asked with an attitude.

"I don't know."

"It better not be no bitch cause I'll put the knife to her ass quick." Ranisha said seriously before going over to check out the boat with everyone else.

Just then, my phone rang.

"Yo." I answered without looking at the caller I.D.

"Peace and blessing star. Happy birfday. Yuh receive your gif?" Prince asked.

"Oh, so that was you. Big Dread you crazy man. What the fuck am I gonna do with a boat?"

"Whu you talk bout bwoy? Yuh ride it, whu you mean?" Prince responded. "Ay mi hafi go now. Mi link up wit you tomorrow. Mi hafi handle someting."

"A'ight cool. Good looking on the gift." I thanked him and was about to get off the phone until I realized something. "Ayo, Prince how you know today was my birthday?" I asked.

"Mi know everyting star. Mi know everyting," he responded with his deep laugh before he disconnected the call.

To this day, I don't know how Prince knew my birthday or my address. He was an ill nigga for real.

Later that night after everybody left Tiesha and Ranisha fucked me and sucked me until I couldn't take it no more. I was lying in the bed ten seconds away from falling in a deep sleep when I felt Ranisha tapping me.

"Nah yo I'm good. Lemme sleep for awhile," I stated thinking she wanted more sex.

"Get dressed. We have another surprise for you," Ranisha ordered pulling the covers off me.

I was getting pissed. "C'mon Re chill. Surprise me in the morning I'm tired!"

Ranisha was relentless. "No, this can't wait get up."

I saw I was in a lose- lose situation, being as though if I didn't get up she wasn't gonna let me sleep, so I got up. "Yo, this shit better be good B. For real."

I got dressed and hopped in the back of my BMW blindfolded with Ranisha while Ty drove us to God knows where. Twenty minutes later the car stopped and Ty and Re led me out the car. When they took off the blindfold, I was astonished. My mouth dropped to the floor. I was at a loss for words. It was a white Bentley Coupe fresh off the showroom floor.

"Surprise!" Ranisha and Tiesha said in unison with their arms outstretched.

I was in shock. "Get the fuck out of here! Who is this for? This is crazy! Nah, y'all gotta take this shit back."

"You don't like it?" Tiesha asked.

"Yeah, of course I like it, you crazy?" I shot back. "But this shit costs too much money. Where y'all gonna get the money for this? I hope y'all ain't spend all ya'll paper."

"Don't worry about that papi just get in. It's yours," Tiesha stated opening the driver's side door for me.

I sat in the car and put my face in my hands. The whip was so sick. It had that new car smell, fresh leather. It had a wood grain dashboard and paneling, TV's in the headrests, 22-inch chrome wheels, and a Play Station 2 in the back.

"C'mon take it for a spin," Ranisha suggested hopping in the passenger seat.

Tiesha joined us and jumped in the backseat and I drove all over Queens. They had all of my favorite CD's in the disc changer and the whole nine. An hour later, I pulled back into the parking lot and asked the question I was dying to hear the answer to.

"Seriously how did y'all pay for this?"

"Don't look at me. This was all Ranisha's work." Tiesha blurted out.

After that first night that Ranisha and I had sex, we went home and told Ty everything. Ty was shocked but happy. After all, it was what she wanted from the beginning. That night, we made a pact that we'd always be together and never let anything or anybody come between us. We were a family. I had two wives. Together they fulfilled every need and fantasy that I ever had. There wasn't even a need to cheat on them because I had two bad pieces waiting in my bed for me every night that were willing to jump in front of a bullet for me. We got along perfectly and hadn't had an argument or disagreement since. The only thing that bothered me a little was Ranisha's jealousy. She would act up if another bitch said as much as hi to me.

"A'ight listen. Remember I told you about that 900 hotline scheme I was thinking about doing?" Ranisha asked.

I nodded my head.

"Well I popped it off. I started a little over a month and half ago and things moved quicker than I anticipated. The calls started coming in so much that I had to rent out an office on Jamaica Avenue. I made a hundred and fifty grand the first month all profit." Ranisha explained proudly.

The 900-hotline scheme that Ranisha was referring to went like this. Ranisha paid for a 900 number and set the price at $49.99 a minute. She then put an ad in the paper looking for part time workers telling them that they could make up to $500 a week dialing phone numbers. After she amassed a crew of thirty to forty different people she set them out all over the city to call the hotline from different peoples houses and places of business and to stay on the line for as long as possible. After that, she went on the internet and put the same ad up and before she knew it, she had workers in different states. The scheme could only last a month or two at the most but by then it would be too late. She would already have all the money and closed up shop before the Feds knew what hit them.

"Word? A hundred and fifty grand? Damn, that's a lot of bread. And, you spent it all on me?" I asked.

"Yup. All for my husband. I hated to see you driving around in that BMW. Mad niggaz got that whip and I wanted my husband to have something that you rarely see. You my nigga now. You represent me. You ain't no regular mu'fucka and you shouldn't be pushing no BMW like you are. And besides all that, every time I get in that car I think about that night you almost died," Ranisha explained.

"Damn, ma that's real! I don't know what to say," I responded.

"Just tell me you love me," Ranisha stated.

"C'mon ma you know I love you," I replied kissing her on her soft lips.

I had never seen Ranisha smile so brightly since I met her.

"Hey-hey, can a bitch get some love?" Ty joked from the backseat. We pulled Tiesha into the front seat and started kissing all over her.

"Ayo, this whip costs a lot of paper. Let's chill until we get to the crib," I suggested.

"I got one more surprise for you baby," Ranisha announced.

"What else you got me, a G4?" I asked jokingly.

"No, even better. I cracked into the police departments' computer. It's a wrap. It's whenever you ready now," Ranisha replied.

I was stuck. "Say word?" Ayo, come here," I called out to Ranisha pulling her on my lap. "I love y'all yo. This is the best birthday I ever had in my life. Real wrap."

I took off Ranisha's sweatpants, put the seat back and had her sit on my face. Tiesha got naked as well and started riding me. We stayed right there in that parking lot in my brand new Bentley

Coupe fogging up the windows. I wasn't lying when I told them it had been my best birthday ever. I was on the way to seeing more paper than I had ever thought possible. I actually found myself falling for Re, and Ty on some other shit. But was it true love or lust?

Chapter 16

New Years Night 05

"Ayo Re… can you hear me?" I asked.

"Clear as day papi. Can you hear me?" Ranisha responded.

"Yeah crystal clear. Everything is a green light. Set ya watch right," I paused to set my watch. "Now."

"Okay gotcha."

"I should be there in one hour flat."

"Take ya time and be careful. It's easy money baby. Do it just like we practiced," Ranisha advised me.

"Yo, remember to holla at me every ten minutes or so to make sure we still connected," I reminded her.

"A'ight."

It was an icy cold New Years New York night. The streets were filled with people from all walks of life waiting for the ball to drop in Times Square, while others were partying away at their local hot spots. Not me though. I had just climbed into the vent from my office and was making the sixty minute crawl to the vent into the Zales safe room beneath me. Ranisha was in a diner somewhere in Manhattan with her two laptops monitoring my every move, and Tiesha was posted up in her whip in downtown Brooklyn waiting for me to get off the train after the heist. I had on a wireless microphone that connected me to Ranisha, and a tracking device in my sneaker that monitored my every movement so that if I got lost Ranisha could direct me. She had the blueprint of the entire building on her computer and made up a program with the route to Zales from my office vent. She saw every twist and turn I made. I had been planning for that moment every day for the last six months. In my mind I had went through every detail of the heist a million times thinking of any and every problem that could arise. People always say that you should have a plan B in case things went wrong and I believed it. So much that I had all the way down to a plan Z. I was prepared physically, mentally, and emotionally for any variable that could possible come in between me and my goal. This was it. Either I was going to get rich or get knocked trying.

I was wearing a full spandex suit top and bottom, with two pairs of thermals over top of them, a black hoody, and jeans, with some Nike Air Shox track sneakers, racing gloves, and a black ski mask. I also brought along with me a duffel bag, the keys to the display cases that Tiesha had copied for me, and some type of electronic box that Ranisha said I needed to put on the safe to open it.

Inside the vent was as narrow as one of the Olsen Twins, and due to the lack of air and dust particles, it was extremely hard to breathe. There was barely enough room in the vent for me and the duffel bag. There were all types of rats, and bugs inside, and it smelled like an old attic. It definitely wasn't the place to be if you were claustrophobic.

I made the long hour crawl from my office vent downstairs into the Zales safe room's vent, that was previously cemented in.

"Yo, Re. I'm here. Deactivate the motion sensors," I said through my microphone.

After about a two-minute wait Ranisha said, "It's done. Hurry up and put the alarm code in at the front of the store. We only have sixty seconds until the alarm goes off."

I climbed out the vent in the safe room and ran into the front of the store to deactivate the alarm.

Ranisha was in my ear. "Hurry up. We only have thirty-five more seconds."

Hearing her in my ear made me panic a little. "The code? What's the code?"

"1681-9403-7925-1438. You got it?"

I punched in the numbers and a green light came on indicating that I had deactivated the alarm.

I was relieved. "Do what you do now Re and I'mma do what I do. Don't forget to loop the video footage," I said.

"I'll holla at you in ten minutes. I gotta hack back into the system to make sure the signal didn't get sent to the police department."

"Do you mami," I responded.

I walked back into the safe room, grabbed my duffel bag out of the vent, and got down to business. I felt like a kid at a candy store. I didn't know what to take first. I decided on the watches. Zales was the biggest store I'd ever robbed. The stores I had ran in previously all had one display case with different kinds of watches. Zales on the other hand had different display cases for every watch the store carried. Rolexes, Cartier's, Movado's, and Frank Mueller's. In total, they had over a hundred-fifty watches. I opened up the Rolex display case first with the key that Ty had duplicated and cleaned it out. All the Rolexes were sick. They had an Oyster Perpetual Collection and a Cellini Collection. They had Yacht Masters, Daytona's, Presi's, Explorers, and Gmt masters. You name it they had it. Gold, Platinum, men's and ladies. I did the same thing for all the watch display cases and moved on to the necklaces and beads.

"Ski, we got a problem," Ranisha said over the microphone.

"Damn! What happened? You couldn't stop the signal from being transmitted to the jakes?" I asked with my heart beating as fast as a crack heads.

"No. What are we gonna do wit all this money?" Ranisha joked.

"Woman don't play wit me like that. I was scared to death up in this muthfucka," I responded laughing.

"You look so sexy up in there stealing all that jewelry. Mmm, mmm. We gonna fuck the shit out of you when we get home," Ranisha replied.

"I bet you I do look sexy taking all this money. Shit, Craig Mack and Flavor Flav would look sexy taking all this cake." I joked back.

Ranisha hacked into the store security system and had all the footage from the camera's being transmitted to her laptop so she saw my every move. The night before she dubbed 1 hour of the video camera surveilling the store and looped it for eight hours so that when the police reviewed the tapes they wouldn't see anything but how the store looked the previous night.

I finished emptying the display cases with the necklaces and the beads and moved on to the earrings. After the earrings, I emptied out all the bracelets, and then the rings. The rings they carried were crazy. The engagement rings looked like something Tiger Woods or Kobe Bryant would give to their wives after being caught in another affair. In addition to that, they had some iced out pinky rings that no one but Diddy could afford.

"Ayo, Ranisha. I'mma keep this one for me," I said walking up to the camera and the putting the ring to the lens.

"Yeah, daddy that shit is off the hook. What you gonna get for ya two wives?" Ranisha asked.

I played stupid. "Two wives? I got two wives?"

"A'ight now don't get stabbed the fuck up," Ranisha warned me.

When I was finished with the rings, I walked around the store seeing if there was anything else of value worth taking.

Inside Zales was huge. Each piece of jewelry had its own section and the display cases were all connected forming a big rectangle.

I decided to leave well enough alone and not take any more shit because my duffel bag was already packed and feeling heavy as hell. I walked back into the safe room for the big grand finale. The safe.

"Ayo, Re this is it right here baby. This is what's gonna make us millionaires," I said excitedly rubbing my hands together as if I was preparing to feast at a Thanksgiving dinner.

"Ready when you are," Ranisha stated.

The safe room was a medium sized room with nothing in it but a 3-foot tall metal computerized safe. If half of what I believed was in there we were set for life. Joke time was over. It was time to get down to business.

"Ski, put the box that I gave you on top of the computer," Ranisha instructed.

I did as I was told and waited for further instructions.

"Just a second..." Ranisha said typing away furiously on her laptop. "A'ight Ski. Take ya time and punch in everything I tell you slowly. We can't afford any mistakes or slip-ups. You ready?"

"I've been ready for this for the last twenty-five years," I said eagerly.

"9859999999999999KDL3984JC," Ranisha read out.

I punched in the letters and numbers just as I was told and an automated voice came out of nowhere and asked me for my thumbprint.

"Yo, what the fuck is going on? This shit is asking me for a thumb print." I replied leery.

"Calm down. Just take ya glove off and put ya thumb on the screen."

"Put my thumb on the screen? Is you out ya fucking mind? You ain't tell me nuthin' about this before."

Ranisha assured me. "Because it was no big deal. Listen, the system is down. It's just asking for a thumbprint because that's how the security program works. It's not gonna be able to read it and it's definitely not gonna be able to save it. Ain't nuthin' going to happen. Trust me Ski."

I wasn't convinced. "Yo, I don't know ma."

"Ski, you know I love you right?"

"Yeah, I know that."

"Do you love me?"

"Yeah, you know that," I answered.

"Ski, I love you. I'd die for you baby. Trust me when I tell you that nuthin' is going to happen to you. I'd never tell you anything wrong or anything I wasn't sure of. You know that," Ranisha explained.

I thought about it for a second and realized that she was right. If there is one thing I knew for sure was that Ranisha loved me. So, out of faith in her, I took my glove off and put my thumb on the computer screen.

"Hello Mr. Klein," the automated voice stated.

I heard a few clicks, and then the light went from red, to orange to green. I put my glove on and opened the safe. When I opened it, it was like the gates of Heaven had opened up for me. Inside the safe there were stacks of money and a small black bag. I took a deep breath and opened it. When I saw its contents, I stood frozen.

"Ski, Ski, what's going on in there? Everything good daddy?" Ranisha asked sounding concerned.

"Yeah. Shit couldn't be better. We hit the muthafuckin' jackpot!" I yelled out in jubilation.

Inside the small bag was nothing but pure diamonds. The store was dark but when I opened that bag, it seemed like it illuminated the whole place. I emptied all of the money out of the safe into my already stuffed duffel bag, put the diamonds in the side pocket of the bag and zipped it up.

"You got everything baby?"

"I just finished emptying the safe."

"Come on back home daddy. Come on back home," Ranisha stated.

I put the duffel bag in the vent, took the small-computerized box off the safe, and climbed back in the vent. After I was in the vent, I put the vent cover back on and began the 60-minute crawl back to my office vent. twenty minutes later, I ran into my first major problem of the night.

"Ayo, Re. We got a problem," I announced. "I made a wrong turn. Where the fuck am I at?"

I got no response.

"Re!" I yelled. "Yo Re, where you at? Re! Can you hear me?"

Once again, I heard nothing.

"Re! Yo, Re!" I continued shouting into the microphone.

I didn't know what happened but I no longer had a connection with Ranisha. I took a deep breath to regain my composure. Panicking wasn't going to help me find my way back at all. One thing that I had miscalculated was the weight of the duffel bag. Crawling through that stuffy ass, blazing hot vent pushing that bag was strenuous. I was sweating and breathing heavily.

I crawled backwards in the vent and tried to figure out where I had gone wrong. Just when I thought, I was going the right way I ran into another dead end.

"Damn. What the fuck," I muttered to myself in frustration.

I'd made the crawl numerous times and never got lost. I couldn't believe I had been so careless. It had been over two hours and I was tired, frustrated, and scared. I was completely lost. I decided to stay still and rest for a while. It was then that I heard Ranisha.

"Ski- Ski- Can- Hear- My-Frozen-I'm- Trying- Where-At-," I heard Ranisha saying in bits in pieces.

From what I could make out, she was trying to tell me that her computer was frozen which let me know that I was really by myself. If I was going to make it out, it was gonna be on my own accord.

three hours later I was no closer to my office then I'd been two hours previously. I looked at my watch and saw that it was 5:30 a.m.. I only had an hour and a half left until Zales opened. The last place in the world I wanted to be when the store opened was the vents. That would be the first place they would look and even if it wasn't by the time I got out the block would be swarming with cops.

At six in the morning, I heard some noise in my microphone. It was Ranisha.

"Ski? Can you hear me? Ski! Yo, Ski!" Ranisha shouted.

"Where the fuck you been at? I'm lost!"

"I see that. My computer crashed. It just came back on. We gotta get you out of there. It's already six."

"No kidding," I replied sarcastically.

"Gimme a minute and I'll have you out of there," Ranisha said confidently.

Hearing Ranisha's voice was like music to my ears. I was so happy I could've shed tears. My previously tired and weak body felt reenergized.

"How did you get all the way over there? Okay, Ski back up and turn left and the-," Ranisha went on directing me.

I followed Ranisha's instructions until I got to the ladder that took me from the ground floor, to the second floor where my office was. I was home free. I made the fifteen minute crawl to my office vent and had my feet on my office floor at 6:45 a.m..

I took a quick shower, changed into a suit, put the duffel bag on my shoulder, and exited the office building at 7 a.m. on the dot.

As I was walking out, I saw the jewelry store manager going inside.

"Good morning and Happy New Years!" he greeted me jubilantly.

"Same to you," I replied.

"Had a late night working?" he asked.

"You couldn't imagine," I answered casually and strolled off.

The whole thing was ironic. There I was walking out of the building with the entire store in my duffel bag and conversing with the store manager as if absolutely nothing had happened. By the time I'd be getting on the subway he'd be calling the police frantically and I'd be long gone.

As I was walking to the subway, Tiesha pulled up in her Benz.

"Need a ride?" she asked with a kool- aid smile.

I got in the car, put the duffel bag in the backseat, pushed my seat back and closed my eyes. I'd done it. I was rich. Life as I knew it was never going to be the same. But not just for the good. You never understand the saying "Mo Money, Mo problems" when you ain't got it but I was about to get a dose of what the true meaning of the phrase really meant firsthand.

Chapter 17

January 05

"Last call for American Airlines flight 227 to Miami on gate 62. Last call for American Airlines flight 227 to Miami on gate 62." the flight attendant announced over the loudspeaker.

"C'mon y'all... This ain't no muthafuckin' catwalk. Hurry the fuck up. Y'all could be cute when we get there," I shouted running to the gate and looking behind me at Tiesha and Ranisha strutting and switching through the airport like they were models.

The reason we were running late was because of them. They'd been in the mirror fixing their hair and changing their clothes for more than a hour. It was enough dealing with just one woman getting ready, but now that I had two it was double the trouble.

We made it to the gate just in time. The flight attendant was just about to put the metal chain up. I gave the woman our three first class tickets and we boarded the plane.

As soon as we got on the plane, Ty and Re started acting up. They both were pissy drunk and acting ghetto as hell. Ranisha started tongue kissing Tiesha and rubbing on her thighs in plain view of everybody. Kids and all. Everyone on the plane was staring at us. Ranisha looked up, saw everyone staring and yelled, "What the fuck y'all all in our faces for?"

The white people got scared, turned around in their seats, and began whispering to one another.

"Ayo. Chill the fuck out. It's kids on this plane B. What the fuck is wrong wit y'all?" I whispered.

"Fuck these crackers and their kids. We paid two gees a piece for these tickets. We should be able to do what the fuck we wanna do for all that got damn money. First Class is a muthafuckin' rip off anyway. What we pay all this money for? Some fucking peanuts and more comfortable chairs?" Ranisha responded loud enough for everyone to hear.

"Just be easy. Y'all drawing unnecessary attention to us," I responded in a low tone. "C'mon let me sit in the middle of y'all."

As soon as we switched seats and I was in the middle Tiesha and Ranisha were all over me, kissing on me, sucking on my neck and trying to play with my dick. They were definitely trying to become members of The Mile High Club.

Enough was enough. "Ayo, yo, chill. Didn't I tell y'all to chill. Y'all buggin' the fuck out! Relax," I shouted. "Go to sleep or something."

"Ski, take me in the bathroom and put me to sleep daddy. I'm mad horny. I always wanted to fuck on a plane," Tiesha whispered in my ear seductively.

"We on a plane with millions of dollars in stolen diamonds. We don't need any unnecessary attention on us. Just chill the fuck out," I shot back aggravated.

Tiesha pouted for a second but eventually sat back in her seat and fell asleep.

Ranisha, Tiesha, and I had just taken off from LaGuardia Airport in Queens on our way to Miami to meet the fence. After the heist, I took all the jewelry to my old fence Ernesto on Jamaica Avenue to sell but it was too much for him. He just didn't have that type of cash on hand. When I showed Ernesto, the diamonds the niggaz eyes got big as hell. He told me he definitely didn't have that type of money to get everything but he had a friend in Miami who he knew would be interested. Ernesto bought a hundred of the watches off me, a few bracelets and took a few rings off my hands for seven hundred- fifity thousand. He gave me half in cash and said that when I returned from Miami he would have the rest. It was no big deal because I knew he was good for it. My niggaz and I had been doing business with him for years.

Ernesto also appraised the diamonds for me. He said that I could get three million for them easy. After I sold a hundred of the watches to him, I had fifty watches, a whole display case worth of earrings, twenty or so bracelets and fifty rings. The cash I had took from the safe came to over five hundred thousand. I figured I should at least be able to get another five hundred grand for the rest of the jewelry, so in total our take was going to be close to five million dollars. We were set.

After the plane landed in Miami, we got our bags and made it out the airport without incident. I was happy because that was what I had been worried about the whole flight. I wasn't going to be happy until all the jewelry was sold and I had all the money.

We took a cab from the airport to the hotel that we were staying at called Loews located on South Beach. Loews was one of the most well-known and expensive hotels in Miami. It was off the hook. The outside of it looked like the White House. They had an indoor and outdoor pool, two bars, a restaurant, and a club. Just sitting in the lobby of the hotel made me feel rich.

We put our bags down in our Presidential suite and walked around in awe. It was two floors; it had a jacuzzi, kitchen, living room, dining room, a 52-inch flat screen TV, a bar, a king sized bed in the bedroom, two guest bedrooms and a balcony with an ill view of the strip. The bar came fully stocked with complimentary bottles of Cristal, and there was even a laptop in the living room. Being in that suite I felt like how the kids felt on The Real World their first day. But I snapped out of my daze quickly. I had business to take care of. Ranisha and Tiesha were running around the suite admiring every detail, so I went into the living room and used the phone.

The first thing I did was call the number to this Jamaican cat that Prince had plugged me in with to get a hammer. There was no way I was going to a stranger's house without a ratchet. Prince's man sent someone to the suite and in fifteen minutes, I had my hands on more than a few guns. A .40 cal, Glock 9, and a .44 magnum.

After that, I called the fence.

"Hello," a female voice answered.

"Yes. How are you? My name is Ski. Is Mr. Coppin available?" I asked in my most professional sounding voice.

"Hold please."

I was on hold for fifteen minutes before he came to the phone.

"Hello. Kevin Coppin here."

"Mr. Coppin this is Ski."

"Hey, so you made it huh? Welcome to Miami. Are you enjoying yourself or what?"

"Well actually I just got here. I was hoping I could reschedule our meeting for today instead of tomorrow."

"Please, call me Kev. You make me feel old when you call me Mr.," Kev responded before continuing. "You just got here. Why don't you go out shopping and partying and let us go with our original plan to meet tomorrow?"

"Well if you don't mind, I'd rather get it over with today. I live by the motto business before pleasure."

"Business before pleasure huh?" he repeated. "Why not have both. You gonna see that it's a pleasure doing business with me. I treat my business associates very well. Where are you staying? I'll send some of my people to come get you."

"Loews."

"Excellent choice. I see you have good taste. See you soon," Kev replied before he hung up the phone.

When I got off the phone, I ran upstairs looking for the girls to tell them to get dressed because I had rescheduled the meeting. I found them in the master bedroom getting it in. Ranisha was fucking Tiesha from behind with her strap on.

"Get dressed y'all I just rescheduled the meeting. C'mon let's go. I need y'all looking professional." I stated.

They paid me no mind. Tiesha was moaning as Ranisha pulled her hair and pounded away at her.

"Let's wait until tomorrow daddy," Tiesha managed to blurt out.

"Yeah, we're on vacation. We're millionaires," Ranisha said backing Tiesha up.

"That's where y'all are wrong. We ain't millionaires until we have the money in our hands. The quicker we get all of this jewelry out of our possession the better," I responded as they ignored me and kept on getting it in. "Matter of fact don't worry about it. I'll go by myself. Y'all stay here," I continued storming out the bedroom.

Ranisha and Tiesha were starting to agitate me. All they ever thought about was fucking. At times, I loved it, but that day it was getting me pissed. I felt like it was nothing to celebrate about until all of our business was taken care of.

I showered, got dressed, and waited in the lobby of the Hotel for my ride. I was taking in the sights of all the beautiful women when a bad ass Chinese woman wearing the top of a bathing suit and a mini skirt approached me.

"You are Ski?" she asked, her Asian accent over-powering her English.

"Yeah, I'm Ski how did you know?" I asked.

"Come with me," she stated with an attitude not answering my question.

I followed the Chinese woman outside to a stretch Benz limo. When I got inside the limo, I was in for the surprise of my life. There were four completely nude naked women of all different nationalities. A chocolate complexioned black woman, an olive skin Latina, a Gwen Stefani look alike and another Chinese woman.

I was like a fat kid in an Entenmann's warehouse.

"Hi Ski,' they all said in unison.

"What's good?" I responded looking around unsure of what was going to happen next.

As soon as the limo pulled off them ho's damn near raped me. They tore off my clothes, sucked my dick, licked my balls and took turns riding me until I couldn't take it anymore and exploded.

By that time, we were pulling up to Kev's mansion on Five Star Island. The outside of Kev's mansion was crazy. It was easily the flyest crib I'd ever saw in my life. It looked like something a famous rapper or actor would be showing on MTV cribs. When it was time to get out the limo, I hesitated realizing I was naked. The girls had practically torn my clothes to shreds. After all the ladies filed out, another woman who I'd never laid eyes on came to the door and passed me a white robe.

"Put this on and follow me," she said.

I put the robe on and followed the woman through the mansion and outside to the pool area. As I was walking through the mansion, I saw nothing but chicks. Bad chicks wearing next to nothing. Kev was sitting poolside with a robe on just like the one I had on sipping a drink. I sat down at the table with him.

"How was the ride?" Kev asked with an all-knowing smile.

"Which one?" I asked jokingly to lighten the mood.

"All four of them," he shot back as we both started laughing.

Kev looked nothing like I thought he would. He was about 5'7 and brown skin, with a stocky build and a low haircut. He was full-blooded Panamanian but looked just like a regular black man. The biggest surprise was his age. I was thinking that he was going to be an older man but he was in his early thirties. I could see why he didn't want me calling him Mr.

We engaged in small talk for half an hour or so and he asked me about my session with the bitches and told me how he'd amassed his fortune. It turned out that his father owned an import/export company that moved diamonds. In addition to that, his father also owned a chain of jewelry stores all over the state of Florida. When his father passed away, he left his one and only son everything making him a twenty-year-old multi-millionaire. Kev told me that he netted over fifteen million dollars a year in profit.

"So is it a pleasure doing business with me or what?" Kev asked with his arms outstretched.

"No doubt. You definitely know how to pull out the red carpet for a nigga," I responded.

"I thought you said that business before pleasure was your motto? You let me distract you with pussy."

"Trust me Kev. I'm far from being distracted. I'm always on point. Don't let my age fool you," I assured him.

Kev looked like he wanted to smile. "Oh yeah? So how did I get all of this?" he asked putting my duffle bag and two guns on the table.

My heart sunk into my stomach. I couldn't believe how stupid and careless I'd been. Not only had I let them ho's take my heaters, but I had let them take the jewelry and the diamonds as well. I'd gotten caught slipping. I was at his mercy.

"That was a test that ninety-nine percent of men would fail. Don't feel bad," he replied. "Do you see all of these beautiful women? They are not just eye candy. These women are all trained security. They specialize in martial arts and can shoot you down from fifty feet with one shot. You see Ski; most people think money is the most powerful thing in the world. But, the most powerful thing is pussy. Everything we men do is to impress women," he went on.

Noticing me shifting around in my seat uncomfortably, he continued. "Ski, I see you are a little apprehensive. Relax, I'm a good guy. I didn't have my girls disarm you to rob you. I had them disarm you for my safety. In the future, please don't bring any weapons with you when you come to visit me. Okay?"

I nodded my head and breathed a sigh of relief. I would've never been able to live with myself if I'd gotten robbed for all the diamonds and jewelry.

"But take this as a lesson learned. Never allow yourself to be so caught up with a woman that you become blind. It's good to fuck pussy. But, don't let pussy fuck you," he schooled me. "Now, let's get down to business. You have some nice pieces here," Kev said putting all the jewelry on the table. "And, these diamonds are exquisite. I'll give you 4 million for everything. What do you say? I think that's a more than generous offer."

I felt like hugging that nigga. "Four mil? Sounds great to me. Deal." I replied shaking his hand.

"So how do you want it cash or wired?" he asked me nonchalantly as if he made deals like this everyday.

"Wired. Could I use ya phone so I can get the account information," I asked sounding a little too anxious.

"Sure, no problem."

Kev had one of his women bring out a cordless phone and a laptop. I called Ranisha at the hotel and got the account number to the offshore accounts that Ranisha had set up for us. After I got the account numbers, Kev pushed a few buttons on his laptop and the deal was done. I called Ranisha back to verify that the transaction was complete and she told me that everything was a go. Just that quick in a matter of seconds I was officially a millionaire. I couldn't believe it. I had the widest smile a person could have.

"Congratulations Ski. May this be the first of many million dollar deals between us," he said smiling shaking my hand. "So when are you gonna pull the next one? That heist you pulled off at Zale's was sweet. They are gonna be talking about that one for years. Who would guess that a black kid so young could pull off such an intricate plan."

When Kev started talking about the heist that we pulled off at Zale's my smile quickly turned into a shit face. No one knew that we were responsible for that.

"Relax Ski. I told you I'm a good guy. Your secret is safe with me. I heard about Zale's being robbed in New York and I just put everything together. You are a bright kid. We could make a lot of money together. Big money. How would you like that?"

"Sounds good to me. What you got in mind?"

"I'd like you to hit one of my jewelry stores in a similar fashion. All you have to do is return my merchandise and we'll split the insurance money straight down the middle," Kev explained.

I was down. "Whatever B. Lemme know when you ready. We can definitely do that."

"Good. Very good. I'll be in contact with you in a couple of months," Kev replied standing up. "I'll have Kim Su drive you back to the hotel. Would you like some more ladies to accompany you for the ride back?"

"Nah, I'm good on that. I'm wore out. I do need some clothes though. I can't go back to the hotel looking like this."

"Sure, no problem."

Kev had one of his ladies bring me some long swimming trunks and a T-shirt. He gave me back my two ratchets and told me he'd be in touch. I left off Five Star Island in the same stretch Benz limo that I arrived in but I felt completely different. I was rich and I felt it. All the uptightness was gone and I was ready to celebrate. For the first time since I'd gotten to Miami, I could appreciate all the beautiful women, weather, and sights. It was time to party and I was in the perfect place to do it.

When I got back to Loews, it was 5:30 in the afternoon. I entered the suite and found Tiesha and Ranisha in the dining room eating room service. When they saw me both of their eyes lit up like Christmas trees and they ran over and began hugging me like I was Santa Claus.

"We're sorry baby. We should've been there to hold you down. I hope you're still not mad at us," Tiesha replied.

"We can make it up to you if you let us," Ranisha added.

I don't know what it was but all of the sudden I was horny as hell. I slobbed Tiesha down and began rubbing Ranisha's ass.

"Come on lets get in the shower," I suggested.

We all got in the shower and they took turns lathering my body up with soap and giving me head. After the shower, we hopped in the jacuzzi, and from the there we took it to the bed. I took turns hitting them from the back, while the other one ate the others pussy. After that, I punished them both in the missionary position until their pussy's were dry and swollen. They didn't know it but I was on my second nut and between that and the excitement that I was feeling from becoming a millionaire, I could fuck for days.

Hours later Ranisha and Tiesha were in deep sleeps. Normally they'd wear me out but that day I'd gotten the best of them.

The next day we got up in the afternoon, rented a Maybach from exotic rentals, and ate brunch on the beach at this restaurant called The Front Porch Café. After brunch, we went shopping. And, when I say shopping, I mean we went shopping. We went on a spree. Our first stop was Bal Harbour mall. Bal Harbour shops carried everything from Prada, Gucci, Emilio Pucci, Louis Vuitton, Ermenegildo Zegra, and Guisepe Zamotti. People at the mall were looking at us like we were celebrities. Even the bourgeoisie ass sales reps at the boutiques jumped on our dick after they saw we were spending big paper. The looks of concern that they had when we first entered the store were now gone. They began treating us like royalty. I noticed that when people know you have money they treat you different. It was like they automatically gave you respect. I was loving every second of it. From the mall we went to the South Beach shopping district and tore up Ralph Lauren, Diesel, and a rack of other boutiques. After we shopped until we dropped at the South Beach shopping district, we went shopping on the strip and hit all the boutiques on South Beach. After it was all said and done, we'd spent a hundred-fifty thousand dollars combined on clothes, shoes, boots, sneakers, and pocketbooks. From there we went back to our suite and went jet skiing and scuba diving on Biscayne Bay. As we were leaving on the boat, we went on Millionaires row and looked at celebrities' houses. Looking at Sylvester Stallone, Gloria Estefan, Jenifer Lopez and Shaquille O'Neal's houses made me even hungrier for success. For the first time in my life, that lifestyle seemed attainable. The only thing that brought my high off life down was the fact that my niggaz weren't there with me to enjoy it. It made it all seem bitter sweet.

After all, of that we went back to the Hotel, and went to the spa at the Mandarin Oriental Hotel and got massages, facials, pedicures, and manicures. From there we went back to the suite and got ready to go party at Club Amnesia.

When the girls came downstairs in their matching Dolce& Gabanna dresses my jaw dropped to the floor. The two girls from the hood had transformed into beautiful, sophisticated looking woman. They looked like they had stepped off the pages of Vogue or Elle magazine. As we walked through the lobby, of the Hotel, and down South Beach all eyes were on us and that wasn't a easy task. Not only did we look like a million dollars, we also had it.

We by-passed the three-block line outside of Club Amnesia and went straight to the V.I.P. to our reserved table. Club Amnesia was rocking. D.J. Khaled had the place in a frenzy. The ratio of men to women was like ten to one and I had yet to see a female who wasn't video material.

Ranisha and Tiesha were in the middle of the dance floor pissy drunk putting on a show for the crowd. While they were kissing, and grinding on each other I played it cool and sat at our table in the V.I.P. drinking Rose. Out of the blue this bad Spanish chick stepped to me.

"Hey sexy. What you doing here all by yourself fine as you are? What's ya name?" she flirted

I looked and was pleasantly surprised at what was standing in front of me. "Ski."

"Ski? Like in ski mask?" she asked letting out a cute giggle.

She had no idea. "Yeah. I guess you could say that. What's ya name shorty?"

"My name is Maribelle," she answered. "Would you like to dance?"

I glanced over at Tiesha and Ranisha dancing on the dance floor and said. "Why not."

At first, we were dancing innocently, just two stepping and what not, but when the DJ put on 50 Cent's "Just A Lil Bit" shorty started wildin' out.

Maribelle was a brown skin, curly haired Cuban Goddess. She was 5'6 and thick in all the right places. She was pretty in the face but her stand out feature was her body. She had some huge D- cup breasts and her ass was fat enough to sit a drink on.

Maribelle turned her back to me, pulled up her tight black mini skirt exposing her bare ass cheeks and started grinding on my dick so good and nasty that I could've bust right there in the club. She pulled her skirt back down, faced me, and whispered. "Let's go back to my room. Me and my girls got a room on the beach."

"Listen shorty I would love to but I'm here with someone. I can't," I replied with regret.

Ranisha came out of nowhere. "Yeah, you heard him bitch he's wit somebody so step the fuck off!"

"Excuse me?" Maribelle asked pushing her hair out of her face. "Who you calling a bitch... Bitch!"

Before I could even attempt to defuse the situation, Ranisha pulled out a razor from inside of her bra, and cut Maribelle across her face two times. Maribelle was screaming and leaking so bad that she drew the attention of the entire V.I.P. I saw security coming our way so I grabbed Ranisha's hand and ran with her towards the exit before the lights came on. We made it out just in time. I was furious. She had no business cutting that girls face for that bullshit. It was all innocent. Once we were back in our suite, I let her have it.

"What the fuck is wrong wit you? What was the purpose of all that? You heard me tell her I was wit somebody didn't you?" I yelled.

"I don't give a fuck! That bitch saw us sitting at that table wit you all night. She tried to do some slick shit! I been peeped that bitch staring at you!" Ranisha shouted back slurring her words.

"So the fuck what? Bitches is gonna holla at me just like niggaz are gonna holla at you. You can't stop it!"

"I can stop it. I did it tonight! You mine! And, any bitch who tries to take you from me will get the same treatment. I don't give a fuck! If you wanted to dance you should've danced with us!" Ranisha shouted back.

"You crazy Re. You crazy as hell B," I said walking up the stairs and into the bedroom.

About ten minutes later Ranisha walked into the bedroom in her panties and bra crying. "I'm sorry baby. Do you still love me?" she asked laying on me.

"Of course I still love you but you can't be wildin' out like that for nuffin' You gotta learn to control ya temper."

"I know. I'm sorry baby. I just love you so much. I don't wanna lose you. Sometimes I don't even like sharing you with Ty. You don't know how much I love you baby. Promise me you'll never leave me," Ranisha responded getting on her knees and sliding in between my legs.

"Re, I ain't going nowhere," I assured her.

Ranisha unbuckled my slacks, sucked my dick for a hot second and began riding me. As Ranisha was going up and down she was crying hysterically and shaking. I just sat back and watched her. Midway through our session Tiesha walked into the room and saw Ranisha bugging the fuck out and walked out. Ranisha was starting to scare me. I had love for her and Ty but I was far from being in love with them and it was starting to look like she may have a fatal attraction for me. Sooner or later I was going to have to break off from them but I was starting to think I was in too deep already. My second night of sleep as a millionaire was terrible. More proof that money wasn't the cure for all problems.

Chapter 18

January 05

Yo, where the fuck you been at B?" Cheeba snarled as soon as I sat down at the booth. I've been calling you like crazy son. I know you had to get all my messages. What you was ignoring my calls or something?" he continued.

Damn homey. That's how you greet me? You sound like one of my broads," I responded jokingly not getting even a smirk out of him. "I just flew back in from Miami. What's good?"

Miami?" Cheeba asked twisting up his face. "That's where you was at all this time? Unbelievable! Unfuckin' believable! You out there laying up on the beach wit them two like bitches while I'm out here dodging bullets! That's crazy! Shit is real out here right now B. The streets is like muthafuckin' Afghanistan right now nigga!"

I was confused and concerned at the same time. "Slow the fuck down son. What is you talking bout? What's going on?"

Cheeba and I were at U.S.A. diner on Queens Boulevard in Queens on an ice-cold day at the end of January. I'd just flew back in from Miami the previous night. After all the drama at Club Amnesia I decided to stay in Miami another week with the girls. They both had been complaining that I wasn't spending enough time with them and I figured I did deserve a week of fun. Once I got back home, I checked the voice mails to my cell phone and house phone and they were both filled with urgent messages from Cheeba. I was tired and thought that he could wait so I called him that morning when I woke up and he told me he needed to see me A.S.A.P.

This nigga Raphael got niggaz up in Kingston wildin' out. They robbed all of our spots uptown and downtown and they shot up Lil Kool. That nigga in Kingston Hospital right now in the I.C.U. They ran up in niggaz apartments, ran up in niggaz bitches cribs asking mad questions and they blew my muthafuckin' car up. If I ain't use my automatic start I would've been dead!' Cheeba explained.

What? How you know it's Raphael? Niggaz seen him up there?" I asked.

Nah, ain't nobody seen that nigga but who the fuck else could it be? Any and everything that got to do wit us they killing."

I was speechless. My mind was racing. I expected Raphael to retaliate but not like that. There were so many unanswered questions. Mainly who the fuck did he have down with him. Raphael never ran with a crew.

So where the fuck is everybody else at? You sent them back home?" was my next questions.

Hell no! Why would I do that? We up there banging out wit them niggaz! Niggaz still gotta eat B." Cheeba replied emphatically.

How much work did they get off of us?"

They only got what was in the spots but you know niggaz don't keep much in there. But regardless they came up on us. They hit the Franklin apartments twice last week. I took all the work and money out the stash house and took it to my momz cribs. So what you wanna do son? We gotta do something and we gotta do it now! Niggaz is gonna start thinking we soft. A few of the lil homies scared to hit the block."

"We gotta find this nigga Raphael B. Once we kill the head the body is finished," stated with a million and one thoughts rushing through my head.

"Nah son, you got it wrong. We gotta kill the body first, then it'll make it easier to get to the head," Cheeba shot back.

I paid his last comments no mind. I'd made my mind up. "Yo, shut everything down. Close up shop."

Cheeba wasn't feeling that plan at all. "For what? Then we gonna look like bitches son. Nah, man that ain't the move."

"Son, we about to go to war. You can't get money and war at the same time," I reminded him. "Go back around the way and grab up as many niggaz as you can. I want niggaz posted up 24/7 at all the spots. The next time them niggaz try something we gonna be waiting for they ass. In the mean time make some calls around and see what's poppin out there in Middletown. See if we can find this bitch ass nigga."

"What about the work and the money?"

"Keep it where it's at. It's time to bring the artillery out. One of us gotta go son. Me or him" I replied seriously.

"A'ight, son whatever. But I ain't really wit waiting on these niggaz."

"We got to son. We ain't got no choice."

"I don't wanna lose this town B. The money is too good. I got shit I'm trying to do," Cheeba explained.

"I know son. I ain't trying to lose this spot either. The sooner we handle this the sooner we can go back to getting money. Holla at me later on," I said getting up and giving him dap. "Stay sharp son don't slip. I need you right now more than ever," I continued before I made my exit.

If it was a war that Raphael wanted, it was war he was gonna get. My paper was up so I could afford to shut down shop, and the money that I'd lost was peanuts so I was good.

I drove to Forty Projects in the South Jamaica section of Queens and hollered at this bitch I knew named Shiny. Shiny was a badass Guianese bitch that I went to school with. Her and her whole crew were dimes. All they did was set up niggaz to be robbed by stick up kids around their way. The niggaz they fucked with paid them pennies, and I was about to give them an offer they wouldn't be able to refuse.

"What's poppin' nigga? Long time no muthafucking see!" Shiny said seeming excited to see me as she opened up her apartment door.

"Damn, girl you still fly as hell. Look at you," I said holding her by the hand and spinning her around to get a glimpse of her whole body.

"Cut the bullshit nigga. I know you ain't bring ya ass over here for some buns so let's get to it. My man is gonna be here in a half an hour. What can I do for you?" Shiny asked cutting to the chase.

Shiny was 5' 5", with a honey brown complexion, C-cup breast, and a petite frame. She was skinny but she still had curves. The feature that stood out the most about her was her face. She was drop dead gorgeous. Besides that, she was just sexy. She had tattoos everywhere from her neck to her back and she had damn near every part of her body pierced. She had six holes in each one of her ears, a tongue ring, lip ring, and she had her navel, breast, eyebrows and clitoris pierced. She was like every thugs dream wife. She as street smart, fly, and down for whatever. I had no doubt that her and her girls were gonna be capable of pulling off the job I needed them to do.

A'ight listen. I got a business proposal for you," I started off.

hiny folded her arms across her chest. "What kind of business proposal?"

I need you and ya girls to go up to Middletown to find this nigga for me."

Find a nigga? In Middletown? What's in it for us?"

$50 thousand," I answered.

50 stacks? Nah, we don't put in that type of work boo."

You don't understand. All y'all got to do is find him and get close to him. I'll take it rom there. All expenses paid and I'mma get y'all an apartment and a whip. I'll pay you alf up front and half when it's done," I proposed.

hiny had nothing but dollar signs in her eyes. "50 thousand? For that? Shit, you know 'm down nigga! Whenever you ready."

ust the answer I was expecting. "Good. I'mma set everything up for y'all up there and 'll holla at you next week. Cool?"

No doubt boo. I'll find him for you believe that. You know how we get down," Shiny aid confidently.

I know you will ma. That's why I came here first," I responded kissing her on the cheek nd letting myself out.

After I left 40 projects, I went to my man in Brooklyn and copped everything from ulletproof vests to teks. It was wartime. Me, and Raphael were set to clash. There vasn't enough room on earth for both of us. Somebody had to go and it damn sure vasn't gonna be me. I'd never been in a beef of that magnitude before but I knew from ny past dealings in the street that experiencing it would be the best teacher.

***

ebruary 05

iesha woke up early in the morning, showered and got her and her son dressed and left ut of the house that she, Ranisha and Ski shared. She got into her candy apple Benz and nade the hour and fifteen-minute drive to Kingston for the fourth time in two weeks. While she was on the thru-way she swore she was being followed, but then paid it no nind figuring that she was just being paranoid. She hated lying to Ski and Ranisha about er whereabouts but it was something she felt like she had to do. She knew they wouldn't nderstand. Especially Ski. She felt relieved that today was going to be the last time she ad to lie to them. It was really weighing on her conscience.

he got off the exit for Kingston and pulled up at the Ramada Inn. She parked her car in he parking lot and walked inside the lobby. Once inside the lobby she walked directly to er destination. She took her room key out her pocketbook and used it to enter the room.

Daddy!" Amir shouted running over to his father who was sitting up on the edge of the ed.

What's up lil man? You missed me?" Rule asked picking him up and sitting on his lap.

Yes. I always miss you. I love my daddy!" Amir responded laying his head on his ather's chest.

See what you doing Ty? How you gonna take my boy from me? Y'all two are all I thought about while I was on the inside," Rule replied.

Ty wasn't going for his sob story. "Rule, don't even start wit the bullshit. I already told you what it is," she said with an attitude. "You should be happy that I'm even here. You don't even deserve this."

"Ty... I love y'all. I still love you. Everything I did, I did for you, for us. You use to be my wifey, how you gonna treat me like this after everything we've been through?" Rule asked.

"Nigga please! You did this to ya-self! You told on them people to get ya-self out of jail. I ain't tell you to rat on nobody. Only good thing that ever came out of knowing you is Amir. I don't have no love for you what so ever. I don't even respect you nigga! Only reason I ain't tell Ski where you was at so he could body ya punk ass is because of Amir. You ain't worth shit! Never was worth shit! The little that I'm doing to help you is out of love for my son. You owe ya life to ya son because if it wasn't for him you'd be a dead man pussy!" Tiesha explained heartlessly.

Tiesha was letting Rule see his son for the last time. Rule was Tiesha's baby's father and an ex partner of Ski. When the Fed's started serving indictments, Rule turned over and became a government witness. He testified against Ski at his trial, and wrote statements on all of his peoples as well which forced them to cop out. He was facing thirty years but due to his cooperation with the government, he only received four years. Rule had only been home for a month. As soon as he got out, he got in touch with Tiesha's crack head mother and begged her to pass his number to Tiesha. When Ty found out that Rule was home from her mother her first instinct was to tell Ski because she knew how bad he wanted to get him back for what he did. Ski was her dude and she felt loyal to him but the more she thought about it she felt like she owed it to her child to let him see his father. She decided to call him and after persuasion, she agreed to let him see Amir one time and one time only. But, after seeing the affect he had on Amir she kept bringing him up. Tiesha no longer had any romantic feeling towards Rule, and even told him that she was in a relationship with Ski. Out of all the times that she had taken Amir to see him she hadn't done as much as shake his hand. Even though she wasn't cheating, she still felt like she was betraying Ski by being in his presence. She felt terrible about lying to Ranisha and Ski. She knew Ranisha knew she was up to something and she didn't know how much longer she could hold her lies together. She knew if Ski found out where Rule was he was a dead man, so she allowed him to see his son for one last time, and agreed to give him twenty-five thousand dollars to get out of dodge. Although she hated Rule, she didn't want to deny her son the decision to get to know him once he got older.

"Ty, leave with me. We can be a family again. I know I did some foul shit but Allah forgave me and I'm a changed man. I'm not the person that I use to be. I know you still love me deep down in ya heart. The Qur'an teaches-,"Rule preached standing up and grabbing her by the arm.

Tiesha cut him off. "Nigga don't touch me! Are you crazy? Get it through ya head nigga, I don't give a fuck about you! You a lame ass, bitch ass rat bastard! Ski is my man and he's better than you in every way imaginable. There will never be no us again," Tiesha said pushing him away from her. "Matter of fact here," she continued going in her purse and throwing the twenty-five grand she promised to give him on the bed. "I'm going to et some breakfast. When I come back you got ten minutes wit ya son and then we out. I in't got time to be sitting up here listening to ya bullshit. Come on Amir. You wanna go o McDonalds?"

Can daddy come?" he asked.

No daddy can't come. He's going to stay here. He'll be here when we get back," Tiesha nswered softly.

iesha and Amir left out the hotel room and left Rule in the room fuming. As soon as ney left he picked up a lamp and threw it against the wall shattering it to pieces. It killed im to know that the only woman he ever loved didn't love him or respect him anymore. le felt like half a man. What angered him the most was the fact that she was with Ski. ust the thought of the two of them together made him sick to his stomach. He knew that f Ski knew his whereabouts he would come and try to kill him but he didn't care. He ated Ski. In his twisted mind, he felt like Ski was responsible for everything that was rong with his life. If he couldn't have his family, he felt like he had nothing to live for. ule made up his mind that he wasn't going to leave town. He was going to follow iesha home and kill Ski. He figured it was the only way he could get his family back.

s Rule was sitting on the bed crying, he heard a knock on the door.

le jumped up and wiped his eyes. "Ty, you forgot ya room key?"

ule was a 27 year old brown skin man with curly hair, that he now wore in cornrows nd he stood 6 feet even and weighed just a little over 200 pounds. In the face, he esembled the rapper XZibit.

Vhen he went to the door, he opened it without looking through the peephole or asking vho it was assuming it was Tiesha. But when he opened the door he saw no one there. ust as he was getting ready to close the door, he felt a strong force push the door open. he next thing he knew he felt himself being stabbed in the stomach repeatedly. He tried o fight off the killer but it was of no use. Rule felt a pain unlike any other that he had ver felt. His eyes were bulging out the sockets and his insides felt like they were on fire. ach time the knife went in and out of his torso he felt the life being drained out of him. he killer was there for a purpose and continued jamming the knife into him repeatedly. ule couldn't even scream. He stumbled back and fell to the floor on his back. The killer nen stood over him and slit his neck from ear to ear killing him instantly. After that, the iller stripped Rule naked and laid him on the bed on his back.

wenty minutes later Tiesha and Amir came back from McDonalds and entered the hotel oom. The stench of blood could be smelled from the hallway. When Tiesha opened the oor and found Rule lying in the bed lifeless with blood all over the room she threw up ll of her breakfast. She didn't know what to think. Her first thought was that Rule had illed himself. She picked up her already crying son in her arms, and put his head on her hest so he couldn't see the mutilated body of his father.

Ohmigod! Ohmigod Rule!" Tiesha yelled starting to cry and shake.

he didn't know what to do. She stood there frozen. She couldn't call the police because ney'd probably consider her a suspect and she couldn't call Ski or Ranisha because then he'd have to explain to them what she was doing up there in the first place. She couldn't ven leave out the room because she was sure the clerk at the front desk would remember er face and tell the police she was the last person to enter the room. She was stuck.

As Tiesha was standing there shaking and crying, she felt the presence of someone behind her. Before she could turn around and look, she felt someone grab her head back and slit her neck. She let out a piercing scream but it was short lived after she started gurgling her own blood. Her eyes rolled to the back of her head and she reached for her neck instinctively dropping her son on the floor in the process.

"Mommy!" Amir called out to his mom.

Before she knew it, Tiesha felt sharp pains all over her body. The knife went in and out of her body repeatedly and each hurt more than the last one. Tiesha was staggering around the room like a drunken person for a while but soon after her legs gave out on her and she went crashing to the ground awkwardly. She fell on her side and the killer stood over her, turned her on her back and stabbed her in the eye killing her instantly. The killer then locked Amir in the bathroom, stripped Tiesha naked, laid her in the bed next to Rule and left. Life as she knew it had come to an end for Tiesha Hilton.

Chapter 19

February 05

"Naked I came from my mother's womb and naked I will depart. The Lord giveth and the Lord has taken away. May the name of the Lord be praised. Ashes to ashes and dust to dust," Reverend Chestnut pronounced, reading the scripture as he sprinkled dust on top of the casket.

After the Reverend finished quoting the scripture, everyone put red roses on top of the casket. After they were finished, I walked Tiesha's son Amir up to the casket and let him put the last rose on top of it.

"Bye mommy. I love you," Amir said sadly.

It was pouring rain and freezing cold on the afternoon of Tiesha's funeral. Everything was surreal. It all still seemed unbelievable. I was dying on the inside but I had to put on a strong front for Amir. He'd witnessed the death not only of his mother but his father as well at the tender age of five. He'd also witnessed Ranisha getting raped the year before. His young eyes had seen way too much too early. His innocence was killed right alongside his mother and father. I knew he'd never experience a normal childhood again. Amir was the strongest five year-old I'd ever met. He took in everything like a soldier. He stood there holding my hand, with his head up watching his mother's casket being lowered to the ground. He actually gave me strength. I knew his mom would be proud of him. When Tiesha's casket was halfway down all hell broke loose.

"No! No! Don't leave me Ty! Don't leave me! Oh my God! No! Take me to Lord!" Ranisha shouted out crying frantically jumping on top of the casket as it was being lowered.

That made Amir start up with the tears. "I wanna go with my mommy too," he stated letting go of my hand and running towards the casket.

I picked Amir up in my arms and passed him to his grandmother, and then ran over and pried Ranisha off the casket.

"Get off me! Get off! It's all your fault!" Ranisha yelled as I picked her up in my arms.

She fell into the wet grass kicking and screaming. When I managed to get her up, she smacked me in the face and then hugged me tightly.

"What are we gonna do now? What are we gonna do without Ty? It will never be the same. I don't wanna live no more!" Ranisha cried out.

"I know baby girl. I know. I'm feeling the same way you feeling but we got to be strong for Amir," I said hugging her.

Out of everyone, Ranisha had taken Tiesha's death the hardest. She'd been passing out and having tantrums since she found out about Tiesha. She didn't sleep. She didn't eat, and she barely spoke. I was worried about her being suicidal. I kept a close eye on her at all times.

"Ski, you are all I have now. Promise me you won't let them take you away from me too. Promise me!" Ranisha demanded.

"I ain't going nowhere Re. We gonna get them niggaz for this trust me. Niggaz gonna die for this," I assured her.

I looked behind me and caught eye contact with Cheeba. He rolled his eyes and looked away from me as if to say I told you so. He'd told me that he didn't think it was a good idea to wait on them to move and he turned out to be right. But in all reality we had no choice.

After the burial concluded, I was opening the door to get in my whip when Cheeba walked up besides me.

"Thanks for coming homey. You coming to the crib to eat right?" I asked giving him dap.

"Nah son all this shit is depressing. I can't take any more of this shit B. I'm out. I'll holla at you tomorrow or something," Cheeba responded. "So you a'ight or what? How you holding up?"

"Honestly this whole shit got me twisted right now son. This shit is crazy! I'm trying to be strong for them though," I answered pointing at the car with Ranisha and Amir inside it.

"Hold ya head my nigga. Lemme get out this rain. I'mma holla," Cheeba replied giving me a dap and heading to his car.

"A'ight be safe son. Stay on point," I said getting into my whip.

Just as I was about to get in, I heard Cheeba calling my name.

"Ayo Ski! Ayo Ski!" he called out. When he saw he had my attention he asked. "So what is this a rental? Referring to my Bentley Coupe that Ranisha had gotten me for my birthday.

"Nah, this is all me playboy," I answered tapping the hood.

"Oh word?" Cheeba said with a funny look on his face. "These shits cost a lot of bread. Lemme find out you holding out on me son," he continued serious as cancer.

I didn't even give him a response. I looked at him, shook my head, and got in the car and pulled off. The fact that he was still thinking about money at a time like this let me know where his head was at. His comment was completely out of pocket. Since I'd gotten back from Miami that nigga had been acting real strange. Something was definitely up with him and I made a mental note to myself to keep a close eye on him.

I drove back home to our crib in Scarsdale after the burial and we all ate and reminisced about good times that we all shared with Tiesha. Ranisha was a wreck. She was anti-social and kept herself locked in our room for most of the night.

After I showed the last of our guests out, I bathed Amir put him in the bed and crawled in my bed next to Ranisha.

"Yo, Re you up?" I whispered as I got in the bed and wrapped my arms around her.

When Ranisha turned around to face me, I saw that her eyes were bloodshot red and she had huge bags under them. Her nose was running, her hair was all over the place, and she just looked terrible.

"I miss her," Ranisha whispered back putting her head on my chest.

"Me too ma. Me too," I repeated. "You ain't have no idea that Ty was fucking wit that nigga? She wasn't acting funny to you at all?" I inquired.

"Nah... I mean maybe. I noticed she was being a little secretive but never did I suspect she was doing nuthin' like she was doing. She betrayed us," Ranisha responded.

"Yeah, I feel the same way but for some reason I think there's more to the story."

"Like what was she doing with twenty-five thousand dollars in the hotel room," Ranisha said finishing my sentence.

"Exactly."

"She probably was gonna run off wit that nigga or something."

"Nah, I don't think she was gonna run away with the nigga cause she damn sure would've took more cash than that with her. Why would she walk away from millions?"

That was the million-dollar question to me. Everything else made sense but that part didn't add up. Rule was Tiesha's baby father and I knew he had a mean hold on her at one time and I knew that Tiesha probably had some pent up feelings for him. I could imagine Rule coming home getting in contact with her some way, and trying to use their child to get her back and I could even imagine Ty falling for it. The funny part was if she was planning on running away with him, why did she only take twenty-five grand?

"Ski, I'm crying because I miss Ty and I loved her but some of these tears are out of anger. How could she betray us like this? How could she go back to a nigga that tried to put you in jail for the rest of your life? It makes me feel like everything she ever said was a lie. Like she was using us," Ranisha explained.

Truthfully, I wasn't that mad about Tiesha fucking another nigga because I didn't look at her or Ranisha as my girlfriend. I wasn't serious about either one of them like that. I loved them but I was far from being in love with them. I was madder at Tiesha for who she chose to cheat with. Rule was a rat bastard who helped put my manz in jail for the rest of their lives and tried to put me in there with them. He deserved to die. I was wishing it could've been me that took him off this planet. However I did feel betrayed by Tiesha. It was a move that was out of her character.

"Word," I agreed.

"Ski, I love you and I want you to know that I'd never do no shit like that to you. I'd die for you and I'd kill for you. Loyalty is everything to me. I almost feel like Ty deserved-,"

I cut her off before she could say it. "Don't say no shit like that! She ain't deserve to go out like that you wildin'! She did some foul shit but she didn't deserve to die for it."

"So what are we gonna do with Amir? Ranisha asked.

I was stuck in between a rock and a hard place. "I don't know man. I ain't figure that out yet. I don't know what to do. That lil nigga has been through some tragic shit. He watched his mother and father get stabbed to death by a masked man. The last place he needs to be is a foster home but I'm not in position to be raising a child. I don't even see my own son enough. I don't know man. I just don't wanna leave him out to dry. I know Ty wouldn't do that to my son," I explained.

"We'll figure out something. Could you just hold me baby," Ranisha requested.

I put my arms around her, closed my eyes and tried to go to sleep. As I was falling asleep, Ranisha said. "Ski, promise me you wont shit on me. I wouldn't be able to take it. I'd probably go crazy and kill you," Ranisha whispered.

The statement that Ranisha made kept me up all night. The scary part was that I believed her. I had to find a way to distance myself from her and I knew it wasn't going to be easy. Ranisha had been through a lot of pain in her life and I didn't want to add to it. She truly did love me.

That night I probably slept a total of ten minutes. I had so much on my plate that I didn't know what to take care of first. I felt like Tiesha's blood was on my hands and I wouldn't be able to sleep until her death was avenged. It was only a matter of time before Raphael and I collided, and I knew that if I didn't stay on point I could easily be the next person in a coffin. The stakes had risen. I got Candy and he got Tiesha. I also had to decide what I was gonna do with Amir and sooner or later I was going to have to break the news to Ranisha that I didn't want to be with her. At the time, I felt like life couldn't get worse. But, you know what they say, just when you think things can't get worse they always do.

***

Right when I was beginning to get a little drowsy I was interrupted by phone ringing.

"Hello," I answered groggily.

"Ski, wha gwon'? Dis Prince."

"Prince? What up? You know what time it is?" I asked.

"Yeah mi own ah clock. Mi need a fava from you. Yu tink ya could do it?"

"Yeah. What's up?"

"Mi daughta jus fly ta New York fa school. Take her out and show her a good time," Prince requested.

If I thought Prince's sanity was under question before that day, he'd sealed it. He was a nut case. It was 10:30 a.m. and this nigga was calling me to be a baby sitter. Even if it wasn't the day after Tiesha's funeral I would've refused. I was tired as hell.

"Yo, Prince I really can't B. A close friend of mine just passed away and I'm taking care of her son. He's a handful by himself. I can't deal wit two children."

"Wha ya talk bout' bwoy? Mi daughta ah grown woman. Mi nah talk bout mi lickle daughta. Mi talk bout mi older one mi haf befoor mi go at jail," Prince replied.

"Oh, I ain't even know you had a older daughter."

"Please bredren. Mi beg ya fa dis fava. Please. The girl is miserable," Prince persuaded.

"A'ight Dread I got you. I'll take her out for a couple of hours. Tell her I'll be there around two."

Prince was excited like a kid at Christmas. "Yes! Yes! Respeck star. Mi owe ya one after dis one ya hear? Da address is-," he went on.

I have no idea why I agreed to take Prince's daughter out. For some reason I couldn't say no to him. I had way too much on my plate to be playing tour guide. Besides that I knew his daughter had to be a beast if she'd been in New York and didn't have anyone to take her out. As I lay in the bed staring at my ceiling, I started to call Prince to cancel but I couldn't. I'd given him my word.

A couple of hours later I pulled up on New York University's campus in Manhattan in my snow white Bentley Coupe. Females were going crazy. They were damn near throwing their panties at me. That day was the first time that I'd brought it out besides Tiesha's funeral and if I would've anticipated all the attention I would've left it home. I was stressed the fuck out. The last thing on my mind was bagging a new chick.

I called upstairs to her dorm room and told her that I was outside. I laughed to myself after I hung up because she had a sexy voice. Ugly women always had the sexiest voices. I closed my eyes and sat back in my seat preparing for my date with the monster.

About five minutes later, I looked out the window and saw the prettiest woman I had ever laid eyes on. She was light skin, about 5' 5" and had the most beautiful flawless face and radiant skin that I'd ever seen. She had long hair that fell down to the middle of her back that looked to be all hers and although she had on a big coat, I could tell that she had some curves. I was mesmerized. Even with no make up, her hair blowing in the wind, and the fact that she was probably freezing her ass off, she still was beautiful. She looked side to side a couple of times and then finally our eyes met. Before that day I though that love at first sight was some shit that only happened in the movies.

As crazy, as it sounds without saying a word to her I felt connected to her in some way. I knew I was looking at the woman who was supposed to be my wife. It felt like we were staring at each other for ten minutes but in actuality it was closer to a minute. She gave me a slight smile and then broke her gaze. My first reaction was to jump out the whip and holla, but I decided against it. I was there to take Prince's daughter out and I didn't want her to come out and see me talking to another girl. I made a mental note of the building I saw her come out of and made a promise to myself that I'd come back the next day. The woman went in her purse and pulled out a cell phone. I couldn't help but wish it was me who she was calling. I knew a woman that fine had to have a man. My cell phone ringing woke me up out of my day dreams.

"Hello," I answered.

"Hi, this is Crystal. I think you went to the wrong complex. I'm out here and I don't see you."

"Nah, I've been here for like ten minutes. I know I followed ya directions right," I responded.

"What kind of car are you driving?" Crystal asked.

"I'm in a white Bentley Coupe."

When Crystal turned around and we saw each other talking on the phone we both couldn't help but laugh. I was amped. Finally, my luck had made a turn for the good. I hopped out the car with the quickness and walked over to her.

"Hey, I'm Ski," I spoke flashing my pearly whites grabbing her by the hand.

"Hi… I'm Crystal," she responded with a smile equally as big as mine.

We stood there for a few seconds just smiling at each other and holding hands like two schoolchildren. Crystal was even more beautiful up close. She reminded me of the late R&B singer Aaliyah. Crystal was the first one to get out of the trance.

"Okay, if we're gonna go get married we're gonna have to let each others hand go and walk to the car. Once we get to the car, we can hold hands again. Okay?" Crystal joked letting go of my hand and walking towards my car.

I followed behind her and opened up the passenger side door for her. "How did you know that was where we were going?"

"It's all in your eyes. The eyes are the windows to the soul. Mouths lie but eyes don't," Crystal, answered confidently.

"Well you must be feeling the same way I'm feeling because your eyes have been smiling at me too."

"I never said I wasn't, did I?" Crystal replied as I closed the door.

I walked over to the driver's side of my car and got in. As I was starting the car, I turned to Crystal and said. "I know this sounds crazy but I feel like I know you. Like we were supposed to meet today, I can't describe it. It's like-,"

"Fate? Love at first sight?" Crystal finished my sentence.

"Yeah exactly. How did you know I was going to say that?"

"Because I feel it too, it's scary. I've barely said two words and I feel like-."

"You've known me for years," I answered this time finishing her sentence.

"Exactly," Crystal said with a smile. "C'mon lets get out of here. I'm starving. I know you're not going to let your future wife starve."

"My future wife huh? I like the way that sounds."

When I started my car 2Pac's song "How Do U Want It" came on.

"Oh that's my song. Do you have the whole All Eyez On Me in here? I love Pac he's the greatest of all time," Crystal shouted enthusiastically.

The last comment she made sealed the deal. Crystal was Heaven sent. The whole ride we held hands and sung along to 2Pac. We didn't even converse. We didn't have to. We had a connection that was unexplainable. I was comfortable around her like I'd known her for years and I didn't know anything about her.

We pulled up in front of Juniors restaurant about 2 p.m. Juniors. People from all around the world came to Juniors just to get a sample of their cheesecake.

"Is this the Juniors that Diddy sent those kids to get cheesecake from?" Crystal asked looking out the window as I parked.

"Yup. This is it. The World Famous Juniors. Welcome to New York City baby."

"I gotta get some of that cheesecake. It must be the bomb if Diddy made them walk all the way here from Harlem," Crystal joke rubbing her perfectly flat stomach.

When we strolled into Juniors all eyes were on us. We were both casually dressed but between my jewelry and her good looks people probably thought that we were famous. And, pulling up in a Bentley didn't hurt either. We got a table in the back, ordered our food and started kicking it.

"So how come you didn't try to talk to me when you first saw me? I saw you clocking me," Crystal joked.

"Only reason you saw me clocking you is because you was clocking me," I shot back. "But honestly I didn't think you were Prince's daughter and I didn't want you coming outside ya dorm and seeing me holla at another woman. That would've been disrespectful."

"Mmm, I see. Good answer. Sexy and respectful," Crystal replied grabbing my hand from across the table. "Where have you been for the last twenty-five years?"

"Waiting on you," I responded kissing her hand. "But, yo lemme ask you something. You saw me in the parking lot as well. Why didn't you think I was me?"

"Well since we're being honest... I thought you were gonna be some fat ugly Jamaican guy with dreads. I didn't even want to go out today. I was going to stay home and do laundry but my father begged me."

"Ya father begged you? He begged me too. He told me that you were lonely in New York and asked me to show you a good time as a favor to him."

Crystal was shocked. "He did what? Oh! Wait until I get home!" Crystal said making a fist.

"Shit you buggin'. I'mma call him and thank him. He's gonna be my father in law."

We both laughed.

"So, what's ya real name? I don't like the name Ski."

"My real name is Isaiah," I said in a low tone.

"What are you acting all ashamed for? I think Isaiah is a cute name."

"If you like it, I love it baby girl. Crystal Thompson has a ring to it."

"Is that a proposal?" Crystal asked after taking a sip of her strawberry milkshake.

"What if it is?"

"Don't answer my question with a question. I asked you first," Crystal shot back.

The waiter bringing out our food cut our conversation off. After we both started eating Crystal came out the blue with a crazy question. "So you're a gangsta right? Do you sell drugs?"

I almost choked on my cheeseburger. "Why would you think that? Do I look like a drug dealer?"

"Actually you don't. But you drive a Bentley and your jewelry looks like it's pretty expensive. And besides all of that, you are a friend of my fathers and all he associates with is gangsta's."

"What if I told you I was. Would that change ya opinion of me?"

"No, but I'd like to know what I'm getting myself into. I hope you don't think I'm corny but I feel like you are my soul mate. I wanna know everything there is to know about Isaiah Thompson. I've never dealt with a street guy before but for you I'd make an exception," Crystal explained.

"Well yeah, I sell drugs amongst other things but I'm not a bad person."

"You must be a good guy because my father has never tried to hook me up with anyone before. He's big on you."

"And I'm big on you," I said leaning over and kissing her softly on the lips.

We sat in Juniors for damn near three hours getting to know each other. It turned out that Crystal was twenty-five years old and born on the exact same date as me. I was only older than she was by a couple of hours. She was enrolled in N.Y.U. to get her Masters in Psychology and she was born and raised in North Carolina. We had so much in common that it was crazy. She loved basketball, and said she even played in high school; she was funny, smart and easy to talk with. I felt like I could tell her anything. I knew from that day on that she was going to be my wife. It's crazy how love finds you when you least expect it.

We went to the movies and walked around in Manhattan arm and arm like we'd been together for years. We even went inside a bridal store and looked at wedding gowns and tuxedos. We were feeling each other heavy.

When I pulled up to her dorm, I didn't want to let her go. I wanted to take her back home with me and never let her leave. She must have been feeling the same way because we sat in silence for almost five minutes.

"So when can I see you again?" I asked.

"Whenever," she spat out a little too quick for her taste. "Damn, did I just sound thirsty or what?" she joked. "But seriously whenever you would like. I don't want to leave you now."

"I know right? This is crazy," I said shaking my head and laughing. "Yo, Crystal right now my life is in turmoil. I don't know what direction my life is gonna take me but I do know I want you by my side. I gotta tie up a few loose ends but I definitely want you to be mine. Like forever," I explained.

"Well I'm here and I'm not going anywhere anytime soon. I feel the same way you feel Isaiah. This was the best day of my life. I've never felt anything like this before and I know it's real," Crystal said.

I leaned over to her and we kissed. But it wasn't a regular kiss. There was something special behind it. Like our mouths were made for each other. I felt breathless afterwards. After we were done kissing, I watched Crystal walk into her dorm and pulled off.

The whole day that I'd spent with Crystal I'd zoned out. I had forgotten about all of my problems. It was like nothing else mattered. I didn't know it, but I was about to get hit with a huge dose of reality.

Chapter 20

March 05

"Cheeba, what it is homey?" I answered my phone.

"Ski, where you at son? I need to see you! Shit is going down right now B!" Cheeba said in a nervous but urgent tone.

"Word? What's poppin'? Talk to me my nigga."

"This ain't no shit I can talk about over no horn. I need to see you. Meet me at the Red Lobster on Sunrise Highway in the hood."

"I can't son. I'm out of town right now," I replied.

Cheeba caught an immediate attitude. "Out of town? Where you at now? How far are you?"

I knew he wouldn't understand my reasons but I told him anyway. "Miami."

"Miami? What the fuck you doing in Miami? Niggaz out here is trying to pop my muthafuckin' top over some shit you done started and you out in Miami taking trips and shit. What type of time are you on son? I mean for real though. Niggaz just killed Ty B. You gon let that ride," Cheeba responded angrily.

"Chill the fuck out son. I'm out here handling some business. Send everybody back home, go somewhere, and get low until I get back. I got something in the works as we speak for that nigga Raphael B. Trust me. Just be patient. I'll holla at you when I get back." I said trying my best to calm him down.

"And, when the fuck is that gonna be?"

"We should be back in a couple of weeks."

Cheeba lost it. "A couple of weeks? We? Who you wit?"

"It's just me and Re. Why all the questions? You sounding like the muthafuckin' D.A. right now B."

He ignored my remark. "Ayo. You need to get ya mind right B. This ain't the time to be taking vacations and shit. Shit is real out here nigga. You out of pocket nigga!" Cheeba barked.

He was trying my patience. "Yo, son what did I just tell you? I'm out here taking care of business! I'll be back in a couple of weeks.

Don't question me nigga. Last I checked you worked for me. I don't work for you. All y'all niggaz go the fuck back home until I get back."

"A'ight big boss man. You got it. No doubt," Cheeba responded sarcastically.

"Son, you acting like a broad B. Word up. You starting to get me tight on some real shit. I ain't in the mood for the bullshit."

"Whatever B. See me when you get home you know where I'll be at. I ain't hard to find," Cheeba said before he hung up on me.

That nigga Cheeba had been acting real ill ever since I had him close up shop in Kingston. It was starting to seem like we were going to have to bump heads because something definitely was up with homey. As soon as I got home, I planned on checking him and putting him in his place. He'd been talking to me like I worked for him and in all actuality he worked for me. He was my man from back in the days so even though he did work for me I never talked down to him or made him feel like it and the salary he was getting was more than generous. He had never tasted the type of money he was tasting until he started fucking with me upstate. Instead of being grateful, he was beginning to become resentful and envious. Instead of being happy with the money he was getting he wanted to count my money and monitor my moves and that was a definite no-no. He didn't know that I came up crazy off the heist and I planned on keeping it like that. In my opinion, it was none of his business. The drug and stick up game were two separate things. Drug money was now peanuts to me. I wanted badly to get back at Raphael for murdering Tiesha but I had no idea of his whereabouts. We could've easily ran through Middletown shooting and robbing everything in sight but all that would have done was put heat on us and put Raphael on point. Shiny and her crew were up there and I knew it was only a matter of time before they'd locate him. I was rocking that nigga right to sleep.

Currently Ranisha and I were outside one of Kev's many jewelry stores. The one he had selected for us to hit was in a small shopping center with a supermarket, Toy's R Us, check cashing spot and a CVS. Kev wanted us to burglarize the store the same way we had done Zales but the landscape was different. Zales was in the Diamond district in Manhattan and the building that it was in had an office building upstairs from it. Kev's store wasn't connected to anything and the only way I could see getting inside was the roof and I wasn't feeling that at all. That was some straight Mission Impossible movie shit. I came to the conclusion at that moment that the only way that we could hit the spot and make it look real was the old fashioned way. The ski mask way, hoodied and masked up with our guns drawn.

I drove back to the Hotel, explained the new plans to Ranisha, and then called Kev to set up a meeting. Kev reluctantly agreed but assured me that I would have full cooperation from his employees. The manager was going to be in on it. I told Kev that I wanted to check out the area for another week before we did to observe police patrols and I'd call him when I was ready. Everything was set.

A week later....

Ranisha came into the jewelry store toting two chrome .44's. She let it be known from the door that she was about her business. She cocked her guns back and announced. "Y'all know what the fuck this is! Put ya muthafuckin' hands in the air and don't move! I want everybody face down with ya hands on ya fucking heads!"

The five employees and two customers all followed her instructions and lay down side by side on their stomachs with their hands on top of their heads.

I came in right behind her. "Who's the manager? Which one of y'all muthfucka's the manager?" I asked pointing my Desert Eagle in the direction of everyone lying down.

"That would be me sir," a white man answered.

"Get up and walk towards me wit ya hands up. If you try and be a hero you will die as one." I explained to him.

The manager got up and walked towards me with his hands up. As soon as he got within arms reach of me, I smacked him in the face with my ratchet. A loud popping sound reverberated throughout the entire store from the blow and blood started pouring out of his mouth like red kool-aid from a pitcher.

"I don't wanna kill you but I will if you force my hand. If you follow my instructions, you'll make it out of here alive, understand?"

He nodded his head.

"Good. What's ya name man?"

"Brian Anderson," he answered barely coherent do to the shot that I had given him to the mouth.

"Brian you are about to help me get rich. You're my new best friend," I replied putting my arm around him.

Brian Anderson was the regional manager of all of Kev's stores in Miami and a close friend of his. If I remember correctly, Kev told me that they went to school together. Brian was a middle-aged slim Italian man in his early forties, with slicked back hair and an expensive suit. To me he looked like a young Pat Riley. I didn't have anything personal against Brian because I didn't know him, but I had to hit him to make the robbery seem real.

"A'ight Brian first things first lock up these doors and put the closed sign up. I don't need no interferences," I instructed like Brian and I were co-workers.

Brian did as he was told and locked up the double doors to the front entrance. After he was finished, I had him help Ranisha tie up the six remaining employees and customers. Once the hostages were tied up securely and out of view from the front door's we had Brian open up all the display cases in the store with his key. Ranisha went to work cleaning out the cases and I took Brian to the back and had him open up the safe.

He was taking too long. "Let's go nigga. I ain't got all muthafuckin' day," I shouted mostly to make it seem real on the cameras.

The safe was stacked even more than the one at Zales was. It looked like there was a million dollars in cash inside. In addition to that Kev had a large pouch full of diamonds. Kev's store was no way near as big as Zales was but they carried pieces that were more expensive. If the average price of a watch in Zales was ten grand the average price in Kev's store was twenty-five grand. Celebrities were regulars at Kev's store and on the walls; they had pictures of everyone from Trick Daddy to Cuba Gooding Jr.

Even the layout of the store was expensive. The store had snow-white wall-to-wall carpet, marble counters, and mad expensive statutes and paintings. The walls were all glass and were so squeaky clean that you could see your reflection in them. The store itself was medium sized and had two separate sides, one for men and the other side for women. The left side was the men's department. It had five separate display cases for watches, rings, bracelets, earrings, necklaces, and pendants. The right side for the women was laid out the same as the men's side except it had an extra display case for rings. The middle of the store was filled with statues. Directly behind the men's section, there was a door that led to a small hallway. The hallway led to a manger's office, repair shop, lounge and safe room.

After Brian cleaned out the safe, I put the duffel bag over my shoulder and led him back to the front of the store at gunpoint.

"You almost done?" I asked Ranisha once we were back in the front.

"Yeah, I got all the men's shit and I'm halfway finished with the women's shit," Ranisha responded snatching up jewelry at a dizzying pace.

"Brian help my lady friend out. I'm warning you though man, don't try anything. I like you, I'd hate to have to kill you," I stated.

Brian went to the women's section and proceeded to help Ranisha empty out the rest of the display cases. When they were finished, we had three duffel bags filled up.

"Okay Brian, we in the home stretch. I want you to unlock this door, go outside, and put all three of these duffel bags into that black Maxima parked out front. I'm gonna be watching you so if you try to alert anyone or run away everyone in the store dies, understand me?" I explained.

Brian nodded his head once more. By this time, the blood that was gushing out of the cut on his lip had dried up and his lips were swollen and purple. I started to feel bad for the cracker until I realized that he was gonna be getting a healthy check for his participation.

He walked out of the store with the three duffel bags in tow, popped the trunk of the Maxima, put all three bags inside, and came back inside.

"Good boy," Ranisha replied as he came back into the store.

She then kneed him in the balls and smacked him with one of her ratchets in the face knocking him out cold. We dragged his body to the corner of the store with the rest of the hostages and tied him up. After that, we played the door and waited for the shopping center security to pass and about twenty seconds later, we came bolting out the door still wearing our masks. We hopped in the stolen whip that Kev provided us and pulled off slowly being careful not to draw any attention to ourselves. We made it back to the hotel with nearly the whole store in three duffel bags. It was a job well done and a plan perfectly executed. Dro would have been proud of me.

"Baby we did it! Ohmigod! We did it! We ain't never gonna have to work after this one. We set for life! We can move somewhere and start our family," Ranisha shouted jumping into my arms with joy as soon as we entered the hotel room.

I was proud of Ranisha. Even though it was an inside job and there was minimal risk involved, she still impressed me. She moved in the spot like a professional and did everything the way I told her to. I could've done the job alone and kept all of the money to myself but I planned on parting ways with Ranisha and I wanted to make sure she had a nice nest egg to fall back on. I wasn't in love with her but I did care about her. She was a ride or die chick to the fullest.

"You did good ma. You handled ya-self like a professional in there. Between this jux and the last one, we should be good. We can do anything we want. Shit, we can go legit," I responded kissing her on the cheek. "C'mon lets count this money."

We took all of the cash out the bags, split it up into two piles and began counting it. When we were done, it came up to 1.5 million even more than we expected. We were ecstatic. We were jumping around and dancing like two fat kids that got locked in a candy store. We started throwing money around and on each other like it was confetti. Hundred dollar bills were everywhere. Amidst all the excitement, Ranisha jumped on the bed got on her knees and disrobed.

"I want you to fuck me on top of all this money." she announced pulling me on to the bed on top of her.

I started to resist because I'd already made up my mind that I was gonna part ways with her and I didn't want to lead her on more than I already had, but Ranisha was a sexy muthafucka. It was hard to tell her no and even though we had sex, numerous times the sight of her body always turned me on like it was the first time. Between her and the adrenaline running through from the jux I was amped the fuck up. I decided that fucking her one last time wouldn't do much harm. I took my clothes off and joined her in the bed and we fucked like two wild animals in a jungle in Africa somewhere.

Later that night we were laying in the bed eating room service when Ranisha came out of nowhere and asked. "Ski, will you marry me?"

I almost choked on my cheeseburger. "What you say? Yo, stop playing."

"I ain't playing. I'm dead serious. I wanna get married and start a family with you."

"Re, you buggin'. I ain't ready to be getting married to nobody."

"Do you love me?" she responded.

"Of course I do. You know that," I answered.

"Have you ever cheated on me?"

"Never." I lied.

"See it's like we married already. What's the difference?"

"That's the question you need to ask ya-self. If there ain't no difference why you in such a rush to get married then?" I shot back.

That line stumped her. I was temporarily off the hook. We ate in silence for the next few minutes until Ranisha broke it.

"I wish Ty was here with us. I miss my boo. She's supposed to be right here in between us. Them faggot niggaz cut her up like she was a piece of meat," Ranisha sobbed.

"I know baby. I miss her too. Them niggaz gonna pay for that shit Re I promise." I responded consoling her as my own eyes began getting watery.

"When you find them niggaz I wanna come too. Fuck that shit! I'm coming!' Ranisha yelled.

"Re, I got this. Lemme handle this. The last thing I need is something happening to you over some shit you ain't involved in. I don't know if I could live with myself after that."

"So what am I gonna do if something happens to you? You are all that I have in this whole world. Without you I ain't got nuthin'. I can't and I won't live without you," Ranisha said crying.

I took the food off the bed, curled up around her, and held her. When she told me that I was all she had in the world, it crushed me because it was true. And, little did she know that I was trying to get rid of her. She truly did love me. The only problem was that I wasn't in love with her and I didn't know how to tell her.

***

The next morning Kev came to our Hotel room to finish business. All was well. We ate breakfast out on the terrace, cracked jokes and just chilled. Kev was in love with Ranisha. He was flirting with her the entire time. He was doing everything in his power to add her to his stable. Surprisingly Ranisha took it in stride and didn't wild out on him. Deep down I was hoping she would give in to his advances so I could get off the hook.

"Okay Ski. Let's get down to business my friend," Kev said placing his briefcase on the table and removing his laptop.

I had Ranisha retrieve the duffel bags with the money, diamonds, and jewelry and passed it to him. He inspected the contents of the bags briefly and said. "Excellent. Everything seems to be here. Listen, Ski we have a slight adjustment with the payout. You guy's were really rough on my friend Brian. I had to up his percentage to keep him quiet so it knocked ya cut down to $2.5 million. You're cool wit that right?"

"2.5?" I asked. "Hell no we ain't cool wit that! We ain't got nuthin' to do wit ya manz cut. The deal was a 50/50 split and from my calculations, that's 4 mil. You trying to jerk us out of 1.5," I shouted angrily.

"Ski, calm down my friend. Don't talk to me in that tone of voice. I did you a favor. I could've fucked you and not gave you anything but I didn't. Please calm down. Let's handle this like gentlemen. I'd hate for this to have to get ugly," Kev said in his calming monotone voice.

"Listen duke you got me fucked up. You ain't do me no favor. We did each other a favor. And as far as you talking about you could've deaded me on the money. That would never happen. Just gimme my money before I get more upset than I already am." I yelled banging on the table with my fist.

"$2.5 million. Take it or leave it," Kev replied.

I stood up and pulled my chrome 44 from my waist and put to his temple.

"Yo, you got twenty muthafuckin' seconds to have my money in my muthafuckin' account before I put ya brains on this muthafuckin' plate nigga!" I said cocking the hammer.

"I wouldn't do that if I was you," Kev stated calmly.

"One... two... three...four..." I started counting down.

After I got to seventeen he gave in. "Okay... okay... you win. You win but it's gonna take me more than a few seconds to send it."

"Ayo Re make sure this cocksucker is sending our money."

Re pulled her chair up and sat down next to Kev as he transferred the money. After a few minutes, the transaction was complete.

"It's done. Are you happy now?" he asked sarcastically standing up.

"Sit the fuck down nigga. You don't leave until I say so!" I ordered. "Re, is it done?" I asked Ranisha.

"Yeah, we good daddy," Ranisha assured me looking up from the computer screen.

"A'ight now get the fuck up out of here pussy," I stated.

"You should've never done this Ski. You fucked up big time. This won't be the last time you see me. You can bet on that," Kev replied as he walked to the door with the bags.

"Whatever nigga. I'll off you and all them stink ho's you got working for you," I responded forcefully.

Kev walked out the room calmly as if nothing happened and shut the door. To his credit, he never seemed scared or nervous. He remained calm the whole time. Kev was rich and had money but he wasn't a threat to me. His words didn't move me at all. I was right and he was wrong, period and end of story. He tried to beat me for my money and then had the nerve to tell me that I was lucky I was getting anything. He was lucky I didn't kill him. I was worried a little about him going to the police but he didn't know what I'd say and I was sure he didn't wanna risk it. Especially for 1.5 million. That was peanuts to him.

An hour after our meeting with Kev, Ranisha and I were boarding our plane back to New York. Even if Kev were plotting on some get back, he wouldn't be able to find me. I had more money than I'd ever dreamed of having in my life but I also had more problems than I'd ever imagined a man could have. So much that I didn't have the chance to enjoy my newfound wealth. I had the never ending all out war with Raphael, Tiesha's death to deal with, a conflict with Cheeba that needed to get resolved and I had to decide what I was going to with Amir. And the cherry on top was that I was stuck in a relationship that I didn't want to be in. The only thing that I had going for me was my wealth, my son and the fact that I'd met the woman of my dreams. But, due to all the drama, I couldn't enjoy any of the three.

Midway through the flight, I started regretting that I didn't kill Kev. The last time I'd slept on a nigga and didn't finish him off I almost lost my life for it. I just hoped history wouldn't repeat itself.

Chapter 21

March 05

I'd been calling my son's mother non stop for the last 4 hours and couldn't get an answer. When I flew back in from Miami, I saw that my mother had left me messages telling me that she hadn't been able to get in touch with Michelle for the last month. Since I'd gotten out of my coma and Michelle came to see me at the hospital and told me she was pregnant by another nigga I cut all ties from her. My mother played the middleman. If I wanted to see my son I'd tell my mother and she and Michelle would meet up somewhere to drop him off. Since Michelle betrayed me, I'd lost all the love I had for her. Being that I was so busy getting money, and dealing with all the drama that was going on, I hadn't realized that I hadn't spoken to or saw my son in almost three months. I wanted to see my son and Michelle not returning neither my mother's nor my calls had me pissed. I called my mother to get Michelle's address, grabbed my jacket and left out the crib. *I know this bitch ain't trying to keep me away from my son.* I thought to myself. I was going up there to let her have it.

It was close to 9:00 at night when I finally pulled up to her house in Albany. She lived in a dingy looking two family house. I wasn't too familiar with Albany but I knew it had to be a bad neighborhood because there was mad niggaz posted up on every corner. The fact that my son was growing up in that type of environment got me more heated. Shit, I was a millionaire. My son had no business living where he was living.

I got out of my BMW, walked up to the house and banged on the door. I knew someone had to be home because all the lights were on and I could hear loud music coming from the inside.

A slim brown skin kid who looked to be no more than 17 years old opened the door.

"What's good?" he replied casually letting me inside.

When I walked inside the house I couldn't believe my eyes. It looked like it was an abandoned house. There was no furniture in the living room, the sink was filled with dishes that looked like they hadn't be washed in years, and the floor was littered with everything from empty pizza boxes to cigarette butts. It smelled like a mixture of dirty wet clothes, and crack smoke.

"Where's Michelle?" I asked looking around disgusted.

"Who you talking about M-Easy. You here to trick too? She upstairs in the bedroom with a couple of my niggaz but I'm next son. You gotta wait ya turn," the kid explained.

I had no idea what the kid was talking about so I ignored him and ran up the stairs in search of Michelle or my son.

The first bedroom door that I opened I found my son lying on a pallet of blankets.

"Daddy!" he shouted with excitement running towards me and hugging my legs.

Isaiah looked and smelled like shit. His hair was nappy and unkempt, his clothes were raggedy and dirty, and his room had no furniture in it and it felt like there was no heat on.

"Where's ya mother at?" I asked picking him up in my arms.

"She's in her room playing with her friends. She told me to stay in my room," he answered innocently.

"Put ya sneakers on, you coming to live wit daddy. I'll be right back okay?"

Isaiah nodded his head and ran to the closet to get his sneakers.

I closed his bedroom door, pulled out my Glock .40 out my waist and kicked open the other bedroom door.

When I entered the bedroom to say I was disgusted would be an understatement. Two young kids were running a train on Michelle. One was hitting her from the back and the other one was getting his dick sucked.

I let off two shots in the air startling all three of them.

"Isaiah, what are you doing here?" Michelle asked in embarrassment trying to cover her naked body with the covers.

"What the fuck you mean, what am I doing here bitch? What the fuck is you doing? How you got my son around this shit?" I shouted waving the gun around as I spoke. I pointed the gun at the two kids and yelled, "Get the fuck out of here before I decide to

pop one of y'all lil niggaz!"
The two scared kids wasted no time getting out of dodge. They grabbed their clothes into their arms and ran out the bedroom ass naked.
"You a smoker now? You out here selling ya body for crack now? What the fuck got into you?" I continued shouting.
Just then a frail looking light skin man came into the bedroom.
"What the fuck is going on in here? Who the fuck is you?" he asked with an attitude. "If you tricking or trying to move something out of here I'mma need something up front," he continued.
"Daryn, no this is Isaiah. My son's father," Michelle notified him.
I took the gun and smacked him with the butt of it knocking one of his teeth out and sending him to the floor. Once he fell to the floor I began stomping him in his face and his ribs.
"Isaiah stop! Stop! You're gonna kill him! Stop! Please!" Michelle pleaded with tears running down her face.
"You crying for this piece of shit? This piece of shit that got you selling ya body to support his habit?" I shouted continuing to go to work on him. "You got my son seeing all this shit? You stupid bitch you, I should kill you! You ain't never gonna see my son again. He's coming to stay wit me for good!"
Michelle got off the bed and fell to her knees in front of me.
"Isaiah, take me with you. Please I'm miserable. I can kick this shit. I don't wanna live like this no more. I know you still love me," she pleaded grabbing the leg of my jeans.
Michelle looked terrible. So terrible that I barely recognized her. She looked like she'd lost thirty pounds, her teeth were stained, her hair was a mess, and she had dark circles around her eyes. She was the complete opposite of what she used to be, but I didn't feel one ounce of compassion for her. She chose that life for herself. Actually, I felt disgusted just looking at her.
I was cocking my hand back to smack her when my son entered the room.
"Daddy, I can't put my shoes on," he said.
"Bitch don't ever try to contact me or my son again or I'll kill you. I swear on everything I love. You don't exist anymore to me or my

son. You hear me?" I shouted picking my son up in my arms and walking out the room.

"Isaiah! Isaiah! Don't go! Lemme hold a hundred dollars!" I heard Michelle shouting as I was leaving.

I meant every word I said. I was mad at myself for having a child with such a worthless bitch. I put my son in my car and drove back home to my crib in Scarsdale. The entire hour drive I was furious. Right when I was getting off the Henry Hutchinson expressway my phone rang.

"Who's this?" I answered with an attitude without checking the caller ID.

"It's me son. I need to see you. We got a problem," Cheeba said sounding serious.

"Meet me in Yonkers in the square in front of the Galaxy Diner," I responded.

"A'ight. I'll be there in a half."

I could only imagine what was so important that Cheeba couldn't wait until the following day. That nigga always called with bad news. I was glad that I was seeing him because the last conversation we had was still on my mind. I needed to know what his problem was.

I made it to Yonkers first. I was waiting for him outside the diner for almost twenty minutes when he pulled up in his Navigator. My son was fast asleep in the back seat. I hopped out my whip at the same time he hopped out of his and met him on the street between our parked cars.

"What happened now?" I asked.

"J. B. and Spazz got knocked by the D's at the spot in the Franklin apartments," Cheeba spat out.

"What was they doing at the spot? I thought I told you to send everybody home?" was my response.

"I know son. I know. I should've listened to you. I'm worried about them two lil niggaz telling B. I don't know how they built."

"You overreacting son. We'll just bail them out and school them. They can't be facing no serious time all they got caught with was hammers right?"

"Nah, B. They got caught wit everything." Cheeba shot back.

"What you mean everything?" I asked.

"They got knocked with a couple ratchets and probably a few O's of crills. Plus I think they sold to a undercover."

"Crills? What was they doing wit crills in the spot? I been told you to close up shop. You knew about that shit?"

Cheeba hesitated then answered. "Yeah. I knew about it. I opened shop back up a couple months back. I told them niggaz to be careful B. I told them."

I was pissed. "You opened the spot back up? What the fuck did you do that for? I gave you specific orders to dead everything until all this drama was dead didn't I?"

"And when the fuck was that gonna be?" Cheeba shouted. "We out here in the trenches dodging muthafuckin' bullets everyday. Every fucking day B! We ain't make a move on them niggaz yet. You act like you shook or something. I can't afford to close up shop. I gotta eat."

"You gotta eat? Nigga you was eating. Everybody was eating. How the fuck you think you got that truck? Or them jewels nigga?" I asked poking him in the chest with my finger. "Them wasn't ya spots to be opening and closing at your discretion. Them was my spots. My work and my connect nigga!" I shouted.

"Nigga, I do all the work. I'm out here in these streets while you home chillin'. Taking them dirty ass bitches on vacations and shit. You had them bitches getting more of a cut than me. You buying Bentley's and shit while I'm out here starving! You treat them ho's better than you treat ya man. You think I don't know you bubbling work somewhere else nigga? I know. And, you ain't even letting me eat, but I bet you had them bitches eating."

"Son, you got this shit fucked up. I ain't ya daddy nigga. I ain't responsible for you. If you don't like the way I do business then bounce nigga. Ain't no chains or cuffs on you. Get ya own money. And what the fuck is you in my pockets for? What I eat don't make you shit nigga."

"Word? That's how you feel? A'ight you gonna get yours B. You gonna get yours," Cheeba said shaking his head up and down.

"What you say nigga? Lemme get mines now nigga!" I said pulling my ratchet out. "You lucky I grew up wit you or I'd leave you here for talking reckless. I'mma tell you like this though son... You cut off! If I catch you out in Kingston I'mma treat you like I don't know you. I'mma have the Feds on my ass all because of ya greed and stupidity. Get the fuck out my face before I change my mind and kill you nigga!" I state pointing the gun at him.

Cheeba ice grilled me for a hot second and then hopped in his truck and sped off. I knew something was up with that nigga. I felt like popping him but I decided against it. He was my man from back in the days and I would only do something to him if I felt like my life was in danger. Cheeba was a thorough nigga and I knew he was tight about the way I carried him but he had to know he was wrong. He deserved it. I didn't know how personally he took it but if he came at me like he wanted to harm me in anyway I'd kill him like I never knew him a day in my life. I really hoped it didn't go there though.

I made the fifteen minute drive from Yonkers to Scarsdale, woke my son up and carried him in to the house. I was exhausted. I had a long day. When I walked in the house, R. Kelly was playing on the surround sound and there were rose pedals all over the floor leading to my bedroom. I put Isaiah in his bed and then went into my bedroom to see what all the fuss was about. The bedroom was dark and candles were lit around the bed. It looked nice and romantic but I definitely was not in the mood, not that day and not with Ranisha. I paid no attention to my surroundings and began disrobing at the edge of the bed. Seconds later Ranisha came out of the bedroom in a see through Victoria Secret lingerie set and heels on dancing seductively. I grabbed the remote control off the dresser and cut the music off.

"What you doing baby? You're spoiling the mood?" Ranisha pouted.

"Not now Re I'm not in the mood. I'm stressed out," I said seriously.

"Guess what?' Ranisha asked sitting on my lap and placing my hand on her stomach. "We're having a baby."

That was the last thing I wanted to hear. "You gonna have to get rid of that. This ain't the time Re. I ain't ready for another child." I responded coldly but truthfully.

Ranisha's eyes got watery immediately. She smacked me in the face and shot out the room.

"How could you say some shit like that? You can't love me!" she cried.

After I saw her reaction, I knew I said the wrong thing and instantly felt bad. It wasn't her fault I was having a bad day. I knew I could've worded my statement better. I ran out the bedroom behind her and found her curled up in the bathroom downstairs crying.

"Re… I'm sorry ma. It's just that a lot of shit is going on right now. I ain't mean for it to come out like that." I said softly sitting down on top of the toilet and placing her on my lap. "A lot of shit went down today. I got a lot of problems ma, you don't even know the half. My life is fucked up right now. I could die or go to prison at any given moment. My life ain't stable enough to be bringing another child into the world. But, if everything was cool I would love for you to have my child. You'd make a great mother," I lied.

"What's going on? Tell me what's wrong so I can fix it," Ranisha said sniffling and then wiping the tears off her face.

I told her everything that transpired that day in full detail. She listened intently.

"Baby, I just got too much on my plate right now. Raphael, Cheeba, Ty's murder, I got my son full time now and I still don't know what I'm gonna do wit Amir. And, on top of that I might have a case coming my way. My life is in chaos right now." I explained.

"I can make it better baby. If you didn't have any of those problems would you wanna have this baby?" she asked.

"Of course I would. What kind of question is that?" I lied again.

"I'mma fix it then. I'mma fix everything," Ranisha replied laying her head on my shoulder. "Make love to me Ski. I wanna feel you," Ranisha requested.

Like I said before her body was so sick and she was so beautiful that it was hard for me to resist her. I knew it was wrong for me to keep fucking her but I couldn't help myself. Just her sitting on my lap had me hard. Her titties were popping out of her bra, she smelled good enough to eat, and I could feel the warmness, and moistness through her thong.

I carried her upstairs to our bedroom and made love to her. Getting Ranisha out of my life was going to be way more of a hassle than I anticipated. She had a hold on me. I wasn't in love with her but I cared about her and felt sorry for her. She gave me all of her all the time. I knew she really loved me and I didn't want to break her heart.

That night I didn't sleep a wink. My head was spinning. I had problems coming from every angle. I never believed the saying money doesn't solve all of you problems until then. I was a multi-millionaire and more miserable than I'd been, my entire life. It was like I was twenty-five going on fifty and the worst part about it was I knew things were going to only get worse.

Chapter 22

April 05

Ranisha was outside of Ulster County jail in her Benz impatiently waiting for J.B. and Spazz to be released. Five hours earlier Ranisha had paid the bails bondman ten thousand dollars apiece to get them out. Luckily for J B. and Spazz the lawyer that Ski had retained for them finally got the judge to grant them a bail and it was perfect timing because the lawyer said he had a feeling the Feds were going to pick up their case. And, everyone knows that the Fed's don't give bails, especially on crack and gun cases. Ski knew this and wanted to get them out as soon as he could so he could school them and get in their ears before they did. If that didn't work Ski was going to threaten them with their family's lives. If they wanted to jump bail and go on the run, he would help them but telling was not an option.

A little bit after two in the afternoon J.B. and Spazz bopped out of the Ulster County jail with big smiles on their faces. They each had on matching Pelle Pelle leathers, jeans and boots.

Ranisha saw them come out and beeped the horn to get their attention.

"Over here y'all. Hurry the fuck up. If I was y'all I would be running out of that fucking place. Y'all niggaz acting like y'all wanna go back," Ranisha shouted out the driver's side window.

When J.B. and Spazz saw that Ranisha was there to pick them up, they sprinted to the car in an effort to be the one who got to seat next to Ranisha in the front. J.B. beat Spazz to it.

"What's up y'all? Y'all a'ight?" Ranisha asked with a big smile.

"Yeah, we good now," J.B. responded looking down at Ranisha's thick yellow thighs.

Ranisha had on a black Chanel mini skirt that was so short that you could damn near see her pussy. Up top she had a matching black Chanel hoodie with nothing on under it and she had the zipper so far down that half of her breast was showing. J.B. couldn't stop his manhood from rising.

J.B. and Spazz were two young niggaz from around Ski's way in Long Island that hustled for him. J. B. was 18 and Spazz was 17. J.B. was Dominican and black and wore his hair in a low fade. He stood 5' 9" inches tall and had a slim build. Spazz was a light skin kid that wore his hair in a small afro and he was the same height as J. B. They were both two thorough young niggaz that were down for whatever and had put in major work before.

"So what y'all wanna eat? I know y'all hungry." Ranisha asked seductively spreading her legs and licking her lips teasing the two kids.

"Uhhhh, it don't matter. Whatever," Spazz said nervously from the back seat.

"Whatever you'll let us," J.B. shot back staring at her crotch.

"I hear that. That's what's up. Relax ya'll, Ski told me to take good care of y'all. Y'all hanging wit me today. I got a half of dro, a bottle of Henny and a suite at the Holiday Inn. Everybody's coming up later tonight," Ranisha stated.

"So what are we gonna do until everybody gets there," Spazz asked nervously.

"I'm sure we'll find something to do after we get twisted. Don't worry cutie I don't bite," Ranisha responded looking at Spazz through her rearview mirror.

J.B. and Spazz were amped the fuck up. They felt like the two luckiest niggaz in the world. They were going to get the opportunity to chill and get twisted with Ranisha all day and by the way she was acting they were starting to get the feeling they were gonna do more than chill. Not only those two, but all of Ski's workers fantasized about her. On the ride to the Hotel both Spazz and J.B.'s dicks were hard in anticipation of what they thought might happen.

Once they got into the suite that Ranisha had reserved for them, she let them order room service and they started drinking and smoking. About two hours later J.B. and Spazz were bent out of their minds.

Ranisha stood up. "Yo, y'all two lil niggaz is thorough. I'm really feeling y'all! Ski, told me to roll out the red carpet for y'all but I wasn't sure if I wanted to do it. But now-," she paused sticking her finger in her mouth. "Matter of fact gimme a minute lemme put on something more comfortable," she continued grabbing a plastic bag off the bed and switching her hips hard as she walked into the bathroom.

When the bathroom door shut Spazz asked. "What you think she gonna do when she come out yo?"

"What the fuck you think stupid?" J.B. whispered smacking J.B. in the back of the head. "She about to give us some cheeks nigga. Ski, told her to set it out for us. Ski is a real nigga son. He about to let us fuck his bitch."

Spazz was excited. "I can't believe this shit son. Ski must got mad love for us."

"Yo, son I saw that bitch pussy in the car B. Her shit is mad fat son. I'mma eat that shit," J.B. responded rubbing his crotch. "I think this bitch been wanted to give me some pussy B. I saw her looking at me at Ski's birthday party. She probably fucking you off the strength of Ski but she been wanted to fuck wit me son."

"Chill son. She's coming out," Spazz whispered.

The bathroom door opened and Ranisha came out ass naked with nothing on but 4-inch Manolos. Her body was oiled up making her look like a goddess.

"You guys like what you see or what?" Ranisha asked spinning around in a circle so they could get the full view.

J.B. and Spazz were in awe. They'd never saw a bitch as bad as Ranisha in their lives. Not even at a strip club. They were young so they were use to dealing with females their age. Even a grown man would be speechless seeing her nude. They both just stood their staring at her with their mouths wide open.

"Nah, I don't like it. I love it," J.B. answered biting his lip.

"Who gonna get this thing wet?" Ranisha asked seductively.

"I can definitely get it wet ma," J.B. volunteered.

"Take y'all clothes off. Lemme see what y'all working with." Ranisha ordered.

J.B. and Spazz wasted no time in disrobing. In 2.2 seconds they were both naked stroking their dicks looking at Ranisha's perfect body waiting for her next command.

"Spazz lay on the bed. J.B. do what you said you was gonna do," Ranisha requested.

She laid Spazz flat on his back, got on her knees and began sucking his dick. Meanwhile J.B. was behind her licking her pussy from the back.

Spazz was in Heaven. His eyes rolled back in his head and veins protruded on his forehead as Ranisha serviced him. She spit on his dick and slid his penis in and out of her mouth while she jerked him off simultaneously. She stared into his eyes the whole time and talked dirty to him.

"You like that daddy? You gonna cum for me?" Ranisha asked in between bobs.

"Yeah!" Spazz moaned out in pleasure.

J.B. was busy feasting on her pussy. "I bet you Ski don't eat it like this!"

"Ohmigod nobody ever ate this pussy like this before," Ranisha lied faking an orgasm.

She backed her behind into J.B.'s face almost smothering him with her massive ass.

When Ranisha felt that Spazz was about to nut she took his dick out of her mouth and began licking on his chest. In one swift movement Ranisha pulled out a gem star razor from under her tongue and slit his neck from ear to ear and put her hands on his face and nose suffocating him.

"ARRGGHGH!" Spazz tried to scream out holding his neck.

J. B. was so busy eating Ranisha out that he didn't even notice that his man was dying in front of him. He heard him scream but figured he was just cumin and kept on doing him. After Ranisha was sure that Spazz was dead, she rolled over him on her back and pulled J.B. on top of her. J.B. was so entranced by Ranisha that he didn't even notice that his right hand man was dead in a pool of blood next to him.

Ranisha reached in between J.B. legs and put his rock hard dick inside of her.

"Ahhh! Damn ma, you got some good pussy," J.B. moaned in pure ecstasy as he entered her.

He'd never felt no pussy as tight, warm, and wet as Ranisha's. He couldn't keep up. His eyes were rolling back in his head and he had to stop pumping because he didn't want to cum too quick. Ranisha was throwing it at him like a quarter back on third and ten.

"Suck my titties baby! Suck my titties!" Ranisha ordered J. B.

As J.B. was licking on her nipples, Ranisha took the same gem star she killed Spazz with and slit J.B.'s neck.

"ARRGGGHH!" J. B. screamed out grabbing his neck.

Amidst all the excitement, J.B. had forgotten all about Spazz, but after he got his neck slit, he thought about him for the first time. He looked around holding his neck frantically looking for Spazz and after a few seconds he realized Spazz was already dead. That sent him into a panic. He started flaring his arms wildly and kicking his legs and managed to fall on the floor. Once he fell on the floor, she got on top of him, covered his mouth, and suffocated him as well.

"You bitch ass lil dick muthafucka!" Ranisha said spitting in his face.

Ranisha got up, took a shower, wiped the room down clean and walked out the Holiday Inn satisfied with her work. She hated that she had to have sex with them to kill them but justified it in her mind believing that she did it all to help the man she loved. She didn't enjoy it, so she felt like it wasn't cheating. Besides, she would never tell Ski that she fucked them anyways. What she did that day to her was all in the name of love. There was nothing she wouldn't do for Ski.

Ranisha drove back home anxious to tell Ski the good news. Ski didn't tell her to kill them but she knew he'd be happy. She'd fixed one of his problems. *Now we can have our baby and live happily ever after* she thought to herself.

***

"Isaiah what do you want for ya birthday?" I asked my three-year-old son as he entered the living room and sat down on the couch next to me.

"I wanna go see Mickey Mouse's house," he answered.

"Mickey Mouse's house? So you wanna got to Disney World?"

"Yeah!" he exclaimed excitedly.

"Do you think daddy is gonna take you to see Mickey Mouse?"

"Yes."

"Why?"

"Because my daddy loves me. He's the best daddy in the world," Isaiah responded giving me a hug.

It made me proud to hear him speak so high of me. "You got that right. Daddy loves you more than anything in the world. What else do you want for ya birthday?" I asked.

"Ummmm… can mommy come with us?"

"No, mommy can't come with us but Grandma and Sable can come. You want to bring them with us?"

He jumped on me and started giving me kisses on my face. "Yeah!"

Just then Ranisha came into the house and walked into the living room and sat down next to us.

"Well if it's not my two favorite men in the world," Ranisha replied sitting on my lap and giving us both kisses on the cheek. "I got a surprise for you Isaiah. I got you a happy meal from McDonalds," Ranisha announced.

Isaiah started looking around everywhere. "Where? Where is it at?"

We both laughed. "It's in the kitchen baby," Ranisha stated.

Isaiah jumped off the couch and bolted towards the kitchen like a sprinter during the Olympics.

I stopped him. "Hey! Come back here. What do you say?"

"Thank you Re, Re," Isaiah said giving Ranisha a kiss and then bolting back towards the kitchen again.

"Hey sexy you missed me?" Ranisha asked rubbing her hands on my face and staring into my eyes.

I was suspicious. "What you so happy about?"

"I'm always happy when I'm around my husband."

"Yeah a'ight. So did you take care of J.B. and Spazz's bail?"

She smiled a devilish grin. "Yup."

"Good. That's what's up. Where they at?"

"Oh they gone. You ain't gonna have to worry about them lil niggaz no more."

I was dumbfounded. "Gone where? Re, what the fuck is you talking about?"

"I killed them," Ranisha confessed.

My eyes got as big as basketballs. "You did what?"

"I killed them baby. I got rid of them for good. You ain't gotta worry about them telling on you. I took care of it. Didn't I tell you I was gonna fix all of ya problems? Now we can have our baby." Ranisha continued rubbing my waves.

"You stupid bitch. What the fuck is wrong wit you?" I shouted pushing her hand off of me forcefully and standing up. "Do you know what you just did? Why the fuck would you do that? Oh my fucking God!" I continued covering my hands with my face and sitting back down.

"Baby... please don't be mad. I did it for you. I just wanted to make things better."

"Make things better? Bitch you just made shit worse. Now I'mma have the fucking Feds on my ass for a double homicide! I can't believe this shit! If I wanted them dead I would've killed them myself," I continued shouting at her.

"Ski, we got enough money to go anywhere that we want. Let's just leave and never come back. Start a whole new life. Fuck all this shit, let's just go and raise our family," Ranisha pleaded trying to wrap her arms around me.

I cocked back and smacked Ranisha so hard in the face that she fell on the floor ten feet away from where she was standing. My handprint was on her face and she laid still on the ground holding the spot where I had smacked her. She got up and tried to come back towards me.

"Don't touch me yo! Don't touch me! Matter of fact stay the fuck away from me! I don't want nothing to do wit you! There Is No Us! There will never be No Us! You got money... Go somewhere far the fuck away from me!" I screamed at the top of my lungs.

"Ski, please no! Please! I'm sorry! Don't leave me like this! I love you! I can't live without you, you are all I have! Please baby I'm sorry! Let me make it better! I can make it better!" Ranisha pleaded crying on her knees crawling towards me.

I didn't want to hear it. "What part of what I'm saying don't you understand? It's over you crazy bitch! I'm done wit you!" I stated coldly.

Just then, the house phone rang.

"What the fuck you want?" I answered.

"Hello… ummm… can I speak to Isaiah?" a sweet voice asked.

"Who's this?" I asked.

"This is Crystal."

She had perfect timing. "This is me. What's up? How are you doing?"

"Did I catch you at bad time or something? I'm sorry for calling your house. I got the number from my father. I lost ya cell phone number. I hope I didn't over step any boundaries," Crystal said.

"Nah, never that. I'm sorry for coming at you like that. I'm just a little aggravated right now."

"Oh, I can call you back."

"Nah. Nah. Matter of fact can I see you tonight? Where you at?"

"Sure. I'm not doing anything but studying. I'm in my dorm."

"A'ight bet. I'll be there in a half hour."

"I'll be waiting."

As soon as I got off the phone, Ranisha was breathing down my neck. "Who the fuck was that?"

"None of ya fucking business!" I exclaimed no longer caring about her feelings.

"I know you ain't got bitches calling my muthfuckin' house!" Ranisha raised her voice.

"Ranisha I ain't gonna tell you again yo. Get the fuck out of my face! Get away from me and stay away from me!" I said putting my hands out in front of me before walking out of the room.

I went into the kitchen, got my son, put some clothes on him, walked out the house and took off in my BMW. Ranisha followed us outside.

"Please baby we can work this out. Don't leave me. I love you. I'm sorry!" Ranisha pleaded with tears rolling down her face.

I ignored her and peeled off. The last sight I saw of her was her standing in the driveway barefooted. After I got a few feet away, I looked in my rearview mirror and saw her drop down to her knees.

I was beyond furious. I couldn't believe that she had killed J.B. and Spazz. I blamed myself for letting Ranisha stick around for as long as I did. The crazy bitch turned a big problem into a gigantic problem. I knew for sure that the Fed's would be knocking at my door asking questions. I was starting to feel like I was cursed. I had a dark cloud following me that I couldn't seem to get from underneath. I didn't have to find trouble; it knocked on my door and found me.

I pulled up at Crystal's dorm at around 8 o'clock that night. I hadn't spoke to, or seen her since the first day we met but she'd been on my mind everyday. I knew she was the one but didn't want to bring her into my life amidst all the chaos. I was gonna wait until I got my life back together and be with her, but at the rate my life was going things were never going to get better. I made up my mind on the drive there that I was going to be honest with Crystal and tell her everything that was going on, and let her decide if she still wanted to get involved with me.

I called Crystal on my cell phone, and she came downstairs and met us in the parking lot.

"Hey, what's ya name cutie pie?" Crystal asked bending down to look Isaiah in the face.

"Isaiah," he replied shyly trying to hide behind my leg.

"Hi, I'm Crystal," she said with a big smile. "And, you Mr. Thompson. Do you know how stressed out you've had me these past few weeks. Were you ever going to call me?" Crystal asked with her hands on her hips looking as cute as ever.

"I'm sorry ma a lot of bull junk is going on right now. I was waiting for things to cool down but shit seems like it just keeps heating up," I explained honestly.

"I understand. Just know that if you ever need someone to talk to I'm here for you," she responded in a comforting tone.

"Well good. That's why I really came here tonight. I need to tell you some things about me and what's going on in my life. Can we come in?" I asked.

"Sure," Crystal answered leading the way.

I was surprised at the size of Crystal's dorm room. It was huge. I was expecting a dorm room with two beds, dressers, and a desk but she had a living room, kitchen, and a bedroom. It was like a miniature apartment. The place was immaculately clean like I expected it to be and she had a few notebooks and textbooks on her coffee table like she had been studying.

After we engaged in small talk for a little while and my son fell asleep, it was time to get down to business. I took a deep breath and began.

"Ayo, Crystal I just wanna let you know that I'm feeling you something crazy. I know it sounds crazy and it doesn't make sense to me either, but I'm falling in love wit you. I fell in love with you from the moment that I first laid eyes on you. I don't know what is gonna happen in the future, but I do know I want you in it. I wanna be with you… like forever. I've never felt like this about anyone." I poured my heart out.

"I've been in love before but it never felt like this before. Since we've met I can't stop thinking about you. When I heard your voice on the phone tonight, it sent chills throughout my whole body. I know you are the one." I continued.

Crystal was smiling from ear to ear. She leaned over towards me, kissed me softly on the lips, and then put her finger to my lips.

"Isaiah, I feel the same way about you. I mean… you are right it is crazy but it feels too right to be wrong. I wanna be with you too. I haven't stopped thinking about you since we've met. I've been practically waiting by the phone waiting for you to call me. Whatever it is that is going on in your life we can get past it. Together." Crystal looked me square in the eyes, grabbed my hand and inter locked them together.

"Listen, I'mma tell you some things about me but I don't want you to look at me different. I have a good heart. Sometimes I do bad shit but I always feel like it's for the right reasons in my heart," I explained.

She sat up in her seat. "I'm listening."

"A'ight... look-," I went on.

For the next three hours, I told Crystal everything about me from being a high school basketball star on my way to college, to becoming a professional stick up kid. I told her about how one of my best friends died during a botched robbery. I told her about the Fed's and how I beat trial, and my manz and them that were still on lockdown. I told her about Raphael and how he had almost killed me. Tiesha, Ranisha, Cheeba, how I met her father, and even told her about all the people I killed and why. Crystal listened intently and only interrupted me to ask questions.

After I told her, everything I felt like a huge weight had been lifted off my shoulders. It was like a confessional. When I was done I sat across from Crystal waiting for her to give me a response.

"So do you still think that I'm the one for you?" I asked her.

"Come here," she said standing up over me and holding her hand out.

She helped me off the couch and led me to her bedroom.

"Isaiah, you've had a hard life. I know you are going through a lot in your life right now but I'd like the opportunity to try and help you make it better. I'd be honored to have a man like you as my life partner," Crystal announced.

Those words were like music to my ears. I hugged her tight, picked her up in my arms, and spun her around in circles. As we stood there kissing it was as if time was standing still. Nothing else mattered. As we kissed, we slowly began to undress each other. After I was down to my t-shirt and boxers, and she was topless and in her panties, I laid her on the bed gently and kissed every inch of her body.

Crystal was beautiful. She was perfect in every way imaginable. She had a golden complexion; she was 5' 5" with soft beautiful dough light brown eyes, and long curly hair that dropped down to the middle of her back. She had sexy full lips and small but firm B-cup breast, a flat stomach and a nice petite curvy round bottom. Her skin was softer than cotton and didn't have a blemish anywhere. She smelled and felt like something refreshing.

I removed her panties and slid down in between her legs. First I teased her by licking the insides of her thighs and after I heard her panting and saw her legs shaking in anticipation I put my hands underneath her and began licking her clit in slow circular strokes. Crystal moaned and squeezed my hand with all of her might and put her head back. She was so wet that that there was a pool of her juices running down from underneath her to the end of the bed. I had my tongue probing her insides like the coastguard looking for Kennedy Jr. I licked the inside of her lips and then stuck my tongue and my face as deep as I could inside of her.

"Baby… This…feels….too…good. I…I can't take it!" Crystal shouted out.

She began wiggling her body, pushing my head off her, and anything else she could do to escape my grasp but I was not having it. There was no escaping me. I had a firm grip on her ass cheeks and the more she fought to get me off of her the more I went in on her. Finally, she stopped fighting and gave into the fire that was building up in the pit of her stomach. She started pushing my head down forcefully in between her legs, and grinding her pussy on my face. Her shoulders hunched, her neck jerked backwards, and she clenched her teeth hard and closed her eyes as her climax steadily approached. Sweat poured down from her sideburns and dropped down to her collar-bone at a rapid pace like tears from the clouds. After she reached her climax, she licked her lips, and a single tear rolled down her left cheek. She pulled me up from in-between her legs and kissed me passionately.

"Please promise me you're the real thing," she said.

I didn't speak a word and I didn't have to. My eyes showed my sincerity. She grimaced in pain as I guided myself slowly into her tight love tunnel but once I was completely inside of her, her body relaxed.

"You feel so good," she whispered into my ear as she started moving her hips in perfect rhythm with me.

"You do too," I whispered back pushing her hair out of her face.

"Wait…I'm about to… Ooh!" she cried out digging her nails in my back.

"Go ahead ma. Let it out baby. Cum for me," I responded stroking her harder and deeper.

Once again her whole body shook but this time she screamed out.

"I love you!"

I could tell that she wasn't as experienced in the bedroom as I was but that was a good thing. After she came, I laid her down flat on her stomach and entered her from behind. As I felt myself about to cum I grabbed her by the neck and began fucking her roughly.

"Ummm!! Don't stop! I'm about to cum on this dick again!" Crystal announced.

I couldn't hold it back any longer. When we climaxed together it felt like the earth stopped spinning and time stood still. We laid side by side sweat, and sticky in pure bliss. There was no doubt in my mind that she was the one. Everything came natural for us. Nothing seemed forced, even our sexual chemistry was crazy. It was the best sexual experience I'd ever had in my life.

"I love you Mr. Thompson," Crystal said laying on my chest and staring at me with her beautiful brown eyes.

"I love you too… Mrs. Thompson," I replied rubbing her back.

"I like the sound of that," Crystal responded with a big smile.

"Me too," I confessed with a smile as equally big as hers.

In the midst of all the chaos in my life, God had blessed me with an angel. Crystal was so perfect that I almost felt like I didn't deserve her. She was so perfect that if I were an atheist she would make believe that there was a God. My life was in shambles, but at that moment, I didn't have a care in the world. I was at peace. I'd found my soul mate. Now all I had to do was get out of all the shit I'd gotten myself into so that I could enjoy her.

Chapter 23

April 05

"Say cheese" Crystal said, as she got ready to snap a picture of Me, Isaiah and Goofy.

"Cheese," we said in unison as the flash from the camera went off.

"Where you wanna go now?" I asked bending down to pick Isaiah up with his hat with the Mickey Mouse ears.

"Ummm-," he thought for a moment then said. "Bumper cars!"

"Again?" I asked. "We just left from the bumper cars. You wanna go all the way back over there?"

"Bumper cars!" he shouted again with excitement.

"Okay, bumper cars it is then," Crystal said pinching his cheeks. "Whatever the birthday boy wants he gets."

Me, Crystal and Isaiah were in Disney World in Orlando, Florida celebrating his third birthday. It was a Saturday, we flew out there that previous Friday morning and were gonna leave that Sunday so that Crystal could make it back to school for her classes Monday morning. Isaiah and I had stayed at Crystal's dorm ever since we'd gotten there that Tuesday. Isaiah and Crystal hit it off from the jump. Being around Crystal and Isaiah gave me a sense of family that I hadn't felt since I was a child. I started to realize that money and material things weren't the most important things in life. Family was. I made up my mind that as soon as I handled all the drama I was in, I was out the game for good. I was a multi-millionaire; I could do anything or start any type of business I wanted. My dream was to be alive and free to raise my son to be a better man than I was. I wanted the opportunity to be a good father and a husband.

Disney World was beautiful. The weather was nice, the employees were friendly and helpful, and just the overall atmosphere was pro family. Everywhere you looked, you saw smiling children and parents. Isaiah was having the time of his young life. Between Friday and that day we'd been everywhere.

We went to Universal Studios and watched all the shows. We visited Snow White's Castle, Epcott Center, the aquarium, and the haunted house. And, in addition to that Crystal and Isaiah had me on damn near every ride that they had in the park. We went on the Batman roller coaster, the slingshot and the Ferris-wheel. I could barely keep up with them. Crystal was just as energetic as my son if not more. If it wasn't Isaiah pulling me somewhere it was her. Her crazy ass even convinced me to bungee jump. The adrenaline rush was even better than pulling a jux. Even though everything was going perfect, I had the feeling that we were being followed. Every time I mentioned it to Crystal, she told me that I was buggin' out and being paranoid but I knew I wasn't wildin'. Something didn't seem right.

Later that night we went to watch the Orlando Magic play against the Minnesota Timberwolves. We had courtside seats and the game was good but the real show as at halftime.

"Yo, Crystal look up at the scoreboard and tell me how many points Kevin Garnett had. I can't see." I said.

"Boy, you can't see them big ol' numbers on that score-board?" she laughed taking a sip of her soda. "We gonna have to get you some glasses baby." she teased.

When Crystal looked up at the score-board, she got the surprise of her life. The scoreboard read: *Crystal will you marry me?* On it in big flashing letters. It took a minute for it to register but when she saw our faces on the teletron, her jaw dropped. She covered her face with her hands, and began stomping her feet in her seat. Tears streamed down her face as one of the security guards passed me a microphone and I got down on one knee in front of her.

"Crystal, you are the most beautiful woman I've ever laid eyes my on. I knew you were going to be my wife from the first day that are eyes met. You are my soul mate and my gift from God and I promise you I will never take you for granted or hurt you. When I'm around you nothing else matters. You complete me. Will you please make me the happiest man on the earth and marry me?" I asked pulling out a 3-karat engagement ring.

Crystal's hands were shaking and she couldn't stop herself from crying. She nodded her head and put her tongue so far down my throat that I could've swallowed it. As we kissed, everyone in the arena cheered and applauded, balloons came down from the ceiling and the words *She said yes* flashed on the teletron. Hollywood couldn't have written a better script.

"I love you so much. You are so crazy!" Crystal shouted as I slipped the ring on her finger. "Ohmigod it's so beautiful." she continued admiring her ring.

"A beautiful ring for a beautiful woman," I responded.

"Isaiah… no one has ever made me feel so special. You make me feel like the luckiest woman in the world. This is the best day of my life. I love you." Crystal stated before giving me a tight hug.

I paid fifteen grand to make all that happen and it was worth every penny. The reaction that I'd gotten out of her was priceless. I wanted that night to be a night that she would remember forever. Crystal was more emotional than I thought she would be. I would've paid a hundred thousand dollars just to see that warm beautiful smile of hers. Seeing her happy made me happy.

As halftime was ending, players from both teams came over and congratulated us. When the game was over Me, Crystal and Isaiah went out for dinner to celebrate.

"CC are you going to be my new mommy?" Isaiah asked.

"No honey. I'm going to be your step-mother," Crystal explained.

"What's that?" Isaiah asked confused.

"See me and your daddy are going to get married. Would you like that?" Crystal asked.

"Yes," Isaiah chimed.

"Well after we get married I'm going to be your step-mother. Ever other little boy has one mommy but you are so special that you are going to have a mommy and a step-mother," Crystal explained tickling him. "Isn't that right baby?" she turned and asked me.

I was in a daze. "What? What happened?"

"You didn't hear a word that I said did you? What's wrong baby you don't like your food?"

I leaned toward Crystal and whispered. "I think someone is following us. I got a bad feeling. Something is up. I feel like we are being watched. Maybe we should get the fuck out of here tonight. I got a sixth sense for trouble."

Crystal grabbed hold of my hand. "Baby, everything is fine. No one is following us. We're all the way in Orlando. Neither one of us knows anyone here. I thought we were going to leave all of your problems back in New York? It's just paranoia. Everything just seems too perfect right?"

I nodded my head.

"That's because we are made for each other. I feel it too. Listen honey, I know that good things in your life always come to a quick and abrupt end but I'm here baby. I'm not going anywhere. Never. That feeling that you're feeling is a feeling of peace and contentment. Get use to being happy baby. Relax," Crystal assured me.

Maybe she's right I thought to myself. Things did seem too good to be true. And, in my life experiences when things were too good to be true they weren't. Crystal had a point but I had a bad feeling ever since we'd gotten off the plane. Something was not right. I constantly was looking over my shoulder and feeling I was being watched. I was paranoid, but I had good reason to be. I promised Crystal that I was going to leave all of my problems in New York and enjoy the weekend so I smiled and told her she was right to ease her mind. Since I'd left for Crystal's dorm that Tuesday, I hadn't spoken to Cheeba or Ranisha. For all I knew it could've been the Feds watching me.

We made love all that night celebrating our engagement and the next day was uneventful. We went to the water park, rode rides and played games all day. We were all enjoying each other's company so much that I began to think that I was buggin' out thinking someone was following us. After we went shopping and got something to eat, we went back to our suite to pack and headed to the airport to make our 9 o'clock flight. We made it there early at about a quarter after eight. Crystal and Isaiah were both burned out and knocked out in the lobby. I smiled to myself looking at them, happy that Isaiah had taken to her so well. I couldn't believe that I was actually going to have a real family of my own.

Since we had a long wait I pulled out my cell phone and checked my messages. Since I'd gone to stay with Crystal I kept my phone off at all times. I didn't want to hear from anyone. My voice mailbox was full. As I waited to hear my first message, my stomach started turning. The last thing I needed was to hear some more bad news. I was praying in my mind hoping that I wouldn't hear that the Feds were looking for me in connection with the double homicide of J.B. and Spazz. I let out a sigh of relief when I found out that there wasn't any bad news waiting. Ranisha had left me ten messages crying, telling me how much she loved me, how much she was sorry and begging me to come home. She sounded crazier and crazier each message. I'd been gone for five days and Ranisha had filled up my voice mailbox up after two days so I realized that I could possibly have some bad news waiting and no one could alert me to it because Ranisha's stupid ass had my shit full.

I sat down away from Crystal and Isaiah to collect my thoughts. The fairytale life that I had been living all weekend was about to come to an abrupt halt as soon as our plane landed in New York. I knew I was going to be hit with a large dose of reality and I began to brace myself for it. I had to deal with Cheeba, Ranisha, Raphael and possibly a murder case. There was drama coming from every fucking angle.

As I was sitting down with my face in my hands my phone started ringing.

I didn't recognize the number on the caller I.D. "Hello." I answered.

"Wha' gwan bredren? Ow mi hear say you ago marry mi daughta en you na call and tell mi or ask mi permission or fa mi blessings?" Prince asked.

"Prince, what up Dred! My bad man, we was gonna come to ya house and tell you in person. Everything just happened so quickly," I tried to explain.

"Yo! Yo! Mi can't hear you bwoy! It a too noisy where you at. Go find someplace quiet so we can chat." Prince requested.

The airport was mad busy. Between the flight attendants on the microphone and people talking, I could barely hear myself think.

"Hold on Big Dread lemme go into the bathroom. Don't hang up!" I said.

Once I found the men's bathroom, I asked. "Can you hear me? Is that better?"

"Yes star. Now whu you say?" Prince inquired.

"Yeah my bad Prince. I'm sorry about that B. Everything is just happening mad fast. We were gonna come to your house and tell you as soon as you got back. We in Orlando right now. Yo, Big Dred I love ya daughter man, and she loves me. I never felt the way I feel about her about anyone before. She completes me man. She's perfect. I'm sorry I didn't call and ask ya permission. I got a lot of love and respect for you. You don't have a problem with me being with ya daughter do you?"

"Naw mon. Everyting krisp. Mi know se you check fa mi daughta and mi know she check fa you. But, lemme tell you dis bwoy if you break mi pickney heart or cause her grief mi ago kill you. You understand me?"

"Of course, It's only right my nigga but you ain't got nothing to worry about. I'm gonna give her the world." I stated.

"Good cause dat's what she deserve. She ah good ooman. Mek sure you watch out and protect mi daughta at all times you hear? And, when you come back come see mi." Prince responded.

"I got you my nigga."

"Peace and blessings." Prince said preparing to hang up.

"Ayo Prince! Yo, how you know I proposed to Crystal? We ain't tell nobody." I asked puzzled.

Prince laughed. "Don't worry bout dat mon. Nuthin' na gwon weh mi na know." Prince said before he disconnected our call.

Prince never ceased to amaze me. I was starting to believe that he really did know everything. Crystal and I hadn't told anyone about our engagement. I laughed to myself and left out the bathroom to wake up Crystal and tell her about her father's phone call. When I walked back into the lobby Crystal and Isaiah were gone. One of Isaiah's sneakers was on the chair so I assumed that Crystal took him to the bathroom so I sat down and waited for them. After waiting about ten minutes, I got impatient and stood outside of the women's bathroom waiting for them to come out. After another ten minutes, I sent a woman inside the bathroom to tell Crystal to hurry up. The woman came out and told me that there was no one in there by that name. I started to panic but calmed down figuring that they were in another bathroom or had gone to the gift shop.

It was now 8:45. I was starting to panic. I went inside all the men's and women's bathrooms and gift shops and there still was no sign of them. They were nowhere to be found. My heart was racing. I didn't know what to think. The clock now read 9:05 and they were calling last call for our flight. I ran to the flight attendant at the gate and asked. "Excuse me did a little boy and pretty light skin woman wearing a sweat suit get on this plane with first class tickets?"

"I'm sorry sir that's confidential information. I am not permitted by law to give out such information," a white man with a bad tan stated as if he was reading out of a handbook of rules and ethics.

"Listen man that's my wife and my son. They disappeared over forty-five minutes ago. We all had first class tickets to this flight." I shouted showing him the three first class tickets.

"Well sir I think you answered your own question. If you have all three tickets there is no way they could've boarded the plane," the white man said in an arrogant tone.

He was right. During all the malay I'd forgotten that I was holding all of the tickets. I knew for a fact then that something was definitely wrong. Someone had kidnapped them but who? No one knew we were in Orlando except apparently Prince. All those questions and a million more were running through my head as I stood there at the gate.

"Sir... excuse me. Sir, will you be boarding the plane?" The flight attendant asked.

"What the fuck you think you stupid muthafucka?" I yelled startling him. "Get the fuck from 'round me!"

As the wide-eyed flight attendant put the gate up and boarded the plane I stood there in a trance. I sat down in the lobby and cried like I never cried before. They had my little boy and Crystal, the two most important things in my life. I was right all along. Someone had to have been following us. It was my fault. I put the blame on myself for not listening to my gut. That mistake could've cost me the life of my child, and future wife. In my heart, I knew it was Raphael. I'd slipped up and let him get the drop on me. The more I thought about it, the more I cried because I knew that

Raphael was playing for keeps and that most likely I'd never see either one of them again. I began to suffer from what seemed like an anxiety attack. My thoughts were racing. I felt like a TV was in my head and someone was switching the channels every three seconds. I couldn't think straight, I was nervous, my palms were sweating, and I felt sick to my stomach. Suddenly my phone rang. I picked it up on the first ring. "Crystal?"

"I have your boy and the girl. If you contact any kind of law enforcement, they will die. I want ten million dollars in two weeks. Go home, I will be in contact with you," a computerized voice explained and then hung up.

After the phone hung up I checked my caller I.D. to see if there was a number and I just like I expected it came up unavailable. They wanted ten million dollars but that wasn't the problem. I would've came up with a hundred million dollars if I knew I could guarantee their safe return. Life as I knew it was over. I was at Raphael's mercy.

Chapter 24

April 05

By the time I made it home, it was past 4:00 in the morning. After I missed my 9 o'clock flight, I had to wait over three hours to catch a red eye flight back to New York. And, I wouldn't have made that flight if someone hadn't showed up at the last minute.

There isn't a word in the English language to describe how I was feeling. My head was spinning and I was sick. And, when I say sick I mean literally. I had a migraine headache, I'd throw up at least six separate times and I felt like I could again at any moment. A million and one thoughts were racing through my head. Raphael had me by the balls. The scary part was that I knew the kidnapping wasn't money motivated. Raphael was asking for a ten million dollar ransom, and I knew that in his mind there was no possible way I could pay it. If we hadn't killed Candy, I wouldn't believe that he'd kill or harm a three year old child. But since we did that all bets were off. Everyone was fair game. All was fair in war.

I came home to an empty house. Ranisha and Amir were nowhere to be found. The lights were on, the flat screen in the living room was on, and all the beds were unmade. It looked as if the crib hadn't been occupied for days. Immediately I began thinking the worst. He probably got them too. I thought to myself. I sat on the bed in my bedroom, grabbed the cordless phone off the charger and hit up Ranisha's cell phone. It went straight to voice mail without ringing. I hung up without leaving a message. Something was definitely wrong. It was unlike Ranisha to be out of the house so late, and it was even more unlike her not to answer her phone. She always answered her phone. Being that I was a pessimistic person by nature, I let my imagination run and create the worst possible scenarios. I had myself believing that the Feds had come to the house and bagged Ranisha because after all she was the one that gave the bails bondsman the money. But, on the other hand I knew for a fact that Ranisha kept a fake I.D. so I couldn't be sure.

The silence of being alone in my thoughts was killing me. I had to call someone but there was no one to call. Dro, Wise, and Boota were in the pen and Snoop was dead. If there was ever a time that I needed my homies it was then. I picked up the phone and called the last homey that I had that was still free. Cheeba. We were going through our little drama but regardless of anything, he was family and I knew he'd be ready to assassinate the president after I told him what happened.

Cheeba answered after the third ring. "Yo."

"Yo, son what's poppin'? Where you at? I need to see you right now son. I can't be by myself right now some ill shit just went down," I explained.

Cheeba sounded apprehensive. "I'm uhhh- out of town right now. Where? Where you at?" he asked stuttering and fumbling his words.

"I'm home. Try to get here as soon as you can. It's an emergency son. I need you more than ever."

"What? Yo, Ski hold on for a second," Cheeba replied.

I heard a lot of fumbling and noise in the background and then I heard him shout. "Ayo. Y'all better shut the fuck up! Don't say a muthafuckin' word! Make them shut up!"

Hearing him talk like that threw me for a loop. "Yo, who you talking too like that? Where the fuck you at son?" I inquired.

"Oh, Ski. My bad son. I'll be there in an hour or two," he stated and then disconnected the call.

I wasn't sure if he hung up on me or if the call disconnected on it's own so I called him back. The first time I called it rang mad times and he didn't answer and then the next time I called it went straight to voice mail. Cheeba was acting strange. He didn't sound like himself at all, but I had too much on my mind to be worrying about what the fuck was wrong with his ass. Someone had my son hostage. Every time I thought about my son being tied and gagged up somewhere it made my heart hurt.

Five hours later I heard a car pulling into my driveway. I looked out the window and saw that it was Cheeba. For the whole five hours I was waiting on him I was pissed the fuck off for him taking so long, but seeing a familiar face in a crisis overruled my previous feelings. I went downstairs and met him at the door.

"Yo, thanks for coming my nigga. Shit is critical right now." I showed my gratitude

"Yo, you look terrible B. What the fuck happened? You a'ight?"

"Son, you don't know the half." I responded noticing a fresh cut on his nose. "What happened to ya nose?" I asked inquisitively.

Cheeba had a big ass scratch the length of his entire nose and it was still red like it had just happened.

"Oh, that ain't nuthin'. I was beefing wit this bitch," he answered and then changed the conversation quickly. "Fuck all that, what happened?"

"They kidnapped Isaiah," I blurted out.

Cheeba looked shocked. "What? Who? How you let that happen?"

"I know it's that nigga Raphael B. He caught me slippin'."

"Where was you at?"

"I was in Orlando. I took Isaiah and my shorty to Disney World for the weekend to celebrate Isaiah's birthday. The whole time we out there I was getting a funny vibe like somebody were following us. I was right. I went into the bathroom to take a phone call at the airport and when I came back they were gone." I explained.

"Word? I can't believe Ranisha let somebody kidnap her tough ass without a fight." Cheeba said shaking his head.

"Nah son, I wasn't wit Ranisha. Me and her got into a argument and I left out. I ain't seen her in like five days."

"So what shorty is you talking about?"

"This shorty named Crystal. But that ain't important. I don't know what to do. This shit is crazy son. We gotta do something." I exclaimed taking a deep breath.

"How you know they got kidnapped?"

"Because they called me with some computer generated voice. They talking about they want ten million dollars."

"Ten mil? Who the fuck do they think you are? They buggin'! How the fuck do they expect you to pay ten mil?"

'The money ain't the problem son. I could get it. If not all of it, damn near close to it. But, Raphael don't know that. Nobody does. I think he's gonna kill them."

When I said that I could get the ransom money Cheeba's eyebrows raised almost up to his hairline. "You really got access to ten million B? That's crazy! How come you ain't put me down B? I knew you were eating on the side son. I knew it. I fucking knew it!" Cheeba stated with an attitude.

"Son, this ain't the time for all that. They got my lil man B. They got my seed B." I stated putting my hands over my face.

"So what you gonna do? You gonna pay the ransom?"

"I got too. I know in my heart that I'm never gonna see them alive again but I wouldn't be able to live with myself if I didn't try." I explained.

Cheeba was still stuck on the fact that I had ten million. "Pardon me son… I still can't get over the fact of you having ten million dollars. That's crazy!"

"I ain't got the whole ten. I got close to half. That's why I need to see Ranisha and ask her for the other half. But, yo son don't ever mention to Ranisha that they got my shorty too. Just act like they only got Isaiah. She'll have a fit if she found out I was wit another bitch and she might not wanna cough up that bread."

"Whatever son."

Cheeba and I chilled for hours trying to come up with a plan and waiting for Ranisha or the kidnappers to call. Cheeba said he was tired from running around all night and was going to go home to get some rest and come back the following day. He advised me to do the same thing but sleep was a lost cause for me. I was stuck in a living nightmare.

As I was walking Cheeba to the door he gave me dap and a hug and then turned around and said. "Yo, Ski I can't believe you was getting money like that and ain't put me on B. We grew up together and you know I would do anything for you. We suppose to be family."

As he was walking away with his head down, I started to call him back and explain to him why I couldn't put him on but changed my mind. After Cheeba left, I went into my living room and replayed our entire conversation back in my head. Once I told him that I had that type of money everything changed. He seemed more concerned about how much money I had then the well being of my son. By the way he was acting I was wondering if he was going to come back.

Twenty minutes later, my phone rang.

I answered it on the first ring. "Hello."

"So far so good. You follow instructions very well keep it up and I might think about letting your people live. Don't try anything I'm watching you," the computer voice stated.

"Ayo! Yo!" I screamed frantically into the phone.

"What?" the voice responded shocking me.

I thought the voice was computer programmed and couldn't talk back.

"Lemme talk to my son. Lemme see if he's a'ight." I requested.

"You don't call the shots. Make this be the last time you speak to me unless I ask you a question. Next time there will be consequences," the voice threatened and then hung up.

As I sat there staring at the phone I felt like I was trapped in a movie. And, it was starting to look like the bad guy was going to win. It made me reflect to when I first got into the game and my girlfriend Paula got kidnapped. I was blaming myself for everything and the whole time I was being set up. It turned out that Paula, who I thought was my girlfriend, had been setting me up the whole time. Dro and I found out where the cat stayed and ran up in the crib only to find him laid up with Paula. I was crushed. Her and her boyfriend were the first two bodies I ever caught. It was so long ago, but the memory seemed so fresh. It was like history was repeating itself.

A couple hours after I got the call from the kidnappers, I heard keys being put into the front door. It had to be Ranisha. I ran down the steps and met her at the door.

"Re! Where you been at? You had me worried as hell!" I shouted embracing her.

"Baby! You're back! I knew you'd come back!" Ranisha exclaimed as her face lit up like a Christmas tree. "I missed you so much. I'm sorry for what I did baby. I'm so sorry. Did you get my messages?" she continued.

"Damn Re, you don't know how happy I am to see you," I replied hugging her tightly.

"Ouch!" Ranisha winched.

"What's wrong?" I asked.

"I lost the baby." Ranisha responded wit her eyes tearing up.

"What-I mean how?"

"I was so upset when you left that I got drunk and took mad sleeping pills and fell down the stairs. I hope you're not mad at me. I just got released from the hospital this afternoon." Ranisha said showing the hospital band on her wrist.

"Damn, baby. Are you a'ight?" I asked genuinely concerned but happy in a way that the baby was gone.

"Yeah," she answered shrugging her shoulders. "I feel much better now that you're back home. Babe, what's wrong you look terrible." Ranisha said noticing my appearance.

"They got Isaiah yo. They kidnapped him."

She asked the same questions Cheeba asked. "What? When? Where were you at?"

"I took Isaiah to Disney World for his birthday. All weekend I felt like someone was following me and then on the way back home I stepped away from him for as second to take a phone call and when I came back he was gone. It's Raphael Re. I know it." I explained once again.

"Did they call you for a ransom?'

"Yeah. They got some computerized voice altering shit. They want ten million dollars."

"Damn how did they know we had money like that?"

"I have no fucking idea B. This shit is fucking crazy Re. they got my boy!" I cried out.

"So it was just you and Isaiah out in Orlando?" Ranisha inquired.

"Yeah," I lied with a straight face.

"Are you sure?"

"What the fuck do you mean am I sure? Re, don't you think I know who the fuck I was wit?" I shouted.

Re apologized. "I'm sorry boo. So what are we gonna do?"

"That's what I need from your ma. All I got is close to five mil. I need your half of the money to pay them niggaz. I promise on everything I love I'll pay you back every penny."

Ranisha looked at me like I'd gone crazy. "Ski, what are you talking about? Isaiah is like my son too. I love that lil nigga. I don't give a fuck about no money. We can make more money but we can't make another Isaiah. All I care about is getting our family back together. You and Isaiah are all I have." Ranisha said sincerely.

I was relieved. "Thank you baby. You don't know how good it feels to hear you say that." I stated hugging her and kissing her on the cheek. "Ayo, where's Amir at?" I asked realizing for the first time that he wasn't with her.

"I had ya moms come pick him up from the hospital."

"Oh, yeah. That's good, he's in a safe place. This is the last place he needs to be."

"Baby, everything is gonna workout. We gonna give them the money, get Isaiah back and start our new lives together somewhere." Ranisha comforted me.

My phone was ringing again. I looked at the caller I.D. and saw that it was Prince. The last person I wanted to talk to.

"Yo." I answered.

"Wha at gwon? Whe mi daughta? Mi can't reach her." Prince asked.

I lied my ass off. "She should be home. Last time I spoke to her she was on her way to class."

"Bloodclot bwoy you better not be lying to mi!" Prince shouted. "When mi daughta ah call you tell her to call her fadda you hear?"

"A'ight, will do."

Prince was suspicious. "You sure nuthin' ago wrong? Yu nah sound like everyting krisp."

He was making me nervous. "Na, everything is good. I'm just tired."

Prince eased up on me. "Yeah, well get some sleep then. Peace and blessings." he replied before hanging up the phone.

I tried to get some rest but it was to no avail. Every time I closed my eyes, I saw visions of Isaiah and Crystal tied up in some dark cold basement somewhere. The worst part was that there was nothing I could do but wait on Raphael. As I laid there, I began to think about how I'd gotten Crystal entangled in my beef. If Prince ever found out that his daughter was kidnapped or harmed in any way, I knew I would be a dead man. I started to call him and tell him the whole situation but I changed my mind. There was nothing Prince was going to be able to do anyways, so I figured there was no use of stressing him and worrying until I had more information. Besides that, I wanted to remain alive.

Chapter 25

April 05

The kidnapper crept down the steps to the basement with a flashlight in one hand, and a brown paper bag with sandwiches and water in the other. With each step the kidnapper took, the wooden steps creaked as if they were going to give way any minute. The basement was cold, dark and gloomy. All that could be heard was the sounds of muffled sobbing, and rats scurrying about. It was completely unfurnished and had no electricity or heat. The walls were cement as was the floor and the ceiling was unfinished. Electrical wires and asbestos were hanging down from every ceiling beam. As the kidnapper cleared the last step, a foul stench could be smelled in the air. It was a mixture of body odor, urine, and feces.

In one corner of the room Crystal was laid out on her side completely naked handcuffed to a radiator bruised and badly beaten. She had a blindfold over her eyes, duct tape over her mouth and her legs tied up together. The kidnapper couldn't help but smile as the flashlight illuminated Crystal. She had mashed up shit on her back and legs, and dried blood smeared all over her face, neck and scalp.

"Don't cry now bitch! What happened to all that tough talk?" The kidnapper asked remorseless kicking her in the ribs.

The kidnapper despised Crystal. When she was getting tied up, Crystal fought back and almost disarmed the kidnapper, and for that, she was beaten until she was unconscious. Crystal got gun butted repeatedly in her face and sustained multiple kicks to the head and body. The kidnapper had plans to kill her but had to hold back. It wasn't the right time and the stage wasn't set for it yet. Ski and Crystal were going to die together.

The kidnapper took the tape off her mouth, bent down, and fed her the sandwich. Crystal hadn't eaten in over twenty-six hours and was so hungry that she gobbled down the turkey sandwich in seconds.

"You was hungry huh bitch? You piece of shit! Don't worry in a little while all of this will be over. You and ya boyfriend can get married in hell." The kidnapper stated coldly.

"Why are you doing this to us? Who are you?" Crystal cried out.

"I'm ya worst nightmare bitch!" the kidnapper answered.

The kidnapper held the bottle water up while Crystal drank and when she was finished, the kidnapper through the water bottle at her.

"Ya boyfriend should've never crossed me! He made it like this. He forced my hand," the kidnapper explained.

The kidnapper walked to the other side of the room where Ski's three-year-old son Isaiah was tied up, and gagged with tape over his mouth. Isaiah was laying flat on his stomach and looked to be sleeping. He was fully clothed, minus one sneaker, and was in the same condition as he was when he got kidnapped except that he had urinated and shit on himself. Isaiah hadn't been a problem at all. He wasn't scared and never cried.

Just looking at Isaiah angered the kidnapper because he looked just like his father. The kidnapper nudged the kid on his side to wake him up but he didn't move. The kidnapper did it again and got the same results. The kidnapper began shaking Isaiah violently to wake him but he never moved. The kidnapper removed the blindfold of Isaiah's eyes and saw his eyes roll to the back of his head.

The kidnapper began to panic. "What's wrong with him? Why isn't he moving?"

"Check his pulse! Hurry up and check his pulse!" Crystal yelled.

The kidnapper put a finger on his neck. "He has a pulse but it's light. What's wrong wit him? What do I do?"

"Untie me! I know C.P.R.! Hurry up! We don't have enough time," Crystal shouted frantically.

The kidnapper was stuck between a rock and a hard place. The kidnapper didn't want to untie Crystal and risk her trying to escape and be forced to kill her. But, on the other hand having Isaiah die was not in the plans at all.

"Okay but I'm warning you if you try anything both of you are dead!" The kidnapper warned.

"Yes! Please… just let me save him! He's just a baby," Crystal shouted with tears rolling down her face,

The kidnapper un-cuffed and untied Crystal at gunpoint. Once she was free, Crystal ran over to Isaiah and checked his pulse. It was light but he was still alive. Crystal held Isaiah's nose, opened his mouth and blew air into it. After that, she began pushing down on his chest. When she was done she repeated the same process again.

"C'mon Isaiah… come back to us baby. Come back," Crystal said as she continued performing C.P.R.

Suddenly Isaiah began to cough and his eyes opened.

"Oh, thank you Jesus! Thank you Lord!" Crystal stated hugging Isaiah and rocking him back and forth.

"You almost killed him! What is wrong wit you? He's a child. You can't keep his mouth covered and not feed him for days! What are you trying to do? Don't you have a conscience? How are you going to enjoy the money after you've harmed an innocent kid?" Crystal asked.

"The same way Ski can live with himself after what he did to me bitch! That's enough put him down!" The kidnapper stated pointing the gun at Crystal.

Crystal put Isaiah down, put her hands up, and walked back to the corner of the room where she was being held. The kidnapper tied, handcuffed, blindfolded, and gagged Crystal, fed Isaiah his sandwich and water and then tied Isaiah back up loosely, this time not putting any tape over his mouth. After the kidnapper was finished, the kidnapper went back up the creaky wooden steps, and locked the steel door leaving Isaiah and Crystal in complete darkness.

Crystal turned to her faith. She kept repeating the Lord's prayer in her head. She knew that Ski would find a way to come and rescue them. She just hoped and prayed it wouldn't be to late.

The kidnapper left the basement realizing that more attention needed to be paid to the hostages. Crystal and Isaiah were no use dead. The kidnapper needed them alive to finish the plan. The kidnapper didn't know how time consuming the hostages were going to be and was trying to figure out how it was possible to give them the attention they needed. It was a tough task because the kidnapper was living a double life.

***

It had been forty-eight hours since the kidnapping. I still couldn't eat or sleep and I was felling worse every day. I was miserable. The two days felt like two years. I couldn't do anything but wait for the next commands from Raphael and pray for the best. Ranisha had been by my side the entire time, comforting and consoling me. Cheeba surprised me and spent the majority of both days chillin' with me at my house.

Currently Ranisha, Cheeba, and I were in my kitchen trying to strategize.

"I'm telling you son, I say we go to Middletown, kidnap some random niggaz and torture them until we get Raphael's whereabouts. There is always a weak link in every crew. One of them niggaz gonna know something B. He the man out there everybody knows that nigga!" Cheeba suggested.

"Word," Ranisha agreed. "He's right baby."

I didn't think so. "Nah, I don't think that's a good idea. If Raphael gets word that niggaz is running through his hood kidnapping niggaz he's gonna know it's me. You gotta remember he got Isaiah, he got the upper hand. I don't want him getting mad, and making him do something crazy to hurt my seed. The goal is to get Isaiah back healthy."

"So, what we gonna do? Wait on them niggaz? C'mon man… If you would've listened to me we wouldn't even be going through all of this. Tiesha would still be alive, Isaiah would be here and we would've still been getting money," Cheeba said frustrated.

I put my head in my lap to conceal the tears that were forming in my eyes. "I know son. This shit is all my fault B. Everything is my fault. They got my fucking boy B!"

"Don't worry baby… we gonna get him back. Everything is gonna be fine." Ranisha said rubbing my back doing her best to comfort me.

I was helpless. The life of my first and only child and my future wife were in my enemy's hands. If anything happened to either one of them, I knew I wouldn't be able to live with myself.

"C'mon Ski you gotta be strong for Isaiah. Crying ain't gonna help nuthin'. We gonna find a way my nigga," Cheeba replied.

Everything that Cheeba said was the truth. I'd slipped up and made mistakes and those mistakes were coming back to bite me in the ass. If I would've listened to him from the beginning none of what was transpiring would've occurred. I wiped my eyes, sat up and took a deep breath.

"You right Cheeba. I gotta get myself together." I stated.

"Everything is gonna be straight son. Trust me. So do y'all have all the money on hand just in case they call and they ready to swap out?" Cheeba asked.

"Yeah and no. We got the money in two separate offshore accounts. I'm waiting for them to tell me how they want it. Hopefully we could just wire it to them." I explained.

"Yeah, that's what's up." Cheeba responded. "Yo Re, what time is it?"

"8:15," Ranisha answered looking at her watch.

"Word? It's that late already? I gotta get out of here. I ain't know it was that late. I'll be back in an hour," Cheeba said snatching his keys off the kitchen table and running to the closet to get his jacket.

"Ayo! What's good nigga? Where you going? You a'ight?" I asked as I watched him sprint out the door.

"I'll be back in a hour," he shouted slamming the door behind him. Cheeba ran out of my crib like a crack head who just copped for the first time all day. I tried to call him to make sure he was okay but his phone went straight to voice mail. Ranisha went upstairs so I decided to watch some TV in the loving room and smoke a L.

Twenty minutes late my phone rang.

"Hello," I answered.

"Do you have all of money yet?" The computerized voice asked.

"Yeah, I got it. Just tell me when you want it, how you want it, and where you want it?"

"Slow down my friend. There's been a change of plans. I want my money wired. Can you make that happen?"

"No problem. All you gotta do is say when and give me the account number."

"Good I'll be in contact soon," the computerized voice said and then disconnected the call.

As soon as I hung up, my phone started ringing again. I picked up on the first ring.

"Yo."

"Ski, what's up daddy? How you?" A female voice asked.

"Yo, who dis?"

"Nigga, you don't know my voice now? This is Shiny."

"Shiny, what up? What's going on out there?" I asked.

"I got some good news for you honey. I found him and I got that bitch ass nigga wrapped around my fucking finger. I live with him now. I just moved in yesterday."

I put my L out. "Say word?"

'Word nigga. I told you I'm the illest bitch in NYC can't no nigga resist this pussy. I got his nose wide the fuck open," Shiny bragged.

All of the sudden I felt alive again. "Shiny, you're a fucking lifesaver B. I got a extra fifty for you when you get back. Where he staying at?"

"Schenectady. He got a big ass crib out there in the cut."

"Okay a'ight. Do he be having mad niggaz in there?"

"Yeah, he be having his niggaz up in here but don't nobody be here after midnight except his two little soldiers but them niggaz don't be on point at all."

"Yo, Shiny I'm trying to run up in there tomorrow. You think you can make that happen?"

"What time?"

"Like one in the morning."

"Yeah, no doubt. The address is…." Shiny went on giving me the address layout of the crib and the plan.

Everything was set. Finally I had the drop on him. The tables were about to turn. It had been a long time coming but I was finally going to get my get back. This time I was going to make sure he was out of my hair for life. *Oh, how sweet revenge is.* I thought to myself.

Chapter 26

April 05

Ranisha rang the doorbell to Raphael's house and waited on the porch to be let in. Raphael lived in an old Victorian style house in Niskayuna Schenectady on Allen Avenue. Niskayuna was a small upper class area in Schenectady that boasted manicured lawns, patrolling neighborhood watches, good schools, and it was so quiet that crickets could be heard chirping in the distance. It was a far cry from anywhere that Raphael ever lived previously. All of his neighbors were professionals and no one but his inner circle knew where he rested his head. He felt like he was untouchable. Little did he know that he'd made a fatal mistake that was going to cost him dearly.

Across the street Ski and Cheeba waited in the backseat of Ranisha's Benz waiting for her to give them the signal. Ranisha had on nothing but a black trench coat and 4 inch stiletto's. Inside her coat pockets she was strapped with two .22's with silencers on them. She was posing as a stripper friend of Shiny's that was invited over to entertain Raphael's two goons. Shiny had brought two of her girlfriends with her upstate but both of them were already locked in with other members of Raphael's crew.

"Who dat yo?" A voice asked from behind the door.

"It's Sunshine. Shiny invited me over here. I'm sorry do I have the wrong address?" Ranisha asked with a fake accent and snapping her gum in her mouth.

When the man looked through the peephole and saw how bad Ranisha was he quickly unlocked the door and opened it.

"You got the right crib mami. Come on in." the man said letting her in sizing her up like she was a piece of meat.

"Hey, papi! How you doing? Shiny ain't tell me you was this fine." Ranisha replied rubbing the overweight man's chest seductively.

The compliment caught the man off guard. He wasn't use to receiving them. "Uhhh... Thanks. You look good enough to eat."

he responded wishing he could've said something smoother.

While they were standing in the doorway flirting, another overweight Spanish man came to the door.

"Yo, Mondo who was that at the door?" He asked.

"Sunshine, this is my partner Punto Con. Punto this is Sunshine... Shiny's friend," Mondo introduced winking his eye at his partner.

"Oh, you fine too! Hi sexy," Ranisha greeted him letting her hand lightly brush up against his crotch.

Mondo and Punto Con were two fat Puerto-Rican men in their mid-thirties that could've passed for being brothers. They were both almost 5' 10", and 300 plus ponds with big bellies and low haircuts. Their one and only job was to serve as security for Raphael's house. Mondo and Punto Con were both dumb as doorknobs and not very lucky with the ladies so they made for perfect vics.

"Damn, you finer than Shiny! Tu muy bonita mami. Mondo did you search her?" Punto Con asked.

"Why would I? She ain't come here to hurt nobody. Did you mami?" Mondo flirted.

"I aim to please papi." Ranisha replied licking her lips.

"Mondo pat her down man. You never know what could happen. " Punto Con ordered playing it safe.

Ranisha was starting to get nervous but she kept her poker face on. If they patted her down and found her two weapons it was no telling what they'd do to her and their whole plan would be ruined. She thought about trying to go for her guns at that moment but decided against it because Mondo and Punto Con were way too big and way to close too her.

Shiny came walking down the steps at the perfect time. "Hey girl! When you get here?" Shiny asked as if they were old friends when in all actuality she had never saw Ranisha a day in her life.

"What's up ma? I just got here." Ranisha answered with a fake big smile giving Shiny a hug.

Shiny nodded her head towards Punto Con and Mondo. "Did you meet the boys?"

"Yes, I did girl and you ain't tell me that they were this fine." Ranisha lied.

"Why you still standing at the door? Come on in girl! Stop frontin' like you shy!" Shiny stated.

"I ain't frontin' they was talking about searching me." Ranisha responded.

"Search you? Are y'all niggaz crazy? This is my friend. Don't be treating her like she's some got damn criminal. Sunshine open up ya coat and show them that you ain't got no weapons on you." Shiny said.

Ranisha un-fastened the belt to her trench coat and opened it up revealing her perfectly sculpted naked body. Mondo and Punto Con were in awe. Their dicks instantly got hard.

"I try to hook y'all niggaz up with some pussy and y'all niggaz wanna search her? What type of niggaz are y'all? That's why y'all don't get no pussy now! Y'all don't know how to treat a bitch," Shiny chastised them.

"I told this nigga there was no need for all that." Mondo shot back in his own defense.

"My bad mami. Do you want a drink?' Punto Con apologized.

"Sunshine if you wanna leave now I'll understand girl." Shiny said.

Mondo fell on his knees in front of Ranisha and began kissing her hand. "No! Please don't go! We're sorry!"

Ranisha acted like she was thinking it over and then replied. "I'mma stay girl. I think they cute."

"Well a'ight. I'mma be upstairs wit my man. Holla for me if you need me. Don't hurt em' girl!" Shiny said with a wink.

"I'll try not too." Ranisha answered with a smile.

Shiny went back upstairs with Raphael, and Mondo and Punto Con led Ranisha into the living room. Once in the living room they fixed her drink and engaged in small talk for a few minutes.

"Listen y'all I'mma real bitch. Y'all ain't gotta front for me cause I ain't gonna front for y'all. I came here to fuck… what y'all tryna do?" Ranisha announced standing up and opening up her trench coat again.

"So, how much is this gonna cost us?' Punto Con asked.

"This is free of charge honey. Take y'all clothes off." Ranisha ordered.

Mondo and Punto Con both got naked in seconds. Ranisha had to hold back her urge to throw up looking at their obese bodies and stumpy little dicks. She was there to do a job and she wanted to do it right to show Ski how much she was really down for him.

After they were both naked Ranisha had them side by side on the couch. "Suck my titties Mondo," she ordered putting her foot on the couch in between them.

As Mondo was sucking on her titties and jerking his dick off, Punto Con began playing with her pussy. Ranisha stood with one foot on the couch with her head back and both hands in the pockets of her trench coat.

Ranisha pulled out the two .22's and started letting off shots simultaneously at their faces. Due to the silencers on her guns only a zipping sound could be heard as she pumped round after round in their faces. Blood and brain fragments flew all over her face, arms, chest, and neck but none of it mattered to her. She was on a mission. She let off ten shots in total. Five into each one of their faces. Each shot seemed like it damaged a different facial feature. Punto Con's eye ball cracked in two and where Mondo's nose use to be was now only one hole and excess skin. When she was done firing shots both of their bodies slumped back into the couch lifeless and began sliding down to the carpet. Ranisha walked outside the front door and put her hand in the air, letting Ski and Cheeba know that phase one of their plan had been completed.

***

"Ayo, come on son. She just gave us the signal." Cheeba announced.

I leaned up in my seat, to see for myself and saw Ranisha standing on the porch a bloody mess. I grabbed the duffel bag out of the front seat, and me and Cheeba jogged across the street and into Raphael's house.

To say that I was excited was an understatement. The first phase of our plan had went smoothly. I thought it was the going to be the hardest part to execute. What we were about to do was the easy part. I was about to kill two birds with one stone. I was going to get my son and Crystal back, and finally get my revenge for what he'd done to me.

When I walked into Raphael's house I was impressed. I could tell he was still getting big money just by the layout of his crib. He had wall to wall white carpet, marble countertops, a huge fish tank, Italian leather furniture, what looked to be some expensive artwork, and flat screen TV's everywhere. His crib was sick. Me and Cheeba ran up the Oakwood steps and went to the second floor and to the left just as Shiny had directed us.

When we opened up Raphael's bedroom door, Shiny had Raphael ass naked with his hands tied up to the headboard, a blindfold over his eyes and was riding the shit out of him.

"Baby... who just came into the room?" Raphael asked nervously. "Take this blindfold off of me and untie me," Raphael commanded.

"Daddy. Mami gotta surprise for you that I know you gonna like. Two for the price of one." Shiny stated continuing to ride him slowly.

"Two for the price of one?" Raphael repeated with a smile.

"Yup. You ready. One... two... three." Shiny counted down removing the blindfold from his eyes.

When Shiny removed the blindfold he was awoke to two .45's in his face.

"What... What the fuck is going on? What's this about? What are you doing here?" Raphael recognizing Cheeba.

I appeared from behind Cheeba and said. "C'mon pa you can't be that stupid. Remember me?"

Raphael's face turned white. The fear that I saw in his eyes was priceless. From the moment he looked me in the eyes he knew he was a dead man. His mouth dropped to the floor and he just gazed up at me trying to figure out how I'd gotten there. Shiny was still on top of him with his dick still inside of her but I'm sure that the fear made him limp.

"So this was all a fucking act? You fucking bitch!" Raphael yelled closing his eyes and turning his head away from me.

Shiny spit in his face and climbed off of him. "All for that paper daddy. You couldn't have thought that I was really feeling ya corny ass. Ya dick game ain't good enough and you ain't thorough enough to hold down a bitch like me. At least you got to get some good pussy before you go," Shiny said coldly putting her robe on.

"Where's my seed at?" I asked getting right to it.

"Seed? What seed?" Raphael retorted.

I pulled my Glock out and smacked him in the face with it two times in the forehead splitting his forehead wide open and blood gushing out of the wound.

"Don't fucking play wit me nigga! Where the fuck is my seed? Don't make me ask you again!" I warned him.

"I don't know what you are talking about Ski! What would I be doing with ya seed?" Raphael asked.

I hit him with the butt of the Glock again in the same spot and then said. "Untie this nigga!"

Raphael was so fucked up that as soon as his hands were untied, he fell to the floor a bloody mess.

Raphael was about "6" feet tall with a very slim build. He was in his mid-thirties but looked like he was in his early twenties. He had curly hair, a straight long pointed nose and sharp facial features. He was the exact replica of the Detroit pistons guard Richard Hamilton.

I wouldn't allow anyone to put their hands on him but me. This was personal. I wanted to inflict all the damage. When he hit the floor, I stomped and kicked him into oblivion. I stomped him repeatedly as hard as I could in the face, stomach, and ribs. Raphael laid there helpless curled up in the fetal position bleeding profusely. I wanted badly to kill him but I couldn't. Not until he told me Crystal and Isaiah's whereabouts.

"Just get it over with and kill me! Kill me muthafucka! You got it… You won!" Raphael yelled in pain and frustration with a mouth full of blood rolling around on the floor.

"Tell me where the fuck you got my son at!" I demanded.

He didn't answer so I shot him once in the foot. The shot was a clean shot so it went right through the top of his foot and exited through the back. He was now left with a hole in his foot almost the size of a fist.

"Ahhhhh! You muthafucka you! " he yelled.

"Raphael you making this hard on ya-self pa. All I want is my son. You know you're a dead man so stop trying to deny it. I know you got him, now where the fuck is he?"

"I told you I don't know what the fuck you talking about!" Raphael shot back.

I shot him in his other foot.

"Ayo, check this crib. See if he got them somewhere in here. Cheeba you take the downstairs, Re check the basement and Shiny you check up here. I'll be waiting in here." I ordered.

Cheeba, Ranisha and Shiny all ransacked the crib in search of my son while I stayed in the bedroom continuing to wild the fuck out on Raphael. After beating him damn near to death, I sat down. As I looked at Raphael writhing in pain on the floor I stared at him and thought about all the problems he caused in my life. He'd damn near killed me, he killed Tiesha, killed one of my workers, had all of my spots robbed and then the icing on the cake was that he kidnapped my three year old son and fiancée. The whole thing was crazy because I didn't understand how it ever got to that point because at one time we were peoples.

After I bodied the two cats that were trying to rob him and saved his life, Raphael took me off the block and put me on. He allowed me to cop off of his connect, and even set me up in a bar to move my work. At the time Candy was my girl, and everything was still love between us. But then Candy started acting up and I had to send her back with Raphael to live. Raphael and I remained cool and continued getting money until one day Candy beat herself up and told him it was me who'd done it. Of course he believed it and called me threatening my life and told me the only reason that my life was being spared was because I'd saved his life. After that he had the connect stop fucking with me, and even had the owner of the bar I was hustling in cut me off. I was bringing in nice paper and was accustomed to living a certain way and after that I was hurting. I ended up going to Raphael and Candy's house beating, robbing, and even pissing on them. After that I didn't see either one of them for years until that almost fateful day after I beat trial. I jumped in a cab to go see my son for the first time and, Raphael who was posing as a cabdriver, turned around and dumped on me almost killing me and sending me into a coma for ten months. Our whole beef was a misunderstanding started by a whore that turned it into an all out war and hate for one another. Fifteen minutes later Cheeba, Ranisha and Shiny all came back into the bedroom.

"What happened?" I asked.

"Nothing," Ranisha and Shiny said in unison.

"I found his stash but that's about it. What you wanna do wit all this work and money?" Cheeba asked.

"Nigga do you think I give a fuck about some money and work right now? This nigga got my seed somewhere B! What the fuck is wrong wit you?" I shouted in anger.

The more and more I waited the more upset and deranged I became. If Raphael wanted to play hardball we were going to play hardball.

I had them tie Raphael to a chair and began torturing him. I cut off two of his fingers with a kitchen knife, and set his feet on fire but he kept on denying it.

"Just kill me man! Please!" Raphael yelled with tears running down his face.

"It's too late to turn into a bitch now nigga. You was a gangsta when you killed Tiesha. You was a gangsta when you kidnapped Isaiah. Don't cry now you bitch ass nigga!" Ranisha stated gun butting him with her .22.

"Tiesha? What are y'all talking about? I didn't kill Tiesha!" Raphael responded.

"Nigga, you gon sit here and lie in my muthafuckin' face nigga! Huh? We know everything B. Don't front, be a man nigga!" I said.

"You killed my sister! She was all the family I had. I can own up to what I did. I shot you! Yeah… I shot you muthafucka! I had my peoples run up in ya spots and they shot and killed a nigga in there but I didn't kill Tiesha and I don't know where ya son is at. I had nothing to do with either of those," Raphael explained with blood pouring out of his mouth. "Please man. Just kill me. You're the better man papi. You win," he continued.

I was starting to believe him. He had absolutely no reason to lie. I figured that even if he did kidnap Isaiah and Crystal and didn't want to tell me he still would laugh and taunt me saying that I'd never find them. He had denied it vehemently from the beginning. But if it wasn't him who was it?

"Ski, I don't mess wit kids papi. Whoever did this to you must be close to you. It had to be an inside job. It' probably somebody you'd least expect-," Rapheal tried to explain but got cut off indefinitely.

Cheeba let off six shots from his two .45's directly into his head mutilating his face and damn near knocking his head off his shoulders.

"What the fuck did you do that for? He's the only nigga who knows where my son is at and you killed him! Why the fuck would you do that?" I shouted putting my bloody hands over my head in disbelief.

"Son. This nigga ain't coughing up shit! We just wasting time! I don't think he had nuthin' to do wit it. I think he was telling the truth," Cheeba explained.

"Maybe because it was you, you bitch ass nigga! Put the guns down!" Ranisha ordered putting her .22's to the back of Cheeba's head. "Ski, it's him. I'm telling you! It's this nigga!"

"Yo, Ski I know you ain't buying that bullshit. Why would I kidnap ya seed?" Cheeba asked kneeling to put his guns on the floor.

"Money! That's all he's ever been concerned about! He's a greedy, conniving, back stabbing bitch ass nigga! Say the word and I'll smoke him baby! Say the word!" Ranisha yelled.

I was at a crossroads. I didn't know what to think. Cheeba had been acting strange for months and he was always concerned about money and material shit. He had every motive in the world to do it. Ten million motives to be exact. And, he did kill Raphael as soon as he said it could be someone close to me. The more I thought about it, the more it became clearer to me that it was most likely him. Every time the kidnapper called, Cheeba was never around and it was funny how Cheeba was asking about what form I had the ransom in, and then twenty minutes later the kidnappers called and requested that I wire it to them. But, on the other hand Cheeba was my man. I grew up with him and we'd spent the night at each others house when we were kids. We'd been through everything together. He had my back and I had his. I knew for a fact that money made niggaz do crazy shit, especially ten million dollars, but I couldn't envision him kidnapping my child. I wasn't sure if he was the kidnapper or not, but I couldn't let Ranisha kill him right then and there because if he in fact was the kidnapper I needed him to find Isaiah and Crystal.

"Ski, this is me son. C'mon B don't believe that shit my nigga, I love you like a brother son. I'd never do no harm to you. You know that," Cheeba pleaded his case.

"Re, put the gun down," I ordered.

"Ski, I know you ain't believing that weak shit this nigga kicking. It's him, I'm telling you," Ranisha shouted still not removing the guns from the back of Cheeba's head.

"Put the fucking guns down Re!" I commanded with authority. "I'm not asking you I'm telling you!"

Ranisha hesitated, but followed my orders and put the guns down to her side. We wiped the crib down, and then set it on fire. Cheeba found two-undred thousand in cash and a few bricks of coke, so I took out fifty and gave it to Shiny and sent her on her way and let Cheeba keep the rest. Cheeba left with Shiny, and me and Ranisha rode back in her Benz. The whole ride neither one of us said a word. When we pulled up in our driveway Ranisha asked. "Do you believe that it wasn't Raphael?"

"Yeah... I believed him. Do you?"

"Yup. It's Cheeba and you know it. How come you didn't let me do him in?"

"Because for one I ain't sure if it's him or not. Don't get me wrong it's a strong possibility that it's him but I'm not one hundred percent sure. And for two, if I let you kill him and he really is the kidnapper we'd never found out where Isaiah is being held. We gonna have to let him think everything is cool, watch him and see if he makes a mistake," I explained getting out the car exasperated. My mind was gone. I didn't know what to think or believe. I was praying that it really wasn't Raphael because if it was I was assed out. All evidence was pointing to Cheeba but I couldn't be sure. All I could do was wait. If the kidnapper called again, then Raphael really hadn't done it. But, the scary part of it was if Raphael didn't kidnap Crystal and Isaiah and murder Tiesha who did?

Chapter 27

April 05

It had been a week since we ran in Raphael's crib and I hadn't received a call from the kidnappers yet. I was starting to believe that Raphael played me and had gotten the last laugh after all. And if that was the case, I knew the chances of me seeing Isaiah or Crystal alive again were slim to none. I was a nervous wreck. I still couldn't eat, sleep, or think straight. All I did was stay in the house smoking trees, drinking and chain smoking Newport's, and fucking Ranisha. Anything I could do to keep my mind off of my reality. Ranisha had been real supportive through out the whole ordeal for me. She was my shoulder to lean on, my psychologist, maid, cook, lover and sometimes the person I took my frustrations out on. Cheeba came through a couple of days but shit wasn't the same. I tried not to show it but I couldn't. It was a possibility that he was the kidnapper. I was watching him and monitoring his every movement like a hawk. My mind was just fucked up in general. I didn't know what to think, who to blame or how to act.

I was lying in the bed staring at the ceiling at 6:00 in the morning when I realized what I needed to get my head right. I needed to see my niggaz. I called Boota's baby mother Shamika up and told her that I needed her to come with me to pull Boota down on the visit. It took a little bit of begging but after I told Shamika it was an emergency she agreed. After that I called Wise's brother Chris and told him the same thing. I showered, got dressed, and had both Shamika and Chris in the car by 7:15, we made it to the jail at around 9:30 in the morning.

Boota, Wise and Dro were all smiles as they walked into the visiting room. I could tell they were pleasantly surprised to see me. I hadn't been up to visit them in over a year and a half. Of course I still spoke to them on the phone consistently and sent them money, but my life had been so crazy that I hadn't had time to check the fam. I on the other hand was serious as cancer. I wasn't smiling at all and I hadn't realized it until then but I looked terrible. I had two weeks worth of stubble on my face and my eyes were bloodshot and had bags around them. I gave all three of them daps and sat back down.

"If it ain't the muthafucking million dollar man! What's up B? How does it feel to be rich?" Dro asked with a smile sitting down across from me.

"He don't look like he rich to me. That nigga look like he smoking!" Boota joked.

"Ski, what's wrong son? You a'ight?" Wise asked.

"Ayo is there anyway that we could all sit down at one table? I need to holla at all y'all about some real shit! I'm fucked up right now, shit is crazy," I confessed.

"Yo, Wise what cop is in the bubble?" Dro asked looking around.

"I think it's Henderson," Wise answered.

"Boota, ain't that ya man? Go ask that nigga if he could bend the rules for us for a hot second." Dro suggested.

Boota immediately got up and went to the officer's station to holla at the C.O. five minutes later he came back and said. "Yeah. We good. But, he says it's gonna cost us."

"Money ain't a problem. Tell him whatever he wants I got him," I responded.

Everybody took the chairs from the tables they were previously sitting at and huddled around me and Dro's table like a football team waiting to hear a play from their quarterback.

"What's good you bird ass nigga? What's all the dramatics for?" Boota asked noticing my apprehension.

I gave a slight head nod towards Shamika and Chris to let it be known what I had to say was for their ears only. Shamika and Chris got up and sat at a table by themselves.

"Ski, what's good fam? Your starting to scare me," Wise announced.

"Ayo, somebody kidnapped Isaiah B," I blurted out with my eyes getting watery.

Everyone at the table's mouths dropped to the floor.

"What? When?" Boota asked.

" Nine days ago son," I answered choking up.

"How the fuck you let that happen? Where was you at?" Dro inquired.

"I was coming back from Disney World. I took Isaiah and my shorty out there for the weekend. We were at the airport waiting to get on our flight, and I went to take a phone call in the bathroom. When I came back they were gone." I explained.

"Who you had wit you Ty?" Wise asked.

That comment reminded me that I hadn't spoke to them in a minute. "Nah, yo. Ty got killed. I was with my girl. I never told y'all about her but she's my connect's daughter."

"Ty is dead B? Get the fuck out of here!" Dro shot back in disbelief. "Who killed her?"

"I don't know son. That's what got my head fucked up right now. Whoever killed Tiesha is probably the same person that got Isaiah. Tiesha got killed in February and my seed just got kidnapped this month."

"Damn, son you got beef out there like that?" Wise asked concerned.

"Word." Dro agreed. "You don't have no idea who it could be?"

"Yo, didn't you say Tiesha had a girlfriend? Whatever happened to that bitch? It's probably her," Boota added.

"You said that ya shorty is ya connect's daughter right? How you know it ain't her pops try'nna come up off of you? The whole shit was probably a set up," Wise voiced his opinion.

Dro, Wise and Boota had so many questions that I had to run down everything that had transpired in the past couple of years. I told them everything. Raphael and Candy, Tiesha, Kev, Ranisha, Crystal, Prince and Cheeba. I didn't leave anything or anyone out. An hour later they were all updated on my life.

"So what y'all think? What should I do?" I asked folding my arms across my chest.

Boota took a deep breath and answered. "I think it's that Jamaican nigga Prince. He was the one that called you from the airport right? He knew you and shorty got engaged before y'all even told anybody and he probably had y'all being followed. It's that nigga son. It ain't no coincidence that he told you to go somewhere quiet while you were at the airport. I don't trust Jamaican's anyway. His daughter is probably down with it too.

Wise spoke up next. "It ain't Prince son. It's Cheeba. Didn't you say that months before all this shit happened he kept asking you asking questions about why you was out of state and complaining about paper?"

I nodded my head.

"It's obvious B. All the evidence is pointing towards him. How you don't see it? The nigga is in ya crib asking you how you got the money and as soon as he leaves the kidnappers just happen to call telling you they want the money wired... C'mon son it's him. Then to top it all off he shoots Raphael when he starts saying that it's probably someone close to you."

Everyone was silent at the table taking everything in. After a couple minutes passed I asked Dro. "So what do you think?"

Dro leaned back in his chair and scratched his head.

I don't think it's Cheeba or Prince. I think it's that cat Kev. Think about it B, he's the only one who knows for sure that you have the ten million to pay the ransom. Cheeba and Prince know you got a little paper but they ain't know you was sitting on millions. You ain't tell neither of them right?"

"Hell no!" I responded.

"Then it has to be Kev. Do the math dawgs. You was out in Florida when it happened and he's from Florida. It's him B, and it's all ya fault. You ain't learn ya lesson from that situation with Raphael? You can't just pull hammers out on niggaz and not finish ya breakfast dawgs. If you would've left him in that hotel room like you was suppose to you wouldn't be going through none of this." Dro explained.

"Visiting hours are now over. All inmates line up against the wall!" the C.O. announced.

"So what you gonna do son?" Wise asked.

"I don't know man. I guess I just got to wait. This shit is some straight movie shit," I replied.

"Stay strong my nigga. You gotta stay sharp I wish I was out there to help you my nigga," Boota said in a rare serious moment for him getting up out of his seat and giving me a hug and a dap before he walked over to say his goodbyes to his baby's mother.

"Ski, it's Kev B. I'm telling you. I'mma call you tonight," Dro said looking me square in the eyes. "Go out there and get that nigga!"
As I watched Dro, Boota, and Wise get escorted out of the visiting room I began to choke up. I felt like I was in the streets all by myself. Whenever there had been a serious problem we always had each others back since we were kids. I needed them then more than ever. Ranisha had my back, and I knew she was going to ride with me come hell or hot water, but it wasn't the same. Dro, Wise and Boota were the only niggaz I knew I could trust no matter what.

Each one of them had valid points. The one person that I had never suspected was Prince. The more I thought about it the more possible it seemed. But, there was still so many unanswered questions. If Prince was indeed the culprit, what would his motivation have been? I'd saved him and his families life, and we were cool. And besides that if it was him who had my son, who killed Tiesha? If Prince and Crystal had set me up money was their motivation but what would be their motivation for killing Tiesha? Cheeba was definitely one of my top suspects. Wise was absolutely right, all the evidence pointed straight to him. He was jealous of me and felt like I was holding out on him. His motivation for killing Tiesha would be jealousy. She was getting more of a cut than him and if he cut her out the picture he could take her spot.

Kev was my number two suspect. He was the only person that knew I had enough money to cover the ransom. Besides that, I remembered after I pulled out my ratchet on him he had told me that, that wouldn't be the last I see of him. If it was in fact Kev, it was all about the money, and I believed he would return Isaiah and Crystal upon receipt of the money. But the more I thought about it I started to feel the same way about Kev that I felt about Prince. If it was Kev who killed Tiesha? Since the whole thing happened I had been under the impression that the same person was responsible for both situations. I'd made up my mind and came to the conclusion that it had to be Cheeba.

After I dropped Shamika and Chris off it was close to 6:30 in the evening. I drove back around my way in Baldwin Long Island to reminisce and clear my head. I ended up driving back to a park at my old elementary school plaza that I use to always shoot around at to hone my basketball skills. When I got there, there was a young kid no older than twelve years old shooting around in the dark just like I use to do. Looking at that kid was like looking at myself years ago before all the street fame and money had clouded my brain. There was a time when there was nothing in the world I would rather do than play basketball. If someone would've told me then, that my life was going to end up like it did I would've called them nuts. Basketball was my first love and I couldn't even remember the last time I touched a ball. After high school I went away to college on a basketball scholarship at a Division 1 school. But after my coach got fired, the athletic director cancelled our season and left me Upstate stranded. I couldn't help but think what would my life have been like if I would've stayed on the right path. Even after I'd gotten into the street, I tried to return to school and play ball after my man Snoop lost his life during a botched robbery of Toy's R Us. I left the streets alone for months taking summer courses to become academically eligible and working to get my basketball game back up to par. But Michelle's mom needed that money for that damn operation. After that jux the Feds got on our ass. We all got bagged one by one and while I sat in jail awaiting my trial I killed my hoop dreams. I ended up beating trial and almost killed by Raphael and hadn't thought about or touched a basketball since.

I got out of my car, and asked the kid could I shoot around with him. The kid said that he had to go so I paid him two-hundred dollars to let me keep his basketball so I could stay there by myself. As I was shooting around my cell phone was ringing off the hook. I looked at the caller I.D., saw it was Cheeba and ignored it. I couldn't fake it any more. I believed he was the kidnapper and had already decided in my mind that I was going to get him before he got me. There was nothing left to talk about with him.

As I shot around I thought about all the crazy shit that I'd been through since I'd been in the streets. I'd done things that I didn't think I was capable of and turned into a monster. I really didn't know who I was anymore. I'd done everything for the money and after I finally gotten it I realized that it was all for nothing. I wasn't happy at all. I shot around at the courts at Plaza Elementary school for close to three hours before I decided to leave. I made up my mind that after I got Crystal and Isaiah back I was out the game for good. I was on a path to destruction and there was only two ways I was going to end up dead or in jail.

I put the basketball in my trunk and started to drive home. Before I pulled off, I checked my phone and saw that I had a message so listened to it.

"You have one new message. The following message is unheard. First unheard message…" the automated voice stated.

"Ayo, Ski. It's me Cheeba man. Yo, shit is crazy right now my nigga. I know you thinking it's me but it's not. I'm calling though because I found out who did it. I just came back from ya crib but you wasn't there. You not gonna believe this son but it's a fact," Cheeba said and then I heard him talking in the background. "It's…. yo, what you doing here? BANG! BANG! BANG! BANG! BANG!" and then the phone line went dead.

I tried to call Cheeba back but his phone went straight to voice mail. I didn't know what was going on but it sounded like somebody had clapped him when he was trying to tell me who he thought it was. I started the car and sped home doing a buck and some change. When I walked in the crib, Ranisha was cooking dinner in the kitchen in nothing but a thong.

"Hey, baby you hungry?" she asked.

"Ayo, did Cheeba come by here today?" I asked.

"Cheeba? No why?" Ranisha responded.

"You was here all day?"

"Yeah, what's wrong with you?"

"Cheeba is dead yo. Somebody shot him. He was leaving me a message telling me how he found out something about the kidnapping when I heard someone shoot him," I explained.

"What? What did he say? Did he tell you who he thought it was?" Ranisha asked.

"Nah, he didn't get a chance too. I heard the shots on my answering machine."

I pulled out my phone and called Cheeba's phone but I kept getting the answering machine. A couple of seconds later, my phone rang.

"Cheeba?" I answered.

"Go to Orlando tonight. Tomorrow we make the switch. I'm watching you. I'm closer to you than you know. Don't try anything or they are dead. Tomorrow," the computerized voice stated then hung up.

"Who was that?" Ranisha asked noticing the panic on my face.

"It was the kidnappers. Get dressed we're going to Orlando. Bring ya laptop," I ordered.

The whole ordeal was getting stranger by the minute. Cheeba was dead, Tiesha was dead and Crystal and Isaiah were next. Maybe even me and Ranisha.

Me and Ranisha went to the airport and got on the first flight available to Orlando. The mystery was about to reveal itself.

Chapter 28

April 05

"That's it... all of our money is officially gone," Ranisha announced sitting behind her laptop in our hotel room.

"You sure it went through? How can you tell?" I asked nervously.

"Because it says transaction complete right here," Ranisha answered pointing at the screen. "And, look... the balance in both of our accounts are zero dollars and zero cents. We broke again," Ranisha replied.

"Fuck it! Easy come and easy go. It's not like we ever got the chance to enjoy none of it anyways. That money was a fucking curse B. Ever since we got it, bad shit started happening." I stated.

"Ski, I don't care about the money. All I care about is us and getting our family back. Nothing else matters. I love you... we can make more money," Ranisha said.

Me, and Ranisha were in our room at the Palm Springs Hotel in Disney World. It was two o'clock in the afternoon and we'd just wired the kidnappers the ransom. All we were waiting for now, was to hear back from them. And, hopefully after they'd gotten the money they'd keep their word and tell me Crystal's and Isaiah's whereabouts. It was no longer a secret who the kidnappers were. I knew it was Kev, and I was pretty sure that Kev knew that I knew it was him. I was playing it cool, and acting dumb but as soon I got Crystal and Isaiah back my plan was to go to his mansion and murdering everyone it, even if it meant I had to lose my own life in the process.

I believed Kev was responsible for Cheeba's death somehow but I still couldn't figure out who killed Tiesha. At the time of Tiesha's death all was well between me and Kev. He had absolutely no reason in the world to have her killed. I didn't have all the dots connected but I was damn sure close. But, the good thing about it was that the truth was on the horizon and it was gonna surface soon.

All that was secondary though at the time. Number one on my agenda was getting Crystal and Isaiah back. I had no idea how I was going to explain to Ranisha that I was in love and engaged to another woman after she gave up her five million dollars. When Ranisha found that out, I knew she was going to flip the fuck out and try to kill me. I wanted to tell her the truth when it first happened but I couldn't because I couldn't risk her getting mad and refusing to give me her half of the money. Without her and her money, I had no chance of getting them back. The worst part about it was that Ranisha had been nothing but good to me throughout the whole ordeal. She'd been there for more than anyone. She'd more than proved her loyalty and dedication to me a thousand times. Truth be told, I loved her too. I just wasn't in love with her. There was nothing I wouldn't do for her just like I knew there was nothing she would not do for me. Somehow, someway I hoped that after all the dust settled we could still be friends and in each other's life. I had a few hundred thousand dollars in drug money that I had Cheeba holding on to for me, I was going to give her the Bentley back to sell, and I planned on selling the boat that Prince had bought me and giving the money to her. I didn't want to lose her as a friend.

Cheeba's death was hitting me hard. I'd been blaming him for everything and it wasn't even him. I had so many deaths on my conscious that it was becoming hard to bear. Everyone was always sacrificing and losing their lives for mine and I was starting to wonder when my time was going to end and why I always managed to escape death. I felt like I had no purpose in life.

"Ski, I just wanna let you know that I loved you. No matter what happens from here on out, know that I loved you more than life itself," Ranisha said standing up and hugging me tightly.

"I love you too Re. Stop talking like that yo. Ain't nuthin' gonna happen to us. Everything is gonna be a'ight baby. Kev ain't built like that. All he wanted was the money and now he has it. Trust me everything is gonna be fine," I stated not really believing it myself.

"Everybody is dying around us. You never know what's gonna happen next Ski. I'm here for you and I'd die for you if I had too. I'm gonna ride this out with you until the end."

"I know ma," I responded rubbing her back and comforting her.

"Make love to me baby. I wanna feel you. We might never get the chance to make love again," Ranisha requested with tears rolling down her face leading me to the bed.

Sex was absolutely the last thing on my mind but once again, I couldn't refuse her. I felt like I owed it to her. She didn't know it but that was going to be the last time we had sex regardless of what.

I laid Ranisha down on the bed on her back, stripped her naked and made passionate love to her. The whole time she was crying hysterically and telling me how much she didn't want to lose me. She was acting as if she knew we were going to die, and those were our last moments together.

Two hours later Ranisha was lying on my chest still crying when she said. "Ski, let's just forget about everything and leave right now. Let's go somewhere we never been and start over. Let's just leave all this shit behind."

I pushed her off of me and stood up. "What? What you mean? You want me to leave my fucking child?" I asked angrily. "Don't nuthin' or nobody come before my child! If you scared you can go!"

"I didn't mean it like that baby. I'm sorry, I just-," Ranisha started to explain but got cut off by the sound of my phone ringing.

"Hello," I answered.

"Ski, you held up your end of the deal, so now I'm gonna hold up my end," a voice said.

"Who the fuck is this?" I asked.

"C'mon Ski you can't be that stupid. Let's stop playing games. You knew who was responsible for all this didn't you? You should've never crossed me man. We could have made a lot of money together. You did this to ya-self," Kev stated in an arrogant tone.

My blood was boiling. "You son of a bitch!"

"Hey, let's not do the name calling thing. I do still have your kid and your woman don't I?"

I was silent.

"That's what I thought. You've been a good victim Ski. Your son and girl are at 15 Freumont Ave. If you're not there in an hour, they die," Kev said calmly and hung up.

I wrote the address down and immediately started getting dressed.

"Where you going? Who was that?" Ranisha asked.

"It was Kev. I should've known it was him all along. Dro was right. I got to go get Isaiah."

"Where is he at?"

"15 Freumont Avenue. I don't know where it's at but it has to be close. I'mma use the navigational system to find it."

Ranisha jumped out the bed. "Hold up! Wait for me. I'm coming wit you," Ranisha said getting up out of the bed and getting dressed.

As we were walking through the Hotel lobby to get to the parking lot where our rental was parked an eerie feeling came over me. Something wasn't right. *Kev can't be letting it go down this easy.* I thought to myself. Ranisha and I hopped in the truck weaponless headed to the address not certain of what was going to happen. I knew I was walking into a death trap and the odds of us making it out were slim and none but it was something that I had to do. My adrenaline was pumping, my heart was racing, and my head was spinning. I was praying the whole ride silently to myself that I wouldn't get there and find Crystal and Isaiah already dead. If it was my time to go I was ready, but I didn't want any more innocent lives dying over my bullshit. It was my beef and my problem. If anyone deserved to lose his or her life, it was me.

Thrity minutes later we pulled up outside a house on Freumont Avenue that Kev had given us the directions to. The house was a modest looking colonial style house with a two-car garage in what looked like an upper middle class neighborhood. A few white kids were playing touch football in the street and another group of kids was skateboarding two driveways down. It was 7 p.m. and the sun had just set. I noticed that all of the lights were completely off in the house and as I parked in the driveway, I turned to Ranisha and said. "Ayo, I want you to just leave yo. Lemme do this on my own."

"What?"

"I don't know what's inside waiting for me but whatever it is I'm ready for it. You've done more than enough for me. This is my beef, I don't want nuthin' to happen to you," I explained.

"Nigga, this is our beef. Whatever is waiting for you inside they're gonna have to deal with both of us!" Ranisha replied defiantly grabbing my hand and kissing me on the cheek.

I took a deep breath, and we both got out of the car and walked to the front door.

I tried to knock on the front door but as soon as I grazed it the door opened as if it was left open for us. The house was pitched black and I couldn't see anything. I walked in with my hands in front of me slowly. I couldn't see a thing. Suddenly the lights came on.

It took a minute for my eyes to adjust to the light, but when they did, I saw that I was in a huge entrance hallway. There was a big expensive chandelier hanging from the ceiling, and a long spiral staircase with a balcony on top of it. In the corner of the room just off from the steps I spotted Crystal and Isaiah tied up and gagged.

"Re, help me untie them!" I shouted hearing my voice echo.

I looked behind me and Ranisha was gone.

"Yo, Re! Re! Where you at?" I shouted looking around still not getting an answer.

I was buggin' out because when we first entered the house Ranisha was right behind me. It was as if she'd vanished. No one could've snatched her up because I didn't hear her make a sound. My thoughts quickly shifted from Ranisha to my son. I ran over to him, took the gag out of his mouth, and untied him.

"Daddy!" Isaiah yelled with joy as I hugged him.

"Are you okay? Did they hurt you?" I asked inspecting his entire body.

Isaiah didn't have a scratch on him. He smelled terrible and looked dirty but other than that, he seemed fine.

"I'm hungry daddy. Really hungry," Isaiah said.

"Don't worry daddy is gonna get you something to eat." I responded running over to Crystal. "Damn baby are you a'ight? Look at you. What did they do to you?" I asked removing the gag from her mouth and beginning to untie her.

Crystal looked and smelled terrible. She was completely nude, and had bruises and scrapes all over her body and face. Dried up blood was smeared all over her, her lip was busted open, and her eye was completely swollen shut. She was so pale that she almost looked white and she looked near death.

"What did they do to you? Did they rape you?" I asked.

"No, she beat me up, but I'm fine." Crystal answered in a barely audible tone and forcing a weak smile. "I knew you'd rescue us. I never doubted you baby," she continued beginning to cry.

"I'm so sorry baby. I'm so sorry that you had to go through all of this shit. It's all my fault. I love you so much!" I responded as I hugged her tightly.

Suddenly I felt a cold steel on the back of my neck.

"Isn't this cute? I love happy endings," Kev said sarcastically. "To bad this isn't going to be one of them," Kev continued smacking me in the back of the head with the butt of the gun.

I fell to the floor on my stomach holding my head. "Ya beef is wit me son. You got the money now let them go. You can kill me, just let my family go!" I begged looking up at him.

"You sound like such a hero," Kev said clapping his hands. "No one is going to make it out of her alive. Not even you little man," he continued pointing the gun at my son.

"No! Please! Not my son and not my girl! What did you do wit Ranisha?" I asked.

"Ski, I begged you not to cross me. When you cross me, everyone pays for it. Didn't anyone ever tell you that you can't win a war with a nigga like me? My paper is too long. But, I can't sit here and front. I can't take all the credit; none of this would've been possible without the help of my special friend. Come on out honey," Kev said.

When I looked up and saw Ranisha walk out and kiss Kev, my heart dropped down into my stomach. I couldn't believe it. She'd been right under my nose the whole time consoling and comforting me. I never suspected her for one second.

"Re... what are you doing? You had something to do wit this? Why? How could you do this to me after everything we've been through? I thought you loved me?" I shouted in disbelief looking up at her.

Ranisha didn't utter a word. She just glared at me with this cold far away look that was full of hate.

"Love you?" Kev asked with a sinister laugh. "Ranisha only loves money and I have plenty of it. Like I said, I can't take the credit for this. It was all her plan. But, this ain't the movies Ski we're not gonna give you an explanation," Kev said passing Ranisha the gun. "Do the honors baby girl."

"I've been waiting a long time to do this," Ranisha replied taking the gun from him and pointing it at me.

"No!" Crystal screamed at the top of her lungs.

"Re, please! Why are you doing this?" I pleaded wide-eyed shielding my face with my hands as if it were going to protect me. Four shots went off. When I uncovered my eyes, Kev's lifeless body was slumped on the floor.

"I never liked that muthafucka!" Ranisha spat. "You're next," she continued pointing the gun at me.

"Re, what are you doing? Where did all this shit come from? Why do you wanna kill me? I thought you loved me, we family."

"No! Get it right pussy we were family! You fucked it up when you betrayed me for this bitch!" Ranisha yelled kicking Crystal in the face. "I loved you. I would've done anything for you. You're the only nigga I ever gave myself to. I killed for you... I rode for you... but you ain't appreciate it. You don't appreciate shit!" Ranisha shouted. "I warned you to never betray me. You told me I couldn't have ya baby because of all the shit that was going on and I fixed it but you still didn't want our baby. All because you wanted to be wit this bitch! Then you had the nerve to ask me for money to save her. When were you gonna tell me? Huh? When, nigga?" Ranisha shouted at the top of her lungs crying hysterically.

"Re... wait. Lemme explain," I tried to say but got cut off.

"Don't say a muthafucking word nigga I swear to God!" Ranisha yelled.

"Re, what would Ty say if she saw us like this?" I pleaded.

"Ty?" Ranisha repeated with a laugh. "Fuck Ty! She betrayed me too! Fucking wit that bitch ass nigga behind my back! She deserved to die! I gave her what she deserved!"

"You killed Ty?" I asked angrily.

"Ty was in the way anyways. I wanted you all to myself and she just gave me a valid reason to kill her!" Ranisha answered heartlessly.

"You're fucking crazy! How could you kill Ty?"

"Not only her nigga. I killed Cheeba too. I had you believing it was him for a minute didn't I. I played you. You're so fucking stupid! Cheeba was just a pawn I had to sacrifice in order to checkmate you. Just like him," Ranisha explained pointing at Kev's lifeless body. "Cheeba forced me to kill him. I was gonna let him live, but he forced my hand. I caught him following me to Brooklyn to feed these two. He didn't think I saw him but I did. He should've just minded his business. I was just using him as a distraction. After we bodied Raphael I had, ya mind so focused on Cheeba that it made it that much easier to maneuver.

I thought you would've been figured me out. Did you forget that I'm a genius on the computer? All I had to do was set it on a timer. Sometimes it was hard to sit next to you and keep a straight face. You are so fucking stupid!" Ranisha said laughing.

I was in a state of shock. She had played the shit out of me. My throat felt like it had bricks lodged inside it. I knew there was no way we'd make it out alive.

"I followed you all the way out here to Orlando. I watched you pretend to be a fucking family man and when you proposed to this bitch, it was the last straw. Before that I was just gonna kill her but after I saw that I came to the conclusion that everyone had to go. I'd just finished losing your baby and you were out making plans to start a family with another bitch. I loved you with all my heart and soul Ski. I would've done anything for you."

"You loved me so much that you kidnapped my seed, what type of fucking love is that? You crazy!" I stated.

"How dare you question my love for you?" Ranisha shouted wiping the tears off of her face. "I killed for you!"

"I killed for you too! Did you forget about that!" I shot back.

"You never loved me like I loved you! I gave my all to you! I can't live without you and after I kill you, I'm going to kill myself. If I can't have you then no one can."

"You loved me so much that you helped this fucking coward kidnap my son? What kind of love is that? What if he would've killed him? Then what?" I shouted.

"Kev ain't have shit to do wit this! I did this to you! Me nigga! I took them from the airport and flew them back to New York. Me! The only thing I needed from him was his private jet. So, I called him and made a business proposal, and just like the dumb fuck, I knew he was he fell right into my hands. Now look at him," Ranisha said pointing to his dead body.

I was feeble. There was nothing I could do to stop that crazy bitch from killing us. As I lay on the floor, I was scanning the area looking for anything I could use as a weapon to get the gun from her but there was nothing in sight. The entrance hallway was completely unfurnished and I couldn't make a move for the gun because Ranisha had smartly kept her distance from me. Isaiah was on the bottom step crying his eyes out the whole time and Crystal was on the floor barely conscious.

"Before I kill you, I'mma kill this home wrecking bitch!" Ranisha announced pointing the gun at Crystal's head.

"NOOO! Please! Just kill me she ain't got nuthin' to do wit this!" I begged covering Crystal's body with mine.

"You love this bitch? You love her. What's so special about her? You used me! Move out the way Ski! Move out the way!" Ranisha demanded.

"I ain't moving. She don't have nuthin' to do wit this."

Ranisha pointed the gun at Isaiah and said. "Move or he's dead!"

"Re, no!" I cried out.

"I'm warning you. Get off of her or he's dead," Ranisha threatened.

From the look that I saw in her eyes I knew she was serious. I loved Crystal but not more than my son, so I got off her with my hands up and stood in front of Isaiah on the step.

"Say goodbye bitch," Ranisha screamed pointing the gun at Crystal preparing to shoot.

Suddenly someone dressed in all black jumped off the balcony and landed on Ranisha. Ranisha crumbled to the ground and fell on her stomach dropping the gun. Before she had the chance to attempt to get up or try to figure out what was going on, the masked person picked her head up and slit her throat from ear to ear killing her instantly.

I picked Isaiah up in my arms and stood in front of the masked person in fear. I didn't know who it was, or what was gonna happen next. Whoever it was had been dressed in all black like a ninja. When the masked man removed his mask and shook his dreadlocks out, I could not believe it. It was Prince. It felt like the whole world had been lifted off my shoulders. I was happy that it was all over but the first thing that came to mind was how he found us all the way out there in Florida.

"Blood clot! Look at mi daughta! Crystal can you hear me? It's ya fadda," Prince asked.

"Pupa? What are you doing here?" Crystal asked in a low voice.

"Don't worry bout dat. How you feeling?" Prince inquired.

"I'm okay pupa. Just a little beat up," Crystal answered.

"Bloodclot bwoy when was ah you gonna tell mi dat mi daughta get stolen? Huh?" Prince asked angrily.

"Prince this whole shit was crazy. I thought I could handle it on my own. I didn't know what was going on. I didn't wanna worry you. I'm sorry bredren," I apologized.

"Mi ah sees you really love mi daughta. You was ready ta die for her. You a good mon. Now you mus ago marry mi daughta and treat her good. We even now bredren. You save mi, and mi ago and save you," Prince replied.

"Respect," I said giving Prince dap and a hug.

"Come now. Weh mus ago at once," Prince announced.

Prince gave Crystal his coat to put on and we helped her up. I wiped the tears off Isaiah's face, picked him up in my arms, and kissed, and hugged him so tight that I almost squeezed the life out of him. Once again, I had narrowly escaped death. But, this time it was different. I'd had an epiphany. I was done with the streets for good. All I wanted to do was be with my family. Money and material objects was no longer my drug. Everything that I needed was in Crystal and my son. Both of my eyes began tearing simultaneously. God had allowed me another shot at starting over and I was going to take full advantage of it.

As we were preparing to leave, I turned to Prince and said. "How did you find us?"

Prince smiled. "Don't worry about dat. Didn't me ah tell mi know everyting?"

All I could do was shrug my shoulders and smile. As we were walking out of the entrance hallway, I glanced at the bodies of Ranisha and Kev and shook my head. It had been a crazy night. Matter of fact I'd lived a crazy life and only through God's grace, I was able to endure it all and walk out the door with my son in my arms and holding Crystal's hand. Little did I know the nightmare wasn't over. It was just the beginning. As we made our way to the front of the house and walked outside we were met with twenty guns pointing at us.

"Freeze F.B.I.! Nobody move!"

The saga still continues…

Ski Mask Way III Coming Soon!

Heaven & Earth
By J.M. Benjamin

The Columbians had Pablo Escobar...The Cubans had Scarface...The Italians had John Gotti...And the Brothers had Bumpy Johnson...But what about the Sisters?

Meet the female Nino Brown and Gee Money, only these two really are their sister's keeper.

New Brunswick, New Jersey native Heavenly Jacobs inherited her beauty and street smarts honestly. Father a top notch go getter, mother a grade "A" dime piece. After tragedy strikes her home her only means of survival is to rely on what she acquired from them both. Her choice to ride for the wrong man ultimately lands her in prison where she is forced to re-strategize her game plan.

Eartha Davis is not your average female. Her eyes as well as her body were exposed to more then they were ready for at a young age. Between her mother, who was a bonafide gangster that loved young pretty females, and the streets of Plainfield, New Jersey, it was hard for her not to fall victim to and embrace all that was going on around her. Her crave for the streets, violence, and women all contributed to her imprisonment in Edna Mahan Correctional Facility.

As fate would have it, these two females are thrown together, in which they form a bond that is un-breakable and spills over into streets. Seeing that everybody got fat while they starved, they put together a team of female hustlers that got all men in the game on edge.

Jealousy, envy, ego's, and pride all come into play unraveling beef between male and female that is far from being a game. Will the brothers sustain? Or will they succumb to the wrath of Heaven & Earth?
AVAILABLE NOW!

The Dutty Way
By J.M. Benjamin

Welcome to Riverton, a ruthless city in Jam-Rock, where some of the most notorious and legendary Jamaican shotas and king pins have emerged. It is also the birth place of Everton Levy aka Dutty.

Dutty had aspiring dreams of becoming wealthy beyond his imagination and being a figure amongst his peers as a bonafide rude boy. His dreams soon become a reality and he finds himself in a predicament that forces him to leave his other half behind in Yard in order to save her and his own life with the promise of sending for her as he flees to America...

David Myrie aka Puff is known in Jamaica for making things happen and getting it done by any means. He is also the right hand man of Dutty. Through his connects and resources he discovers some information that is detrimental to his best friends health. With that, Puff's top priority becomes Dutty's safety as he does everything in his power to get him out of the West Indies before it is too late...

Now in America for the first time, Dutty quickly realizes the only way he will be able to survive is by doing what he does best. Linking up with some of his country men, Dutty embraces the under world of New York City where he catapults himself in the streets of NY, becoming a force to be reckoned with. He wastes no time establishing his name and reputation in The Big Apple as a Jamaican Don.

Dutty decides to trade in the street life for the family life. But someone has other plans for him. Because he was an illegal alien Dutty is deported back to his homeland and loses everything in America...Even his family. Now on a war path he returns back to the U.S. with a vengeance... And he intends to make everyone involved pay for all that he has lost the only way he knows how...The Dutty Way!

SUMMER 2010

BREAKING LONDON
BY J-ROD NIDER

London Smith's life went from rags to riches overnight like that of a ghetto fairytale after meeting Jamar Jones aka Mar Buckz, one of the streets of Plainfield New Jersey finest.

This was all London ever had dreamed of, what more could a woman ask for she thought... But just when she thought it couldn't get any better... She was absolutely right because life as she once knew it took a drastic turn for the worst.

Blinded by love, London finds herself caught up in the middle of an abusive relationship full of drama, lies, betrayal and decent all in which begin to take a toll on her.

One smack too many and discovering she was now carrying a child, causes London to make some decisions... But will she stand strong and remove loves blindfold or will she continue to let her man break her down?

SUMMER 2010